ISLAND TALES

CARIBBEAN FOLKLORE STORIES

Amber Drappier

Island Tales (Caribbean Folklore Stories)
Written and published by Amber Drappier
Copyright 2018 Amber Drappier
Cover Design by ©grandfailure - stock.adobe.com

Without limiting the rights under copyright reserved above, no part of this publication may be reproduced, stored in or introduced into a retrieval system, or transmitted, in any form, or by any means (electronic, mechanical, photocopying, recording, or otherwise), without the prior written permission of the copyright owner and publisher of this book.
This is a work of fiction. Names, characters, places, and incidents either are the product of the author's imagination or are used fictitiously.

ISBN: 9781730965371

For my mother and my brother.
Both of whom inspired my love for folklore from an early age.

It may all be true, it may all be untrue.
But I'm not willing to test the fates to find out.
And that is why you will never find me alone outside at night.
Once the sun goes down,
I'm safely locked away from whatever may be out there.
As for what might be in here with me, well,
that's a different story!

TABLE OF CONTENTS

Introduction	Pg 01
Meet the Legendary Characters	
A Brief History of Caribbean Folklore	Pg 05
Baccoo	Pg 07
Bush Dai Dai	Pg 08
Changelings	Pg 09
Churile	Pg 11
Dee Baba	Pg 12
Douens	Pg 13
Gang Gang Sara	Pg 14
Heartman	Pg 15
Jacakalantan	Pg 16
Jumbies and Duppies	Pg 17
La Diablesse	Pg 19
Lagahoo (Loup Garou)	Pg 21
Mama Dglo	Pg 23
Mama Malade	Pg 25
Massacooramaan	Pg 26

Mermen and Fairy maids	Pg 27
Moongazer	Pg 28
The Obeah Man	Pg 29
Papa Bois	Pg 30
Raakhas	Pg 32
Rolling Calf	Pg 33
Silk Cotton Trees	Pg 35
Soucouyant	Pg 36
Three-Footed Horse	Pg 38

Short Stories

Water Baby	Pg 41
Sun and Rain means more than Monkey Wedding	Pg 50
Moongazer Found	Pg 58
Sonny	Pg 66
Going for Gold	Pg 71
The Legend of Gang Gang Sarah	Pg 83
Tipping the Scales	Pg 86
Driver	Pg 95
House of Chimes	Pg 102
Buck-Buck-Goose	Pg 108

Until Death Do Us Part	Pg 121
Fairy Garden	Pg 126
Council of Elders	Pg 128
Wayward Children	Pg 137
The Sculptor	Pg 147
Mother Knows Best	Pg 154
The Offering	Pg 170
The Plea	Pg 172
Who Don't Hear Go Feel	Pg 176
Endless Cycle	Pg 185
Dark Angel	Pg 195
Whitey Don't Know No Better	Pg 202
I Heard a Cry	Pg 209
Hidden Treasures	Pg 210
Ah Bit of Obeah Go Fix That!	Pg 223
Slight Complications	Pg 241
Piggy Back Rides for Mr. Gundy	Pg 246
Glossary of Term and Phrases	**Pg 265**
About the Author	**Pg 285**

INTRODUCTION

This book is dedicated to the wonderful melting pot that is the Caribbean, and in particular to my home island of Trinidad and Tobago. It was there that my love for Caribbean culture and the myths and legends of the lands developed.

From a very young age I was introduced to the horrors brought about by supernatural beings. Like most children, I eagerly gulped up the stories and put on a brave face in front of my friends, cousins, and especially the adults. But once I was alone and the sun went down, I would always take that extra peek over my shoulder to make sure there wasn't a jumbie lurking behind me. It was a precaution you see. The rational part of me *knew* better, but the practical part of me just needed to be sure.

Do you remember the terror of lying in bed at night when the house was silent only to hear a noise? In those moments even though you told yourself that it was just the house settling or your mind playing tricks on you, there was always that voice in the back of your mind assuring you that it was most certainly the *soucouyant* that was coming to suck your blood, or maybe even a *douen* hiding outside your window. And worse of all would be when the neighbourhood dogs suddenly began barking for no reason, you would cower for you knew the *lagahoo* was likely about!

These stories and legends are something that stay with you, they are something that has been passed down through the generations, and even as you age into adulthood they linger in the back of your mind.

The Caribbean culture is immensely diverse as a result of our history, so for those not familiar with the Caribbean's folkloric characters, you may notice as you read through this series that many of them share a likeness to other more mainstream folklore characters (such as the soucouyant who is a vampire, or the lagahoo who is a shapeshifter).

I sincerely hope that I've been able to do justice to the beautiful culture of Trinidad and Tobago and to the Caribbean as a whole.

We'll begin where I think is most appropriate—an introduction to the various characters of Caribbean. So without further ado, let's…

Meet the Legendary Characters

A Brief History of Caribbean Folklore

The origins of many of the folklore characters of the Caribbean can be found seated within the history of the islands. The colonial era saw the introduction of African slaves, many of whom arrived with the French-speaking slave masters and thus developed their own French-based language known as *patois*.

Considered heathens, since their religious practices were not based on Christianity, the slaves were not allowed to recognize or partake in their culture and religious observances. However, despite the threat of being killed for acknowledging their religion and heritage, many slaves continued to practice their traditions in secret, in an attempt to preserve their identity and carry forward their unique culture.

For these Africans, their culture is deeply rooted in the beliefs of nature and wildlife, many of which holds heavy superstitious significance. As a result, many of the local folklore's origins have been derived from a variety of African beliefs and superstitions.

Over time, and with the abolition of slavery, many other ethnic groups such as the Europeans, the Chinese, and the East Indians, arrived on the shores of our islands under the idea of indentured labour. These groups, along with others who have migrated to the Caribbean islands over the years, have all lent their culture and traditions, along with their unique elements of folklore and superstition, to our nations.

It was through this process of assimilation and acculturation that these various ethnic groups have not only retained their identities but have also contributed facets of themselves to our melting pot society that currently stands as the rich and diverse Caribbean culture.

BACCOO

A *Baccoo* (pronounced *bah-koo*) also known as a *Baku* or simply a *Buck*, is a term used to refer to the members of a tribe, whose heritage can be traced back to the Yoruba people, who are well known for possessing magical powers and abilities.

Though Bucks are reportedly from Guyana, many Trinbagonians and Bajans have reported their presence within their island nations. In the Guyanese folklore, the Baccoo is known to be a spirit that has been trapped in a bottle that was then thrown into the sea. Once freed, it is difficult to trap the Baccoo in its prison again and the owner usually ends up indebted to the spirit for life.

Often described as short in stature, many of those who have seen a Baccoo report that the creature's only humanoid feature is the fact that it walks upright. Those who find or are given a Baccoo often take ownership of them as they are known to bring wealth and prosperity to their masters. However, the only way to guarantee continuous wealth is to feed the creature milk and bananas every day, (though some legends tell that some Baccoos require fresh meat) and allow it to live on their property.

Should the owner cast it out of his house or stop feeding it, bad luck (sometimes in the form of death) often plagues the family. If the Baccoo is unhappy or disgruntled, it is known to rain stones down onto your roof, an act that is said to bring malady to the family who lives under that roof. In some reported instances, the Baccoo beats his master since it is known to possess superhuman strength.

BUSH DAI DAI

This forest spirit is well known in Grenada and Guyana and among the Amerindian peoples. The *Bush Dai Dai* (pronounced *bush die-die*) is said to protect the lands and any treasures or precious stones (diamonds) and metals (gold) it contains.

Though its natural appearance is short, squat, and hideous, it often takes the form of a beautiful woman who appears within the camps of miners. She flirts with the men and share in their feast before seducing the weakest man who would be the most susceptible to her charms.

After getting intimate with him, she waits until he drifts off to sleep before transforming herself into a wild beast that kills and eats her victim, leaving behind nothing but a few bones.

CHANGELINGS

[Author's note: I have heard of several stories occurring within the Caribbean that describe this creature, though it doesn't call it by name. However, research shows that reports and sightings of Changelings occur all over the world. With this in mind, I felt compelled to include it as a part of our folklore. Here is what I know of them...]

A *Changeling* is a popular folklore character that is said to be either a troll or a fairy that has the ability to take the shape of a human child or baby. Stories of their existence can be found throughout the world. In African society they're known as the *ogbanje*, in Spain they're referred to as the *xana*, and in England and Wales they're known as the *plentyn*.

Despite being known by a variety of names the similarities are all striking and point to the same character.

A Changeling lures unsuspecting human children away and returns in their place. They have also been known to steal into nurseries in the dead of night and take the place of a newborn baby.

Though it's not certain what happens to the human child, many believe that the child is either put into a sleep-like state while others believe that the child is watched over by the "parent" of the changeling.

In some cases the being would integrate into the society though it would often be mute. However, if the human parents begin to distrust or mistreat the creature it slowly begins to revert to its original form, and as it does, its behaviour and features begins to transform into something ugly. It begins with disobedience, then graduates to fits of anger and finally ends with murderous violence.

The older legends state that the creature is afraid of iron and fire and many people often keep a pair of open iron scissors or a metal cross over their child's crib or bed or even on their person. Elders advocate that to rid yourself of the changeling you must be cruel to it by beating it or killing it. There have been reports of people who burn the creature alive, however it's important to remember that everything you do to the being will be done to your child in return. Instead, it is recommended that you calmly take the creature back to where it came from and if you're lucky and you've been kind enough, your own child will be returned to you in exchange.

CHURILE

A *Churile* (pronounced *choo-rile*) also known as *Churail* (pronounced *choo-rail*) is said to originate from the Indo-Caribbean folklore. She is said to be a bhoot – the spirit of the deceased. In this instance, the churile is a pregnant woman who has either died during childbirth or committed suicide while pregnant. She is often depicted wearing all-white clothing with her long dishevelled hair hanging in her face. Her screams and screeches are said to be like that of a banshee.

She roams the streets in the dead of night with her foetus in her arms. Often it is said that the foetus cries for milk and the sound resembles that of a wailing cat.

In a fit of rage, and grieving over the loss of her life, as well as the life of her child, she possesses pregnant women and attacks them, causing miscarriages or harming newborn children.

In other legends, she manifests from a woman who has done evil but whose child has survived her death. It is said that being apart from her child is what drives her to wail and howl.

She has also been known to seek revenge on her former husband if he ever abused her during their marriage, or if he ill-treats or neglects any of the children she has borne for him, by striking him with a crippling illness.

In some legends she manifests as a vampire-like creature who seeks vengeance on every being she comes across regardless of their affiliation to her or her family. She can morph in to a woman for short periods of time, and during this time she reportedly lures men to their death.

DEE BABA

Dee Baba (pronounced *dee bah-bah*) is a benevolent Indo-Caribbean spirit who is believed to be the protector of the lands against evil and danger and is known to some as the incarnation of Lord Shiva. He is often sought by farmers wishing for a bountiful harvest, or by people who wish to have their homes protected. Some people offer sacrifices to Dee Baba in exchange for health, prosperity, and happiness.

Traditionally, he is given offerings in the month of January. These offerings can be of two varieties. Either a vegetarian offering referred to as *sadaa* (salted crackers, butter, rum, cigarettes, bread or fruit, and flowers) or a non-vegetarian offering referred to as *satwick* (canned sardines or a black rooster or a goat, pig, or fresh fish).

DOUENS

Douens or *Duennes* (pronounced *dwenz*) are the souls of children who have died before they were baptized. They are forever confined to roam the earth in a state of eternal limbo and are known to play in forests and near rivers, especially around dusk.

They are distinguished by the fact that they are sexless beings who possess no faces with the exception of a small O-shaped mouth. To hide this fact, they wear large dome-shaped hats that have been woven from coconut fronds, straw, vines, or whatever materials they have at their disposal. Another distinguishing feature of the douen is the fact that they walk with backwards turned feet.

Forever looking for more playmates, these spirits will approach children and lead them astray in the forest until they are lost. At times, they will approach people's homes in the dead of night, crying and whimpering or laughing and shouting in order to get the home owner's attention. Those who have encountered a douen will tell you that they are not malicious spirits. They are simply mischievous "forever children" who enjoy playing pranks.

Legends tell that the only way to prevent douens from calling your children away into the forest is to never shout your children's names in open places, as the douens will take their names and call to them in your voice to lure them away. Baptizing your children is also a highly recommend solution as it does not allow the child to be tied to the earth with the other douens but instead allows the child to ascend to heaven in the event of their passing.

GANG GANG SARA

Gang Gang Sarah, the African witch of Golden Lane, is perhaps one of Tobago's most famous folklore legends. According to legend, she arrived on the isle of Tobago in the latter half of the eighteenth century after flying from Africa to the village of Les Coteaux, Tobago.

She landed and ventured towards Golden Lane in search of her family who had been brought to Tobago long ago on slave ships. Upon finding them, she opted to remain in Tobago for many years and is remembered for her great wisdom and kindness.

She married Tom, who, according to the old tales, she knew as a child in Africa. When Tom died, he was buried under a great Silk Cotton tree in Runnemede, and in her grief, she decided to fly back to Africa.

Gang Gang Sarah climbed the great Silk Cotton tree and tried to fly, not realizing that she had lost that ability as a result of eating salt. As she leaped from the tallest branch of the tree, she plummeted to her death much to the dismay of villagers.

To this day, there are two gravestones under that Silk Cotton tree upon which the names of Tom and Sarah are inscribed. There they've both been resting in peace for over two hundred years.

HEARTMAN

The Heartman is a folklore character native to Barbados, and unlike any other folklore character, the Heartman is the only one who is human. According to the legend, the Heartman carves the beating heart out of a victim's chest as an offering to the Devil. It is not known what he gains in return for his offering though many claim he is granted an extended life.

According to many local Bajans, there are several Heartmen who live on the island from St. Lucy to St. Phillip. Their preferred victims tend to be children since they are easier to lure away with promises of toys and candy and shiny baubles due to their naivety and impressionable nature.

JACAKALANTAN

A *Jacakalantan* (pronounced *jack-ah-lan-tan*) is said to be a mysterious light or glowing orb that appears in the dead of night. It is often said to resemble the lanterns used by hunters, and it is known to attract and lead many people (usually those who find themselves walking home alone) away from their destinations and deep into the heart of the dense tropical forests.

As the weary traveller follows the light deeper and deeper, they soon become lost, and just when they think they've caught up to it, the Jacakalantan vanishes, leaving them stranded in the darkness.

JUMBIES AND DUPPIES

Known throughout the Caribbean, *Jumbies* (also known as *jumbees*, *ghosts*, *phantoms*) and *Duppies* (also known as *Bakru* or *Bageede* on some islands) are said to be mostly malevolent spirits that roam the earth at night.

In the Caribbean, it is believed that a person possesses two souls—the good soul that ascends to heaven, and the earthly soul that remains with its earthly body for three days after death. If proper precautions are not taken, the earthly spirit can appear as a jumbie. It also should be noted that some of these spirits possess the ability to shape-shift into the forms of various animals such as pigs, hogs, snakes, dogs, and cats. Caribbean parents will often warn children about the dangers of playing with stray animals as you can never be certain if the animal that's following you home is a jumbie or not.

There are various ways to keep a jumbie or duppy out of your house. One such way is to walk home backwards if you are returning home late at night. This ensures that the spirit cannot follow you home. Another method states that you must place a pair of shoes outside your door at night. Since the spirit does not have feet, they will spend the night trying to get the pair of shoes to fit them before they attempt to possess you. However, some people contend that this is not an effective method as some jumbies simply disregard the pair of shoes or shape-shift to give themselves feet.

The best method to protect yourself from a jumbie is to sprinkle either grains of rice or salt around your house, as the jumbie must first count each individual grain before entering. By the time they've almost completed the task, the sun will have risen and they will be called back to the spirit world.

It is also important to note that many of the characters mentioned here (from the churile to the soucouyant to the douens) are all jumbies since it is an umbrella term used to classify malevolent or mischievous spirits.

LA DIABLESSE

La Diablesse (pronounced *la-jah-bless*), is known as the *Devil Woman* or *Cow Foot Woman*. She is believed to possess eyes that glow like burning coals, and the face of a corpse that she either transforms into a beautiful woman for short periods of time, or more simply keeps hidden under a wide-brimmed hat she often dons.

Dressed in a white puffed-sleeve blouse with very meticulously detailed embroidery and a long petticoat skirt that hides her one cloven foot, she often shows up at village gatherings at nights. All women who see her immediately grow jealous, whilst all men become entranced by her hypnotic charm.

Usually, at the end of the night, she asks one of the men—usually the best dressed one—to accompany her on her journey home.

She is also known to appear before men who find themselves walking home alone at nights. She steps out from behind a tree and asks the man to see her to her doorstep.

If one listens carefully they will hear the jingle of chains mixed with the rustling of her petticoat, and if one looks carefully they will notice that only one of her feet ever touches the road while the other (her cloven hoof) stays in the grass. Regardless of how she finds her victims they all meet the same fate. They are led deeper and deeper into the woods until she suddenly disappears, leaving the man lost and alone. Unable to navigate the usually lush and dense forest, the man stumbles around in the dark until he either falls into a ravine and breaks his neck, falls into a river and drowns, or is attacked by wild boars.

The La Diablesse is also known to cast a spell that makes her young and pretty and often wears a heavy perfume that serves to mask the smell of death and decay that lingers around her. But she has two tell-tale signs that make her stand out from anyone else in the area. The first thing is that she will be carrying a dirty old gris-gris bag with her that contains bones, shells, balls of herbs tied up with twine, and dirt. The second and most telling sign will be the fact that she will be wearing clothes of days gone by that are heavily adorned with lace and embroidery.

Legend advises those who believe they have encountered a La Diablesse to take off all their clothes, turn them inside out (with the seams facing outwards), and put them back on again.

LAGAHOO (LOUP GAROU)

The *Loup Garou* (pronounced *loop-gah-roo*), also known as *Lagahoo*, *La Gahou* (pronounced *lah-gah-hoo*), or *Lugarhoo* (pronounced *lur-gah-hoo*), comes from the French word for "werewolf." Like the soucouyant—his female counterpart—he feeds on blood, though he is said to be content with feasting on only animal blood if no human blood is available. He is a shape-shifter who can transform himself into an animal and can vary his size in an instant from large to extremely tiny.

The loup garou is typically a male village elder of creole descent whose shape-shifting abilities have been passed on to him throughout the generations of his family. Sometimes known as the village obeah man, or even as a scholar and a man of science and higher education, he has the ability to create charms and spells, both good and bad, and is often revered and feared by all.

At night, he transforms into a great beast and roams the streets with a series of massive chains and sometimes a large black coffin that drags and rattles behind him—or in some legends the coffin is carried upon his head. In his hand the lagahoo holds a bunch of dried sticks and reeds, most of which are used in his practice of obeah (black magic).

If one wishes to see the lagahoo but not be seen by it, they must take the yampie (eye boogers or rheum) from the corner of a dog's eye and place it in the corner of their own eye. Then at midnight, peek through a keyhole.

. To protect yourself, you must carry a crucifix on your person and recite the prayer *L'Oraison* to ward off the loup garou (and evil in general). However, if you wish to catch or trap the loup garou, you must open a pair of scissors and place it on top of a bible at the head of your bed. It is important to note that the scissors must be made entirely of metal for this to work. The loup garou will be forced to revert to his human form if he enters your bedroom and you will then be able to catch him.

Mama Dglo

Mama Dglo, (pronounced *Mama Duh-Lo*) also known as *Mama Dlo*, *Mama Glow* or *Mammy Wata* is derived from the French "Maman de l'eau" which translates to "Mother of the Water" in West African culture. She is known as the protector of all bodies of fresh water. Her upper body is said to be that of a beautiful woman while her lower body loops into that of an anaconda whose coils remain hidden below the water's surface.

At times she is known to take the form of a beautiful woman who sits at the water's edge, basking in the sunlight and singing silent songs to herself until she suddenly disappears in a flash of bright green.

There is suspicion that she is the true lover or wife of Papa Bois, and there have been many hunters who report coming across them in the high woods.

Men who commit crimes against her waterways, such as polluting her rivers and lakes, causing harm to her animals or abusing the natural resources in any way may find themselves married to her for two lifetimes and will be unable to take any other mate except for her for the duration of their marriage.

Hunters who come across Mama Dglo usually find her sitting at the water's edge. Spellbound, they are immediately attracted to her immense beauty as she sits combing her hair in the sunlight and singing to herself.

Should you encounter Mama Dglo, be very polite if she asks you anything. Subtly flatter her about her beauty, and under no circumstance should you mention that you enjoy eating anything that lives in her waters as she considers every living thing in her watery world to be her children. Instead, as you make small talk with her, take off your left shoe, turn it upside down with its tip pointing towards her, and leave the scene by walking backwards all the way until you reach home or else *you* may find yourself married to Mama Dglo for two lifetimes.

MAMA MALADE

Similar to the Indo-Caribbean Churile, *Mama Malade* also known as *Mama Maladie* (pronounced *Mama Mah-luh-dee*) is a character derived from the folklore of Grenada. She is the spirit of a woman who has died during childbirth. At night, she roams the streets and tends to linger outside houses, crying like a baby. Unsuspecting victims often fear that an infant has been abandoned and they tend to look out of their windows to see if any child is in need of help.

Those unfortunate enough to look outside find themselves overcome with illness, and those who dare to open their front doors find themselves being whisked away by Mama Malade, never to be seen or heard from again.

MASSACOORAMAAN

Well known in Guyana, the *Massacooramaan* (pronounced *mah-sah-coo-rah-man*) is a massive beast-like creature who possesses sharp teeth and powerful arms that he uses to capsize boats that carry *pork-knockers* (local miners in Guyana). Once the boat has been flipped, he captures the men aboard and tears them apart and eats them. He is known to reside in and around the rivers of Guyana, and his ability to swim long distances and stay underwater for long periods of time lends to the theory that he may also be aquatic.

Based on the history of the island, it is said that the massacooramaan was once a runaway slave who escaped his plantation and fled into the dense jungle, using the rivers and waterways to guide and protect him from the trackers (*curabans*) used by the plantation owners (*massa*). His rage transformed him into an insatiable beast, who, to this day, holds a great disdain for any and all ships as they are said to remind him of the slave ships and colonial ships that once dominated the Caribbean waters.

MERMEN AND FAIRY MAIDS

Mermen and *Fairy maids* are a deep-rooted part of Tobago's folklore. The mermen possess the upper body of a handsome and rugged man and the lower body of a fish. They often ride the rolling waves of the deep sea and are dressed similarly to kings of years past. They are very friendly towards humans and are often said to grant a wish to any human who encounters them. They mate with the fairy maids who live within the rivers, beneath bridges, within mountainous pools, or behind waterfalls and waterwheels.

Fairy maids are beautiful creatures with long, lush hair and a foot in the shape of a deer's hoof. They are fond of smooth-skinned men and have been known to pursue the men they are attracted to onto land. They enchant the men by using their powers to turn his head in their direction and have been known to steal a man's shadow, thereby rendering him insane. The only way to retrieve their shadows once more is to go to the water's edge where they encountered the fairy maid and plead with the water for the return of their shadow.

For those men who find themselves involved with a fairy maid and who wish to end the relationship, they must make an offering of two pairs of shoes. The first pair must be burnt on the shores of the beach. Once this is done, the fairy maid will then rise out of the water and ask if she is to be paid for past services. The answer given by the man must be, *"No fair maiden, nothing but this pair of shoes."* He should then cast the second pair of shoes into the water and leave the water's edge immediately.

Moongazer

The *Moongazer*, also known as the *Phantom* or *Phantome*, stands between forty and sixty feet tall, though other accounts say he's only as tall as the tallest tree in the region. He is known to appear when the full moon is out and has a habit of standing with his legs poised on either side of the roadway as he gazes up at the moon. If anyone is unfortunate enough to be noticed as they pass between his legs, he unleashes a sharp, shrill whistle just before he clamps his legs shut and crushes the person to death.

Origins of this character remain unknown and the legends surrounding him have, for the most part, been lost throughout history. However, some claim that he is an invisible entity who can only be seen by his shadow, while other stories tell that he is an opaque, wavering form. Even older stories lay claim to the fact that crossroads tend to attract him and that that is where he can mostly be found on any given night if the moon is out and visible.

THE OBEAH MAN

Obeah (pronounced *oh-bee-yah*) also known as *Obi*, *Obia*, or *Obea* in the African culture, or as the *Canaima* in the Amerindian culture, is a term that is used predominantly within the Caribbean to refer to the practice of religious spirituality. It is associated with both benign and malignant magic, and bears similarity to Santeria, Voodoo, Hoodoo, Rootwork, and Palo Vodou. It should also be noted that the term "kanaima" is known to refer to the spirit of justice amongst the Amerindian people and many believe that those guilty of misdeeds will suffer from mysterious ailments (most commonly a knot within the intestines) which leads to a slow and horrible death.

The obeah man is usually a revered man (or woman) of considerable age who resides in the village. Believers often visit the local obeah man for spiritual readings or for charms and spells relating to matters of love, revenge, wealth and money, luck, health and healing, power, etc.

Based on the request, the obeah man recommends a series of rituals that must be performed to the strictest of instructions in order for the charm or hex to work. He also specializes in reversing such charms or hexes should the victim require it. During these rituals, the obeah man will invoke a number of spirits with the request. In return, he offers the spirits a payment which can vary from herbs to blood sacrifices.

It is also believed that he can call on these spirits to do his own bidding and that he often invokes the ability to change and transform himself into many shapes, sizes, and forms, though he seems to have a particular fondness for transforming himself into that of a jaguar.

PAPA BOIS

Papa Bois (pronounced *Papa bw-ah*) also known as *Maître Bois*, or *Daddy Buchon* (pronounced *Daddy Boo-shon*) is the guardian of the forest and protector of all the animals who dwell within it. His name can be translated from the French patois to mean "Father of the Forest," "Master of the Woods," or "Hairy Man".

He is described in a variety of ways and is mostly seen by hunters and people who live near the forest. Some describe him as being an old, hairy man with gnarled and thickened joints, who wears a pair of timeworn, ragged trousers and a bamboo horn on his belt which he uses to warn animals of any approaching hunters. Other more traditional depictions of him show describe as a creature that possesses the muscular upper body of a man and the lower body of a four legged cloven-hoofed animal. His beard is said to be made entirely out of leaves, while the rest of his body is covered in hair, like that of a wild animal. In some legends, hunters report seeing two small horns protruding from his forehead.

Papa Bois is said to be the long-term lover to Mama Dglo, though he has also been known to court the La Diablesse. By transforming himself into a large buck (deer) and sprinting away, he lures habitually disrespectful hunters deeper and deeper into the forest. Once the hunters catch up and move in for the kill, he either reverts to his true form and issues them a stern warning, disappears entirely leaving them lost and alone, or hexes them by turning them into some wild animal. Other times he takes the form of a deer to observe the habits and patterns of hunters without alerting them to his presence.

Earlier legends depict him as being very mean and ill-tempered, but more modern encounters describe him as being kind and friendly. Regardless, he has no tolerance for those with malicious intent, or those who abuse his lands. When angered, he can be quite dangerous and has been known to cast spells over bad hunters, turning them into wild hogs, or to lead them to the riverside where he forces them to marry Mama Dglo.

Should you encounter Papa Bois in the forest, it is advised that you greet him politely by saying, *"Bonjour vieux, Papa,"* or, *"Good day, old father,"* and under no circumstances are you to stare at or comment on his hooves, as he considers this action to be unforgivably rude.

Raakhas

Originating out of East Indian folklore, the *Raakhas* (pronounced *rah-kaas*) is born when its human mother or father has committed a wrongdoing that has brought bad karma upon them. The child is born demonic in nature with jet black skin and eyes as well as a full head of hair, sharp teeth, and long fingernails. In some cases the creature has been said to bear the resemblance to a monkey or rat and it may even have a long tail that it whips around itself.

Alert and able to navigate the world immediately after its birth, the raakhas will attempt to escape its mother and the clutches of the midwife in an effort to seek higher ground. Though it will attempt to kill its parents for their wrongdoings, it has a limited lifespan of three to five days in which to do so.

To kill the creature, a large brick or stone needs to be placed upon its chest at birth, or the less preferred method is to strangle the creature before it comes into awareness. Just before the raakhas attacks, it is said to emit a high pitched wail that is reminiscent in syllabic nature to its mother's or father's name.

ROLLING CALF

The *Rolling Calf* (also known as the *May Cow* in the Cayman Islands and similar to the *Steel Donkey* of Barbados) is said to emerge from the spirit of a deceased butcher who had been dishonest in his business practices.

In one recollection, a butcher in a small village near the edge of Kingston, Jamaica became very wealthy by tampering with his scale. With the scale deliberately giving the incorrect weight in the butcher's favour, he was able to rob each and every one of his customers by charging them more than they owed. One day one of his patrons discovered his dishonesty by asking a passing fisherman to weigh his purchase. Soon the villagers descended upon the butcher and stoned him to death. Upon his death, his spirit was destined to roam the rolling hills of Jamaica as a massive bull. Clad in chains with fire burning behind its empty eye sockets, he sought his revenge on the villagers who had killed him.

In another telling of the creature's tale, it is said that the rolling calf can also take on the shape of animals who roam the lands at night. The Rolling Calf seems to have a fondness for molasses and often spend its days under silk cotton trees or in bamboo patches—a place of strong spiritual energy where duppies/jumbies are known to enjoy and exist.

Those walking home late at night can tell if a Rolling Calf is approaching because the ground begins to shake and vibrate with its anger. This allows the person to seek immediate shelter. If no shelter is available, the person should run to the nearest crossroad and stick any sharp straight object that can penetrate the ground, into the middle of the intersection. In the rare event that the person is carrying a whip on them or can quickly attain a whip, they can fend off the demon by turning to face it head on and whipping it with their left hand as hard as they can. If the person is caught by the beast and unable to escape, the Rolling Calf tramples them to death until their bodies are unrecognizable.

SILK COTTON TREES

Silk Cotton Trees are looked upon with fear and reverence and it is extremely difficult to find anyone who would be willing to cut one down since they are believed to host spirits, such as Jumbies and Duppies, that reside inside the tree. Cutting one down is said to release these malevolent spirits into the world.

Obeah men are known to approach the Silk Cotton tree to cast their spells by driving a long iron nail into the tree which allows a small amount of spirit energy to be released.

Legend tells of colonial masters who learned of the power of the Silk Cotton tree. It is said that they would force a slave to bury portions of their wealth at the base of a Silk Cotton tree. Then they would kill the slave so that his spirit would be trapped within the tree and he would be forced to guard the treasure for all eternity.

Soucouyant

The *soucouyant*, (pronounced *sue-coon-yah*) also known as *Old Hag*, *Ole Higue* (pronounced *old hig-you*) and *Wangala lady*, is said to be the female counterpart of the Loup Garou. She is an old woman who has made a pact with the devil which allows her to shape-shift into various forms including animals as well as her most common form, a ball of fire.

She is a creature akin to the vampire who assumes the form of an old village woman. She often lives at the edge of the village in an old wooden house set high up on posts which, in some accounts, is sealed tight by day since she cannot live in the sunlight, while other accounts merely paint her as a recluse who is typically seen overlooking the village from the vantage point of her front porch.

At night, however, she strips off her wrinkled skin and places it into her mortar, or sometimes a hollowed out calabash, and assumes the shape of a fireball that streaks through the night skies, looking for a victim. The soucouyant is able to enter the home of her victim through any keyhole, crack, or crevice.

Once inside, she proceeds to suck the blood from her victims, going for their arms, legs, and other exposed soft parts while they sleep. Her inflicted wounds heal instantly but tend to leave behind dark bruises that can sometimes be mistaken for love bites.

Should she draw too much blood out, the victim either becomes a soucouyant or loses their soul, allowing the soucouyant to assume her victim's skin as her own.

Oftentimes, she will fly to the nearest Silk Cotton tree and exchange her victim's blood with the demon known as *Brazil* in exchange for more supernatural powers.

She must slip back into her skin before the sun rises or the cock crows. If not, her spirit remains earth bound and powerless without its body once the sun comes up.

Legend says that you must empty a one hundred pound bag of rice at the village crossroad if you wish to discover who the soucouyant in your village is. Due to her nature, she will be compelled to pick up the grains one by one, and once you discover who she is, you can kill her by beating her to death. Or you can wait until she leaves her skin. Once she has, you can fill it with a rub of salt and pepper—bird pepper is said to be the most effective. The salt will cause the skin to shrink while the pepper will ensure that she dies writhing in agony all the while calling out to her skin, "Skin, skin, why you don't know me? Skin, skin, let me in!" in an effort to plead with her old skin to recognize her form and allow her to resume her original shape.

In the rare instance that you come across her in her true form, a crucifix must be made and can be constructed from any objects around you. Once she is paralyzed by the crucifix, you must recite Psalm 23 and attack her by kicking and punching at her with all your might until she goes still. Only then will you be able to capture her and chain her up. It is highly recommended to place her chained form in a barrel and seal both ends with tar and cast the barrel into the sea. You must also go to her home and destroy her skin so that no other spirit can reside in it.

THREE-FOOTED HORSE

The *Three-Footed Horse* is a spirit that is native to Jamaica and is known to be a large black horse with only three legs. Despite its malformation, it is said to be able to run faster than any creature on this planet and often travels along lonely roads at night stamping at the earth and neighing. Its breath is toxic and is said to be the stench of death and will kill anyone who breathes it in.

Many people who live in remote parts of various island have reported hearing the three-footed horse go galloping past their houses, and in one report a man retold his encounter whereby he was forced to climb out of his lover's window after her husband came home unexpectedly early one night. As he sat in the bushes below the window waiting for her to give him the all-clear sign, he heard a soft neighing and peered through the bushes to see a massive, black three-footed horse standing in the yard and bobbing its head as its single front leg scoured the earth.

When the woman called out to him from above, to tell him that the coast was clear the horse mysteriously vanished!

SHORT STORIES

WATER BABY

I stood on the rocks above, holding on for dear life to the rough tree trunk while the wind blew about me in an attempt to pry me loose and cast me towards the open sea. Tightening my grip, I watched as she climbed down and dove headfirst into the deep, dark water. Her form shimmered then blurred as she swam out deeper and deeper, and as she did I could see the flurry of parrotfish that had been lazing about near the rocks dash away to safety.

Mama swam deeper still and my lungs burned as I held my own breath, anxiously waiting for her to surface again. The seconds dragged by before her circling form appeared in the murky water, and as her head broke the surface she grinned up at me with her perfectly straight white teeth. "Come swim with me nah," she called, and I shook my head and held on to the tree trunk so tightly I could feel its bark biting into the skin on my arms.

Her grin widened as she laughed. "You is your father child self. He 'fraid water too bad." And with that she was gone again, her body disappearing below. This time she didn't dive down but instead kept close to the surface as she swam out to an unimaginable distance with her extended hands placed on top of each other and her legs kicking together in a wave-like motion.

When she surfaced once more I could barely see her. Her head was nothing more than a small black dot bobbing up and down in the water. There were sharks and God knew what other terrifying creatures that lurked in the depths of these waters, yet she seemed oblivious to the dangers that I, a mere child, could conceive.

In all the stories of my mother's childhood she always seemed to be near the water. Whether she was diving in the ocean, or collecting chip-chip on the beach, or setting crab traps along the muddy river banks, every one of her tales involved her love for the water, and even then, when I was growing up, she would often slip away to the river or to the beach and return hours later with near impossible catches. Things that I knew even the most seasoned fishermen in the village often whispered about. How could a woman her size wrestle a shark, even a small one, in the water and bring it to shore without being torn apart. How could someone of her age swim so far and fight the current without ever losing their breath or getting pulled under and swept away by a riptide. She was brave and fearless while I was the exact opposite. What a disappointment I must have been to her, though if I was, she never let on about it.

I was born at the stroke of midnight on March 1st 1971. My birth was a strange one not only because I was a month early but because I was born in a drum. My mother always told me that story with a certain degree of fondness, and with a smile she would cup my face and whisper, "You is my water baby."

According to her, she knew when the moment was upon her and without a word she went outside and climbed into the black drum we used to catch rain water. She said she submerged herself into the water while my father stood beside the barrel with one arm immersed so that he could hold her hand. I never knew if this was something they'd agreed upon beforehand or something that just happened, but whenever they told me the story their eyes would light up with a glimmer of mischief. With a single push and minimal pain I was brought into the world.

My mother says that the moment I came into this world I swam to the surface of the drum on my own, and when I broke the watery seal, I let out a cry that sounded musical. My mother named me Nerida Margaret Bartholomew, a name I carry with pride.

I'd been so lost in my thoughts that I didn't even notice her reappear at the base of the cliff. A thrashing movement caught my eye and as I looked down she winked at me and hoisted up her net which was filled with fish and other things. Today she'd caught a cavalli, a few snappers and several hard-headed catfish all of whom were grunting in annoyance. The fish wriggled in desperation, trying in vain to get back into the water but in their efforts to do so they only managed to wedge the net and themselves between two rocks. The cavalli's mouths opened and closed in an eternally looping O of surprise to reveal sharp jagged teeth as they sucked in our air, and I briefly wondered if air to their lungs would be like water to mine. I felt sorry for the fish but before I could grieve too deeply my mother picked up her knife and swiftly ended their misery.

She hoisted herself up and I gazed in awe at the sun touched the water droplets that shimmered and glistened as they rolled off her smooth muscovado-coloured skin and tight kinked jet black hair like diamonds. She climbed the cliff with ease and sat beside me. "You know..." She began and I already knew what was coming next. "...You is my water baby…look, you even have the fish scale mark on you." She traced the U-shaped birthmark that lay upon my right thigh. "One day you will get into the water and realize how much you love it just like your Mammy."

I smiled at her but shook my head. "I 'fraid."

"It ent have nothing to 'fraid." She kissed my head and stood up. "Come on, let we go and check the crab traps. Daddy will be home soon and I still have to make the dough for the dumplings."

Life was so simple back then. But now, now it had no meaning. It had no flavour. It was like a callaloo without crab. Like a mango chow without pepper. Like a pelau without Golden Ray. It was just bland and flavourless and I was tired of it.

Without even realizing it, I'd returned to the very bank she and I had spent so many years on. Her sudden death had caught me off guard. She had never been sick a day in her life, and after losing my father only a week before… It was more than I could bear and I wasn't sure how I was meant to process any of it.

As I strolled along the muddy banks I allowed my bare feet to sink into the warm clay soil, watching as the crabs all scampered back into the safety of their holes and peered out at me from behind their gundys with curious uncertainty as I moved past. My preoccupation with their burrows had brought back memories of my mother so strong that I could almost hear her laugher around me, coaching and encouraging me as I poked and prodded a stick or leaf into the holes, hoping to make a valiant catch of my own. She always knew it was a fool's mission but she never discouraged me, instead she would arm herself with a stick of her own and join me, and together we'd go sprinting off after every crab we spotted.

As I neared the spot we used to set our traps, the area where the river's mouth French kissed the sea, and where the waters licked the shores at high tide, my journey ended. I sat down in the cool, silty sand and allowed my mind to drift away. There had to be more to life than this. There had to be a reason for it all. As the water slowly creeped up to lap at my sunburned toes, I gazed into its frothy white foam and remembered the day that Mama went out so far that I could no longer see her.

I'd stood on the shores panicking. Wondering who I should go call to help. Wondering what I would tell Daddy, how could I explain that something terrible had finally happened to Mama? I was nearing hysteria when I heard her call out to me and there on the horizon with the fire of the setting sun behind her she rode on the trail of some large fish. I'd never seen anything like it in my life. Mama had encountered a school of wild bottlenose dolphins and had swam with them. "Come take a ride with us, doux-doux!" she'd called. But of course I hadn't. I couldn't. I knew if I would have set foot in those waters they would have eaten me alive. "You can't be afraid," she'd told me. "You have to go brave. And once you're in the water you'll understand the language of the sea. You have to let it speak to you and it will tell you what it wants, but most of all, you have to listen. Harden children don't listen, but you not harden, ent?"

I'd shook my head and stood on the land, shaking in fear and amazement. I would never be anything like her.

"Come swim with me, doux-doux..." I could see her in the water calling to me but like always I remained landlocked. I was not a water baby, even if in my heart I so dearly wanted to be.

***

Unaware that I'd drifted off, I awoke with a start to find myself laying in the sand and roasting under the heat of the sun. There was still about an hour of solid daylight left, and as I sat up I had to shield my face against the glory of the soon-to-be-setting sun. My clothes—my good work clothes—were caked and with grit and soaking wet. But I didn't care. I had no intention of going back there anyways. If it hadn't been for that job, if it hadn't been for my longing to fit in and be societally successful I would have been with *them*. I might have been able to help. They might have been here still. Mama would often scoff at those who would work themselves to death for the profit of others and yet still barely get by themselves. She'd even turn up her nose with a wicked glint in her eyes at those who she thought were living a lie by pretending to be free and happy. "Live for yourself. Then you are truly free," she'd say.

The tears stung my eyes. If only Mama could see me now she'd be so disappointed to know I'd turned into one of those people. Or perhaps she'd already known. Had she died ashamed of me? A lump formed in my throat at the thought.

I needed to get out of the thing that had become my life, but where could I go? I didn't want to go back to that miserable apartment in the concrete jungle of town, and my childhood home was now nothing more than an empty house filled with memories. Home was where the heart was, they said, but my heart was nothing but broken.

I looked up just in time to see a fish, a tarpon by the looks of it, breach the water some ways out. The world was teeming with life beneath the surface and so few people knew or cared, but my mother knew. She knew better than anyone. My tears finally broke their banks much like the riverbank I was sitting on did in the rainy season. Leaning forward, I gave in to my sorrows and allowed the choked sob to escape. Losing all sense of hope I allowed myself to fall to the side and curled up into the smallest ball I could.

But my sorrow was short lived. As my saltwater tears burned my eyes and obscured my vision, my sobs drowned out the world. And that was the reason why I didn't hear the men who'd been watching me exclaim as they ran towards me. They were shouting at each other and as they came well within earshot I finally realized I was no longer alone.

But it was too late and without warning or explanation they threw their cast net over me and ensnared me. Thinking back, I know to myself that even if I had I seen them coming I would have simply sat frozen, staring up at them with my mouth open like the fishes Mama would set upon the rocks. However it was because I was caught off guard that I was able to fight out of sheer surprise. Summoning a strength I never could have guessed I had, I jumped up, found my footing, and began to tear at the net.

"Hold it!"
"Don't let she get away!"
"Grab it! I have the rope!"
"Don't let it fairy maiden foot kick you!"

They called at each other as they frantically tried to contain me.

Breaking free of their trap I backed away frantically searching for a way out. There were six of them and they had formed a tight semi-circle around me and were trying to block every path including the one to my back...the sea. I turned towards it before they could encircle me completely and one of the men called out, "Don't let it get in the water! If it get in we will never get it back!"

I turned back towards them, suddenly aware that I was being referred to as an "it" not as a "she" and as I turned I noticed something odd. Something that shouldn't have diverted my attention under the circumstances but it was so strange, so out of place, that I stared down at it.

A hoof print. A single trail of them. And they were following me.

Confused I looked down and was dismayed to see that my right leg was no longer there and in its place was a delicate cloven leg like that of a young deer. My blood ran cold as I reached down to examine it. Moving backwards in an attempt to get away from the leg, I found it following me. One of the men took that opportunity to spring an attack. He threw himself on top of me and dragged me to the ground. I kicked and screamed as I tried to break free and the other men surrounded me.

He held onto me, scrabbling to grab anything he could for purchase. As his hand rooted themselves around the waistband of my pants, I bucked and wriggled so hard the clasp broke and I was able to drag myself away from him. With my pants around my ankles, I looked down at him over my leg which was covered in short, coarse brown hair that trailed all the way down from my hip to my ankle. Instead of seeing my bare foot, I was now looking at an oily black and perfectly shaped hoof that I knew would leave an imprint that resembled my fish scale birthmark. My world stopped as the realization came to me. But before I could wrap my mind around what was happening the men began to pile on top of me, struggling to contain their prize.

Using my now transformed leg, I kicked as hard as I could

and I sent one of them flying a few feet backwards. Suddenly the men eased up on their attack and backed away. As one of them ran for their net, another drew his machete, but it didn't matter, I'd already seen an opening in their defence and it was right where I needed it to be.

I sprinted towards the sea and the second I felt the waves wash against my feet something happened; I was no longer afraid of the water. Stepping out, I ran along the sandy bed and kept on running until I was waist deep. A few more meters out and I was no longer standing on solid ground as the shelf gave way to the deep sea. I allowed myself to sink deeper and deeper no longer caring about the men, my job, or my life.

The water hugged me from all sides and as I opened my eyes and kicked my limbs, I found that I could see and move through the water just as easily as on land. There was nothing to it. Looking ahead I saw a glittering shimmer of silver and as I swam closer I saw a large school of fish swarming as they spun themselves into a massive ball. Kicking as hard as I could, I propelled myself directly into the core of their shape and as I entered I could feel them open up and swallow me within their world.

I floated along with the mass of fishes as they moved through the water, safe and hidden in my own personal fish bubble. My chest burned and my lungs screamed for air, and with no option I opened my mouth and gulped the water in, fully prepared to give into the deep, dark depths of the mysterious ocean.

The briny saltwater rushed into me and I could taste the powerful tang that reminded me of when I used to dip my finger in the liquid of the pigtail bucket in my uncle's shop. The memory bubbled up and burst forth onto an even more powerful one: the massive pots of my mother's salty and rich pigtail soup, a treat she made for us when she could. I was sure that I was slowly drowning, but instead of the pain and panic I expected, I felt peace unlike anything I'd ever felt. And as my lungs adjusted to the water I could feel my mind let go of all my worries. The minutes rolled by while I remained with the fishes who kept pushing further and further out. I closed my eyes and gave in fully to the ocean. I'd heard her call and now I could hear her promise to me, her promise to hold me in her bosom and to protect me, a promise of true freedom, a promise to be the person I'd always dreamed of being—the person that I knew would make my mother proud.

I was a water baby, I understood that now, and as I left it all behind I made a resolve to never go back, to never be seduced onto the prison of the land by anyone or anything. Instead, I would keep on swimming forever within the magical world that exists right below the surface of the water.

Sun and Rain Means More than Monkey Wedding

John-John made his way through the bush, following the barely discernible path that he'd trodden over the years. The parcel of land he was on his way to had been an inheritance from his father, and though it was meant to be divided between him and his four sisters, the land stood untouched and unwanted for years. Two of his sisters were away in foreign having tea with the Queen herself—or so they made it sound—and the other two had lives of their own with husbands and children and their own lots of land.

John-John's land was almost ten acres in size and was only accessible by foot. The terrain was undulating, and at one point it even had a deep precipice that snuck up on you if you weren't paying attention. But on the eastern side, the side furthest away from civilization, there was a river that flowed well in the rainy season and even though it tended to dry up into a smaller stream during the dry season, it always produced enough water for John-John to grow his garden.

It was more than out of the way, but times were hard, and with the little section of land he'd cultivated he'd been able to feed himself and gain some surplus to sell outside the market when he needed it. The soil here was rich and untainted, and after the heavy rains that had fallen last night John-John knew that now was the perfect time to go turn the soil in preparation for some corn and dasheen. The river would be flowing strongly and the earth would be rich, loose, and well-saturated.

Shifting the bundle of tools he carried over his shoulder, he wiped the back of his hand over his forehead and cursed the humidity that had taken hold of the day. Stepping over a knobbed and protruding tree root, his muddy black garden boots squelched in the mud that sat pooled on the other side.

With the knee high grass rustling around him he pressed on, pausing only once as a lone drop of water splattered itself against his arm. As the cold drop soaked into his shirt John-John cast his gaze upwards to gauge whether or not it was just a passing cloud—he was sure that it was—and as he did he suddenly noticed the prismatic sweep of the rainbow that arched over the treetops.

"But a-a, look thing, it reaching in my garden!" He exclaimed. "Ah wonder if it have a pot of gold waiting for me at the end of it!" He laughed at himself, and though it was silly, the idea held a certain level of enchantment to it. John-John soon got lost in the thought of what he would do if there was indeed a pot of gold waiting for him. Then, minutes later, John-John reached his garden and though there wasn't a pot of gold that he could see, he was delighted at how well his crops were doing. They had thrived with the rain and stood lush and green. He could smell the cool crispness of the air and could almost taste the clean moistness of the earth in the back of his throat.

Laying his tools down, John-John decided to go take a look at the river first before he got to work. The last time he'd been here he was slightly concerned that its banks might have needed reinforcing. The last thing he wanted was for one good rainfall to flood his land and drown his crops.

Making his way over to the river, a shimmering sight caught his eye and John-John stopped dead in his tracks. Not far from where he stood the rainbow ended in the river and just a little ways away from it, an anaconda, the largest one he'd ever seen, lay with its coils looped around some unfortunate animal. As the snake's body throbbed and flexed, two cloven hooves popped out followed by the animals' large, muscular flank. The buck, much like the anaconda, had to have been the largest he'd ever seen! John-John observed the sight before him, his mouth agape. Never before had he ever witnessed such massive beasts in his life! And for not just one but *two* of them to be here...

The hairs on the back of his neck stood up as his mouth went as dry as a sucked piece of sugar cane. This was a terrible omen, this land was surely cursed.

The moment the thought formed in his mind he heard what sounded like a soft, husky chuckle followed by the sensual moan of a woman.

John-John's eyes bulged out of his head as he realized that the sight before him was worse and more impossible than he ever would have thought it to be. He began backing away and was already fleeing towards the safety of civilization in his mind. But in that moment poor John-John's heel caught on an upturned root and as he tried to brace himself, his boot sank into the muck of the mud and sent him catspraddling to the side and into the bushes where he fell with a loud rattle and a wet squelch.

As he looked up in fright he found two larger-than-life pairs of eyes staring back at him. The beasts each bore the upper bodies of a man and a woman, and though their gazes began as surprise, the man-buck's gaze quickly dissolved into black rage, whilst the serpentine-woman held seemed to regard the situation with mild amusement.

The being known as Papa Bois got to its feet, and in three steps it stood towering over John-John who cowered in fear, aware that death was surely upon him.

"What are you doing here? How dare you intrude in our affairs! Are you a hunter? Have you come to claim a prize? I will make you sorry you ever set eyes on me!" Papa Bois snarled as he lifted his mighty fist and pointed his finger at poor John-John.

A light chuckle came from behind him and as he glanced over his shoulder, Mama Dglo, clearly giddy and basking in her afterglow, slithered forward. John-John found himself almost hypnotized by the fluid shimmer of her beauty and by her brown and amber-coloured scales that seemed to flow like the river itself.

"You think he is a hunter? Surely you can tell that he's not. Don't let your anger cloud your ability to see clearly. You're just embarrassed at being caught!" She cackled and playfully slapped his arm.

Papa Bois snorted and stamped his cloven feet as he looked away. "He has no right to be here. If you want to spare him from my wrath and take him as a husband, then so be it, but if not, step aside and let me deal with him."

"P-please. No!" John-John wailed as he tried to crawl away. "Ah sorry. Ah so sorry. I didn't know. I didn't know!"

Papa Bois cast his eyes upon him once more and John-John immediately froze.

"He's clearly just tending his garden," Mama Dglo said as she pointed to the neatly arranged patches of crops that dotted the clearing, and as she slithered over to the tools that John-John had laid down she picked up a sickle and slashed it through the air.

Whoosh! Whoosh!

"Whether or not it was an accident he must pay for his crimes!"

"Stop being such a child," she chided. "Clearly he's broken no rules. We are in his land…"

"HIS LAND?!" Papa Bois screeched. "THIS IS ALL MY LAND! HE OWNS NOTHING!"

"…and his intent is clear," she continued as though he hadn't spoken. "He means to till his plots and tend to his crops. He's taken nothing from us or our home, he hasn't disrespected us in anyway and his regret at seeing us genuine. Plus," she added, "he has no weapons on him and he doesn't even have one of those picture boxes with him. This misunderstanding is all your fault for getting so carried away." Her tone was pleasant and teasing. Papa Bois snorted and stamped his feet against the ground.

"Since when you does take for *them*?" Papa Bois spat but his anger was less than it had been moments ago.

"Since you're so very ashamed and embarrassed at getting caught and being seen with me. Besides, he's cute."

"So take him as your husband then!" He scowled.

Holding her hand out to John-John she smiled and nodded as her coiled body continued to flick and flex.

Taking her hand, he allowed her to help him to his feet for fear of insulting these mythical beasts any further. He swallowed the lump in his throat and felt his bladder threaten spill its contents. Shaking like a leaf, he tried to stand before them knowing that he was about to be taken as Mama Dglo's husband. He was already imagining what it would feel like once she ensnared him in her body and dragged him down into the waters of the river. Without moving his lips, he began to pray and recite every bible verse he could think of.

She moved closer towards him and he braced himself for the inevitable, hoping that his end would be quick and painless. But instead she leaned forward and pinched his chin between her delicate hands, an act that while seemingly innocent made Papa Bois glower and smoulder with barely disguised rage and jealousy.

"Don't worry," she said as she stroked the side of his face. "There's no need to be afraid of me for I mean you no harm and you certainly don't have to worry about becoming my husband as you don't qualify." She winked at him.

John-John's eyes widened as she nodded. "Yes I can," she answered his unspoken question. "And it's how I know your heart is pure and your intent is true. So take your tools and run on home," she told John-John.

John-John stood there, teeth chattering like a chac-chac as he gazed up at her in awe. Mother of the waters they called her, she was feared by all but maybe she was nice to those who were respectful to her and her lands and waters.

"That's very accurate," she once more said in response to his unspoken thoughts.

She pulled him to his feet and leaned forward and kissed him lightly on the lips, grinning as blood rushed to John-John's face and made it as red as a newly bloomed hibiscus.

"Take this and keep it with you always." She placed a small copper bell in his hand and closed his fingers over it. "Now go on home and come back tomorrow to tend to your garden."

Clutching the bell tightly in his hand, John-John turned around and silently returned to his garden, gathered his tools, and disappeared into the bushes without ever looking back at the two lovers.

"You were much too nice on him. I was going to turn him into a quenk." Papa Bois shook his head.

"He's sweet and meant us no harm. If anything we probably scarred him for life!" she said with a grin.

"You didn't have to kiss him though." The tinge of jealousy was evident in his voice.

"If I hadn't he would remember this incident and us…and what we were doing." She raised an eyebrow at him as she lightly trailed her fingers up his muscular arm. Feeling him instinctively flex, her grin widened.

"And what of your gift to him?" His voice was calmer now.

"The bell is enchanted. It has no ringer but I can hear its rattle so it will tell me when he's near. I really like this river and I might stay here for a while so it will be good for him to have it. He will believe it to be only a good luck charm and will keep it close to him and guard it with his life though he will never recall where it came from or why it's of such importance to him."

"You is one hell of a woman, you know!" Papa Bois chuckled as his mood changed entirely. "I never knew you could work magic like that!"

"There's many things you may not know about me Daddy Buchon!" she said with a twinkle in her eye as she wrapped her coils around him and drew him into her.

John-John could hear their chattering and laughter as he

made his way back to the main road but he dared not look back in the event that Papa Bois kept true to his word and turn him into a wild hog. John-John hurried on, eager to get home and share his tale with his wife or with the fellas who would surely be posted up around the bridge outside the local bar. And to think that he had something as proof of his encounter! Clutching the copper bell in his hand, he paused to quickly tear a piece of vine down and fashioned a make-shift chain upon which he secured the bell. Tucking it into his shirt, he hurried on.

But by the time he got back to the main road he'd already forgotten everything. He stood on the roadside, tools in hand, absentmindedly stroking the bell as he wondered what he'd been planning to do. His head felt foggy and he was sure he'd just been on his way to do something. To see someone? To pick up something? Collect something? Figuring that it would come to him in time if he didn't think too hard about it, he turned in the direction of his home and began daydreaming about what delicious prospects his wife had made them for lunch.

The months rolled by and John-John's garden was thriving enough for him to have his own spot in the market instead of being made to set up just outside its gates. And it was all thanks to the river who flowed strong and, even in the dry season, was filled with fish—the sign of a thriving eco-system. Whenever he came near the bank to collect the water for his crops he could hear them splashing and could see them making the surface ripple, and once he'd spotted a large fish leap out the water so high that he wasn't even able to see where and when it entered the water again!

With a full bucket in his hand he unconsciously touched the bell that he wore under his shirt and felt his contentment soar. Turning, he carried the water and poured it into the large drum that he kept to water his crops with. John-John was enjoying riding the wave of good fortune that had come his way and as far as he was concerned, life had never been better. Wiping the sweat off his brow he splashed some cool water on his face and gazed upwards at the semi-overcast skies. Noticing the resplendently translucent arch of the rainbow he exclaimed in delight as a tiny tingle of déjà vu swept over him. "But a-a, look thing, it reaching in my garden!"

Moongazer Found

The suspension of the old Datsun bounced up and down and groaned in protest as Junior pelted down the empty road. His headlights sprang to and fro and each time he would try to manoeuvre around a pothole and fail he would let loose a loud steups. Junior knew some of the potholes by heart, but as of late there seemed to be more and more of them appearing and he suspected it was due to all those big trucks that were using this road to transport their loads of material to the Point Fortin development.

His window was down and the chilliness that came with the five a.m. hour seeped into the car but Junior didn't mind. The smell of the dew and the wet earth calmed him. With his arm hanging out the window and his half-smoked cigarette clamped firmly between two fingers his journey continued.

Suddenly an unexpected hole appeared before him and Junior dropped his cigarette onto the road as he let loose a yelp and jerked the wheel to the right. As his back tire crashed into the hole and the back bumper scraped against the road Junior sucked his teeth and cursed.

"This blasted road go mash up meh car!"

As he adjusted the radio to hear Richie Spice singing that the world is a cycle, he felt his nerves calm down as he settled back into his seat. Working night shifts wasn't ideal but he liked the silence and the fact that the night-time pushed away the sweltering heat of the day. Plus there was no traffic...not that there ever really was much traffic on the oilfield's winding back roads.

He was coming up to a crossroad when he sensed a static charge in the air. His pores raised as a chill flushed through his body, leaving him gripping the wheel with both hands until his fingers ached. Looking out the windshield at the cloudless night he felt his stomach drop. Something was wrong. Something was about to happen. Stories about the number of accidents and tales of the ghosts that lingered in the area waiting for unsuspecting drivers ebbed into his mind.

Wasn't there something about this crossroad? About an old woman who hated men? Or something about her having no head? Something about her appearing in the backseat of cars, causing the driver swerve off the road when he looked up into his rear-view mirror?

Junior swallowed and braced himself to look into the mirror. His foot hovered over the brakes, and as his breathing quickened, he glanced up as quickly as he could into the mirror, fully prepared to see *her*.

The backseat was nothing but darkness. If she was there he couldn't see her. But he had to know for sure. Stealing a glance over his shoulder he confirmed that there was nothing there. Breathing a sigh of relief, he turned his attention back to the road just as the large dip he didn't even know was there appeared before him.

He jerked the wheel to the side, screaming as his car spun out towards the approaching crossroad.

"AH CHUT!" he bellowed, as he reflexively whipped the wheel from left to right and pumped the brakes which only caused the car to fishtail across the roadway and into the intersection.

Then, out of nowhere, something white flashed before him and hit the rear driver side with enough force to send his car careening off the road in the opposite direction. Even though he could see his world spin and then jolt violently once more as the car came to rest against a tree with an ear splintering metallic crunch, it felt as if time had slowed down and his world had gone completely silent and still.

Junior pushed against his car door and found himself unable to get out. As his head throbbed, he felt panic rising in his throat, acidic and bitter like bile. He was going to throw up and he needed to get outside. It didn't matter that he'd just been in an accident, all that mattered was that he had cleaned his car just last week and he was not about to sully its interior with vomit.

Freeing himself of his seatbelt, a nasty habit his bird had nagged into him, he climbed over to the passenger's side and crawled through the open window just as a jet of sour Chinese food forced itself past his lips. As he wiped his mouth on the back of his hand he straightened up and winced at the pain that was now blossoming on his chest and neck where his seatbelt had been.

He stood looking at his car in disbelief as its headlights illuminated both the ground and the night's sky. Overcome with a sense of helplessness, his anger erupted as he stumbled back towards the crossroad, ready to confront the driver of the white car that had hit him. He'd never seen the car coming so it had obviously been driving recklessly with its lights off. That driver was in for the licking of his lifetime regardless of what state he was in, Junior thought to himself.

At the edge of the road Junior scanned for the car under the gleam of the moonlight but found nothing. The place was eerily calm and serene. Walking over the spot where the broken glass and fragments of his car had been torn off, Junior was preparing himself to scream when the whiteness of a nearby electricity pole caught his attention. The pole seemed to glow almost ethereally and as Junior stopped and stared upwards he immediately began backing away as his mind reeled.

There had been no white car. There had been no other driver. And had he not already been out of control, there would have been no more Junior. The reality seemed utterly unbelievable for there stood the creature known as Moongazer, or Phantome to those who had never seen him, at the crossroads with his legs poised on either side, ready to crush any man, child, or beast that had the misfortune of passing through. Like a surreal scarecrow, he stood taller than any building Junior had ever seen, limbs long and lingae with his gaze cast towards the almost suede-like darkness of the night's sky.

Junior sat down at the edge of the road unable to function anymore. The pain in his chest began to ache and lance as his adrenaline slowly wore off, and he thought that he was about to start screaming at any second. And if he did, he knew that moongazer would notice him and likely crush him to death.

Man, get a hold of yourself and go get help. It was a logical thought but it was easier said than done under the circumstances. The nearest police station was, well it was out of the question. Which left the nearest house. Since Junior was on foot, there was nothing else he could do except go back, because if he went forward, moongazer might notice him, and if that happened…

As the world darkened, Junior looked up just as a cloud drifted into place and blotted out the moonlight. Moongazer seemed to come alive in that moment and Junior cringed and tried to make himself as small as he could in the hopes of going unnoticed.

The tall creature shifted and stepped one foot onto the road and causing the asphalt to warp and crack before he was off, and without allowing rational thought to set in or chewing over what he was about to do, Junior set off after him.

The idea of following this being did not pan out as Junior's limited imagination had envisioned it would. The sheer darkness of the forest as Junior stumbled into it was suffocatingly overwhelming. In his mind he'd always imagined that the trees would be black marks against the navy blue sky while the dark green shrubbery and undergrowth would be dotted by silvery kisses of rocks bathed in the sheen of white light. It was an arguably romanticized notion no doubt influenced by Hollywood itself. As it stood, the canopy above was immediately dense two feet in and the idealistic notion of his night-time forestscape was quelled as the lands stole his senses and disoriented him to a near dizzying effect that was heightened by the crackling static screech of the night-time insects that surrounded him.

With no choice, Junior moved back to the roadway whose cut path provided him with relief. Gazing up at the trees ahead he could trace the path of the creature as it stalked through the forest simply by listening to the rustle and cracking of the foliage as it moved.

Without trying to understand his need, Junior followed the road, trailing behind Moongazer hoping to gain some insight as to why he'd done what he was famed for doing, but more than that, Junior felt as though he needed to see him again, needed to know that he hadn't completely lost his mind.

That wish came to fruition as Junior found him standing at yet another intersection, looking up at the sky as he was known to do. He could hear him now, humming softly under his breath a slow and sad song that made Junior's eyes water. Suddenly, Moongazer stopped and sighed as he stepped off to the side of the road. The skies were growing lighter now and Junior listened to the sounds of the phantome's movements.

As the birds began to stir and the faintest light touched the sky Junior took off, delighted that the long path was not hard to follow. It was easier than tracking any small and wily critter at any rate.

The trail of disturbed brush stopped at the base of an incredibly large tree whose smooth trunk held an ivory shine to it. As Junior touched the trunk he could feel a deep pulsing warmth coursing below the surface and his eyes followed the bark upwards to where it split and trailed down into a separate trunk on the other side of him.

He knew it then that he was standing before the legs of Moongazer and in knowing what could happen he felt a queasiness boil in his belly. But the tree stood firm and rooted.

Junior tried to spot its face but soon saw that there was none. Instead Moongazer had transformed into the tallest tree in the forest with a mass of dark green waxy looking leaves that formed a wide spread crown. The sheer size of it reminded him of the famous Silk Cotton tree along Northside Road in Tobago but this tree stood much taller. Maybe even twice the height.

As he stared up in awe from between the giant arch of legs Junior knew he had to do something. Moongazer had apparently been plaguing this area for some time now and after what had happened to him he was sure that the numerous reported deaths, accidents, and even disappearances in the area had to have been because of this being.

His option was to go back to the town and gather a group of people. Perhaps they could chop the tree down before nightfall. But the more he thought about it the more absurd the idea sounded. No one would believe him. Maybe he could bring the group and they could wait until nightfall and see for themselves. That plan seemed reasonable but brought to mind a host of other problems, the main one being, what if Phantome killed them all?

That left Junior on his own. He had to act fast least this beast awaken from its slumber. But what could he do? He couldn't possibly chop down such a massive tree on his own. And what if Moongazer came to life once more as he was doing it?

There had to be another way. Junior reached into his pocket for a cigarette to help him think and as he lifted the lighter to its end an idea took hold. Looking around he began gathering the dried brush, hoping that the dew hadn't dampened it too much. As he formed a pyre of sorts around both legs of the tree he set about lighting them with the lighter that was mercifully still in his pocket. Junior was in luck as the kindling caught with little effort and soon the smoking tendrils curled into the morning air as the fire crackled and came to life.

Suddenly the massive tree shuddered and its trunk and

branches popped and groaned as the tree began to sway back and forth; a noise that sounded eerily akin to bamboo being pushed around in the wind.

A low moaning sound began all around him and as the deep cry grew into a howl Junior pressed the heels of his palms against his ears, creating a vacuum that could blot out only a fraction of the sound. Suddenly the tree spoke.

"Creature, I beg of you, put me out please!"

Junior shook his head feeling braver now than he had ever felt before. "No, Phantome. You have caused us people too much trouble and your habit of crushing us between your legs must come to an end."

The fire was spreading and Junior retreated as the tree shuddered and moaned once more.

"I do not mean to, creature. We are a peaceful kind. Our only purpose is to go home, it is why we look to the night's sky. Please, have mercy, put me out and leave me be."

The fire was spreading upwards and splintering outwards as a draft blew through the forest. There was nothing Junior could do and nothing he would have done even if he could. As he made his way back towards the crossroads he could hear Moongazer screeching in agony as the flames consumed him.

It would only be later, as Junior sat at the local corner bar with the warmth of the Puncheon burning in his belly, that he would give thought to Moongazer's final words.

Junior poured out another drink for himself and swallowed it in one whole gulp. He felt his head swirl, and as a hand clamped down on his shoulder, he looked up into the face of Mootoo.

"I hear you get into a big accident on the Oilfield Road!" he declared, and a miserable Junior nodded.

"You hear about the bush fire? It happened not too far from where you crash. Hundreds of acres just up in smoke. They still trying to put it out!"

Again Junior nodded as he poured one more drink. "I know. I was there."

"Eh-heh?" Mootoo took the bottle and poured a drink for

himself with a grin. Setting the almost empty pint on the table he patted Junior on the shoulder. "Doh worry, man. You go get the car fix up."

Junior nodded yet again in the hopes that Mootoo would just go away now that he'd gotten his free drink. The car was a write off but he didn't care about that anymore. It was the sheer weight and magnitude of Moongazer's pleas that wore heavy on his mind. The implication of who or what moongazer was, was almost more than he could bear to comprehend. Junior planned to drink until the words were blotted out of his memory.

As he poured the last of the clear liquid into his glass he nodded and motioned to Moonan, who stood behind the counter, for another bottle. Moonan produced the bottle with a frown as he examined Junior, but as they locked eyes the unspoken words that often pass between patron and barkeep were understood and Moonan nodded as he cracked the bottle's seal.

Sonny

Sherene awoke in a cold sweat, alert and aware as the loud pop reverberated within the recesses of her sleep-heavy mind. Had it been a noise in the house? In her dreams? Lying as still as she possibly could, she clutched the coverlet to her chest and strained her ears in the darkness of the night. When a full minute had passed without a sound she felt her muscles relax slightly, and as her courage built itself up she lifted her head and peered over the edge of the sheet and through the half-opened door that led to the living room where the harsh streetlight cast its ominous orange glow. Nothing moved.

In the kitchen the ancient, yellow fridge groaned and popped again and Sherene felt the tension ebb from her body entirely as she relaxed against the pillow. *Just that goddamn fridge protesting against the heat of the night.*

Her eyes drooped, heavy with sleep once more as the silence carried on, disturbed only by the soft white noise of the oscillating fan at the base of their bed, and just as she was in between that delicate state that lay somewhere between sleep and wake, another unexpected pop rudely drew her out of her drowsing just in time to see the massive shadow of the beast slink past the open doorway.

Her heart lunged itself into her throat and her chest ached

under her attempt to conceal her rapid breathing. For a moment she tried to convince herself that it had been all in her mind. That she'd conjured up the image in the dead of night in a self-destructive manner.

Looking to her right, she saw that Salman was dead asleep and as peaceful and utterly unaware as always. Trying to match her breathing to his she found it all but impossible as she could hear the creature's snuffing and chuffing as it moved back and forth across the living room. The soft clattering of a plate in the dish rack caused her heart rate to drum erratically, and with it her bladder throbbed. *Jesus Christ, Lord Almighty, grant me the serenity to not pee myself tonight!*

Easing up at a snail's pace, least the movement make the bed squeak, she peered over the edge and gazed out at the thick salt circle, hoping and praying that it was intact. She knew that it was, she had checked it herself before they'd gone to sleep but there was always that little niggle of doubt that had a habit of squirming its way into your mind, much like people wonder if they left the stove on, or the door unlocked after they've left their homes. But this was far more serious than that, and right now she needed that ring to be intact. If not…she didn't want to think about what would happen.

Squeezing her thighs together she was about to lay back down when the creature let out a small growl. The sound was amplified by the echo within the sparsely filled concrete walls of the house and the silence of the night. Without meaning to, she jerked in surprise and the metal springs of the bed creaked in response.

As the air stilled and went thick, Sherene clasped her hand against her mouth to stifle her scream as the creature rushed into the room. It badly wanted to get at them but the salt ring stopped it dead in its tracks.

Annoyingly enough, Salman still remained undisturbed. *That man could sleep through the end of the world,* she thought to herself as the thing, the thing that affectionately called her *Mummy* by day, paced around the circumference of the ring, testing for a way in.

In the beginning they'd tried getting help after being awoken by the opening front door. They'd rushed out to see the beast leaving the house dressed in the tattered remnants of Sonny's pyjamas. When they found Sonny, hours later after the sun had risen, he was sound asleep on the sandy base of the savannah's cricket pitch, and awoke with no recollection of what had happened to him. They immediately took him to the doctor who'd found nothing wrong. *Sleepwalking.* That's what they'd told the doctor had happened, and in turn he'd told them that it was more than a common occurrence for children of Sonny's age to sleep walk.

They went home and the conversation was heated as they tried to decide who they should seek for help. Sherene suggested the pundit. Clearly the child had demons in him and needed a good puja to exorcise the spirits plaguing their boy. But Salman disagreed. He believed that the boy had been hexed, that what was needed was a visit to the obeah man.

They couldn't agree on a course of action and as night drew near, a fearful Sherene had agreed to let Salman put the salt ring around the child's bed, something he said he'd learned from his grandfather's stories when he was a boy.

It was almost one in the morning when the howling and screaming began. The salt ring had worked but the beast was clearly distraught at being caught in such a confining space. The wrought iron bed trembled against the floor and made the house vibrate as the beast leaped up and down in rage. Never had they heard such sounds in their life, and soon enough all the neighbours had heard it too, and that was when the pounding on the front door began.

There was no way they could explain away the events and at first the villagers had been convinced that it was Salman, that he had been the one to transform into the beast. And Sherene had to admit, it was a logical choice. Salman was a big man, dark as pitch, with a deep voice and a shock of hair. On the outside he was fearsome, but the truth was that he was as mild as a kitten.

That one incident had been the real start of trouble though, and as sure as Captain goat had a traitor on his boat, trouble had found its way to their house.

Sonny didn't have any more incidents for the next week but word spread quickly as it tended to do and Salman began to find himself being pelted with little stones and sticks from the children who would hide in the culverts as he walked past. Within days the shopkeepers and bartenders refused to sell him and the neighbours no longer greeted him when they saw him. Everyone was afraid.

The worst blow came at the end of the week when TTPOST told him that there had been too many complaints and that they had to let him go. People didn't want him coming into their yards to drop off the mail anymore and no one wanted to say why. A plead to be reassigned had gone unanswered with a sullen shake of the head and that was it. Just like that the family had lost their only source of income.

Salman had cried that night and it was the first time Sherene had ever seen him so distraught. They'd packed up and left a few days later without a word to anyone. Sherene knew that if they stayed it was only a matter of time before someone tried to kill her husband, or worse yet, they figured out it was Sonny and killed her only child.

For four years they moved around, taking whatever odd job they could find to get by. And once Sonny's episodes became known they would pack up and move to another town. To say life was hard was an understatement. At first their money had been spent towards the men of the cloth; pundits, priests, imams, even obeah men and women, but none of them had been able to cure Sonny. This had become their curse to bear, and so they began working towards building a house in the middle of nowhere, one that would serve to contain and protect their beloved boy.

Now here she lay, locked in their big concrete house that stood isolated on the lot of land and far away from any neighbours, the house with steel bars over every external door and window, the house that had become her prison.

The beast stamped its feet in a rage and she looked up into

its eyes searching their depths for any sign of her boy, any trace of her little choonkaloonks, but the black, murderous hatred that stared back at her made her heart ache. Whatever it was he turned into, it took him over completely.

Testing the ring again, it paced around the bed and Sherene could smell the stink of sulphur that rolled off its body in hot waves. The fan circulated the smell and Salman's nose twitched in his sleep as he grunted, rolled over and buried his face into his pillow.

The beast growled, low and deep, a feral sound that came from deep within and bore the threat of death. With her bladder lancing she reminded herself to buy a posey to keep under the bed. This was pure agony in more ways than she cared to count.

With an annoyed grunt, the beast glanced through the curtained windows, pausing for a moment as it considered some unknown, before it dropped down to all fours and began slowly counting the salt grains one by one, hoping to count its way through an opening in the ring so that it could get at its prize.

Watching the beast sitting hunched over in the darkness, Sherene knew it would never make it through the ring. Yet still she continued to watch over it until her eyes grew fatigued and her mind began to wander. Feeling like the grit of the salt was in them, her lids drooped lower and lower and she once more fell asleep without even realizing it.

As her breathing evened out Sonny looked up at her and sniffed the air before he resumed his counting. One day he was bound to make it through, and if his calculations were right, tonight would be the night.

GOING FOR GOLD

With our boots squelching against the slick forest floor we made our way back to camp under the quickly fading daylight after having what I would call a rather successful day. With Artho in the lead, I slipped my hand into my pocket and caressed the small golden nugget, one of three we'd uncovered today. It was a more than promising sign that the spot we'd chosen was a good one and I could almost feel it in my blood that tomorrow we'd be even luckier.

My mind was on getting back to camp and on checking up on Yams who'd left us to head back around lunch time after complaining of a headache. The truth of the matter was that he was sweating more profusely than any of us, and though none of us wanted to even think it, I was sure he'd contracted the dreaded malaria.

As the light faded further, like a curtain coming down or a heavy eyelid slowly closing on itself, the forest gradually slipped into an almost disorienting shroud of darkness. We trudged on, talking and laughing and recarving our path as we went. To say we were a rowdy bunch was an understatement. We were greenhorns, all of us, and this was our first time mining for gold in the deep depths of the Guyanese rainforest. We were friends, a group of misfits hunting for that big payout, the one that would let us all retire early, and it was close, I could feel it.

Though it was our first gold run, we'd all grown up in the area. We all knew how to hunt, how to navigate the forest, and how to listen to the sounds around us and move to suit. We were born on the forest outskirts, played at its edge as children, hunted its outer sanctum with our fathers when we were teenagers, and now that we were men ourselves, we'd entered into its inner layers almost as a rite of passage.

With a solid two weeks' worth of supplies and a Region 8 base camp a mere two miles away we were set and sitting nice and easy. This was honestly more like a camping trip than work, but at night we tended to be louder than usual as if our boisterous laughter and cantankerous cackling would hold the crushing darkness of the forest and all the dangers it held at bay. I think for some, being extra loud was a defence against our own fright, as well as a warning to anything that may have been around.

As we broke the wall of green and stepped into the circle that served as our camp a roaring fire greeted us with a crackling welcome, and the thick, black blanket of mosquitoes that had been following us fell back against its heat and smoke so suddenly I could almost sense their disgust and disappointment.

"Aye, Yams! Where you?" I called out but the head that emerged from the other side of flames made us all take a sudden step back.

Artho's grip on his gun tightened as he lifted it slightly, and though his initial reaction had been to size up the intruder, mine had been to wonder if we'd stumbled into the wrong camp. A quick glance around at the six hammocks confirmed that this was indeed our camp so who was this strange face peering at us through the flames?

"Hello!" Her voice was like golden syrup, thick and sweet and rich. She came around the fire with a brisk confidence that made it seem as though she belonged.

"What yuh want? Yuh lost or something? Yuh need help?"

Artho's voice was cautious, but we were all spellbound by her beauty and Artho himself was no stranger to being led astray by a gorgeous woman.

"Help me?" A soft and melodic laugh ebbed out from between her full lips. "Actually, it's the other way around. I'm here to help you boys out."

"Where Yams?"

"Who?" She scrunched up her face for a moment before she nodded. "Oh, you mean the skinny lil one! He gone."

Artho's grip on his gun tightened once more. "What you mean *gone*?"

She saw him growing defensive and placed her hands on her wide hips and arched an eyebrow at him. "Listen mister, don't think I don't see you there with your gun, if you going to shoot me, then shoot me, but don't play around with me, you hear? Now, your friend came out to the base camp because he wasn't feeling well and the doctor there called in the boat to take him to the hospital. He told us where you were so I came over to make sure you boys were doing alright. If you don't want me here just say so and I will leave."

Her words were sharp and direct and it was clear we'd upset her so I spoke up. "I'm sorry, it's just surprising to see you here. This is no place for...for a woman, you know? It have dangerous things in these forests so forgive my friend here and please feel free to stay. My name is Kadeem, but everyone calls me Bush."

"Let me tell you something, I know more about what living in this forest than all of you put together, you hear me?" Her voice was no longer stern and her admonishment was good natured. She smiled. "I am a woman, but trust me when I tell you I know my way around, so never you mind about me, mind yourself first!" She turned and moved around the fire. "Now, I make a stew, so if you want some come and eat, if not, fix up for yourself. I is not your mother."

She hiked up her skirt and bunched the fabric between her shapely legs and I couldn't help but stare at her soft features and her smooth skin. She seemed to be about our age, no older than mid-thirties, yet her movements felt almost maternal. Flicking a strand of hair so dark that it was almost iridescent over her creamy shoulder, she looked up at me with brown eyes that spoke of the wonders of the warmth of a late afternoon sun. Patting the empty space on the log next to her, she invited me over, and as I sailed to her and sat down I relished at the jealous tutting that came from the others.

Dipping her pot spoon into the large black cauldron-like pot, she handed me a boiling bowl of stew and indicated that I should pass it around as she began filling another bowl.

With our bellies unreasonably full, we sat around the fire whose flames seemed intent on licking the canopy that lay high above us, and smoked our cigarettes.

We'd learned that our new guest's name was Maria and that she, much like us, had lived on the outskirts of the forest all her life. Her father owned a large lot of land deep within the jungle and so she learned how to not only survive but to mine gold herself. As she relayed some obscure tips and tricks to us we sat in rapt awe and I found myself wondering why she was working at the base camp instead of making her living mining like we were trying to do. It was clear that she was far more knowledgeable than we were on the matter. But as the talk went on, we learned that she seemed content to simply exist and that was astonishing to us all. Never before had I met anyone who was so close to the allure of mining but hadn't been touched by the fever of it. Lost in her words and stories we listened as she spoke of the jungle and its many secrets.

As the time slithered on by, I felt my eyes suddenly grow heavy and my body tilt forward. Drunk with the darkness and the food that sat in my stomach, I yawned and drew in a deep breath.

"Aye fellas, I think I calling it a night, oui. I tired fuh so."

Heavy-headed nods and murmurs of agreement rippled through my friends, and with sluggish resolve we all made our way over to our hammocks and settled in for the night leaving an amused and still bright-eyed Maria sitting by the fireside.

The night was over in the blink of an eye and we awoke to

the sounds and smells of frying fish. Sitting up in my hammock I looked over at the fire that was either still burning or had been rekindled, and saw Maria squatting next to it with a handful of skewered sardines.

Going about our morning ritual, we ate our meal and drank our bitter instant coffee, relishing as our energy levels slowly rose. Our chattering was even more energetic than usual, save except for Mouse who seemed unusually quiet.

"What happen to you?" Artho asked him.

With a shake of his head he shrugged. "I don't know, nah. I not feeling too good." The corner of his mouth trembled slightly as if he were suppressing a smile.

Maria looked up at him with a frown. Reaching over she rested the back of her hand against his forehead and her frown deepened further. "You should go see the doctor at the base camp."

Mouse made no protest and simply nodded as he picked at his fish but Artho grunted as though he knew something the rest of us didn't. I looked to him with a questioning expression but he softly snorted and shook his head—his way of telling me to just leave it be, whatever it was.

Our mood fell away as we packed our bags and knocked out our shoes against any unwanted squatters before slipping them on. We were ready for the day ahead and so we set out, our six man team now down to four.

The first mile out we kept the silence until Theo spoke. "Allyuh feeling it to, ent? That something wrong with that woman somehow. Like she too good to be true."

Artho nodded. "I was feeling it since yesterday."

"You think she…?"

A sudden sharp snap from behind us made us all turn around with a jump. The path stood empty but it was clear that we'd all heard it.

We stood stock still for minutes, looking around, alert to any noise or sounds, but the surrounding foliage held its secrets. Another snap in the distance made me jump and I found myself questioning if the sound we heard hadn't been further than we thought. The forest has the ability to do that, to mask sounds, to cast them outwards in all directions, and out here it was sometimes hard to trust your own ears and eyes.

Artho lowered his gun and we continued onwards but before long he stopped and turned around in one swift motion, drawing the barrel of his shotgun upwards and firing off a round. We all went deaf in that moment having had no chance to plug our ears against the blast that ricocheted off the trees around us. I knew I was yelling, that I was screaming at Artho, asking him what was wrong, what he'd seen, if he'd lost his bloody mind, but all I could hear was the shrill high-pitched hissing of my stunned eardrums. It took some minutes but the hissing mercifully subsided and the sounds of the woodlands slowly returned. I found myself feeling dizzy and disoriented, but Artho stood firm and so too did I as I brought my own barrel up and scanned the surrounding area. "What is it?" My words sounded wet and muddy.

"I not sure, but whatever it is, it following we for a while now."

"Maybe it's Mouse?"

Artho shook his head. "I caught a slight glimpse, it wasn't Mouse. Besides, Maria will be keeping him plenty busy."

I looked at him but he kept his gaze forward.

"So what was it?" Akeem asked, having heard our conversation. Theo who had been standing closest to Artho's gun still hadn't recovered his hearing.

"A forest cat, and by the looks of it, a big one too."

My mouth dropped open as my eyes frantically scanned all around us. I hadn't heard anything, hadn't seen any signs. Chills ran through my body as I considered how utterly unaware I'd been. I thought my little experience hunting would have proven useful in knowing if I were the one who was being hunted.

"You think we should head back?" Akeem's voice was almost a whisper.

Artho seemed to consider for a moment before he shook

his head. "No. I think we just need to be alert and make our way to the dig site as quickly as possible, but we will be going back earlier than usual, I'm not chancing darkness catching us out here tonight, and you can be sure we will be sleeping in shifts from now on."

The day dragged by and though our haul of gold was even more than the day before no one felt like celebrating. By the time we got back to camp there was still plenty of daylight left. Mouse's belongings were gone except for his hammock and there was no sign or trace of Maria anywhere. As we got the fire going and prepped for the night, Artho seemed troubled. Popping open a jar of pickled pork's feet I gnawed on what would be our dinner and wished I could have one more bowl of Maria's stew.

The night wore on and our usual talk fell away as each man seemed to be preoccupied with their own thoughts. I found myself wondering just what had become of our expedition and more importantly, what tomorrow would bring.

When it came turn for my shift, I sat up with a groggy head, almost forgetting to knock out my shoes. The fire was going and Artho clapped me on the shoulder and nodded before he went to his hammock and zipped himself in. Sitting before the fire, I listened to the sounds around me, trying my best to be alert to anything that sounded unusual, or worse yet, approaching, but without realizing it I slowly drifted off and fell asleep, leaving us all vulnerable and exposed to the beasts of the forest.

The hand that covered my mouth was soft and slender. It staunched my blood-curdling scream as I fought to sit up against the heavy weight that sat on my chest. A familiar laugh bubbled up from my assailant and I instantly relaxed as the fire-lit silhouette of Maria came into view.

She slowly moved her hand away from my mouth and shifted her weight so that that she was no longer suffocating me.

"What-?"

She pressed a finger against my lips to silence me. "Shhh,

don't wake the others."

I sat up and she leaned back, angling herself so that her features were cast into a soft glow by the light of the low-burning fire.

"You walked through the forest in the middle of the night by yourself? You mad or what?" I whispered.

Her form shook with her silent laughter. "It have no need to worry about me. I know what it have out there and how to keep myself safe." Her hand slid up my chest and cupped my jaw as her expression melted into want.

Like a confluence, my lust and unease flowed together, but as she leaned forward and pressed herself against me all thoughts ceased. Her breath was hot against the side of my neck, and as I strained against her I heard a mumble come from one of the hammocks.

With a soft snicker she retreated and stood on the outskirt of the fire's light with her head cocked. "Come on, let's find a more *private* spot before we wake up the others. I know one not too far from here."

Common sense told me that this wasn't a good idea. Given that a jungle cat had been stalking us, just walking off into the dense vegetation in the middle of the night by ourselves was the height of stupidity. But as any man can tell you, when your blood is singing with heat common sense tends to fall to the side.

Taking her hand, I followed after her and together we left the light of the camp's fire behind and made our way through the dense jungle, utterly oblivious to the pair of eyes that trailed along after us, watching, stalking, waiting for the right moment to strike.

We emerged about ten minutes later into a clearing where another fire was burning low. Looking around, it seemed like this camp was relatively new. I had no idea there'd been one set up so close to us.

"Is this yours?" I asked as I spotted the large black stew pot and utensils near the fire.

She nodded as she looked at my face, trying to read my

reaction but I had none. My mind was blank as it tried to figure out why she'd have her own camp in the middle of the forest…one that was strategically set up so near to us.

Pressing herself against me she sighed and nuzzled the side of my neck. "I wanted to join you boys at your base, but it didn't seem like you all wanted me around." She whined softly against me and I felt my heart melt. We'd been so rude and unwelcoming to her that she'd opted to face the dangers of the forest by herself just to be near to us…to me.

"You…you can join our camp. I'm sure the others would love to have you, I know I would." My breathing was coming in hard and fast now as she ran her fingernails along my back.

"I'd like to have you too…"

With her face still buried against my neck I could feel her lips brush against my feverish skin. Running her tongue up to my ear she bit my earlobe as I wrapped my arms around her and began leading us towards the fireside. She was the aggressor, pushing me to my knees and pressing me back into the heady earth as she climbed on top of me, the lengths of her skirts piling up against my hips. I reached out to touch her and she threw her head back, her long locks whipping around her as though they had a life of their own. She leaned forward and smiled at me and in that moment I knew I was hers. I would do anything for this woman, and in turn I knew she would lead me, us, towards a golden life. This is who and what I'd been searching for, not some shiny, glistening rock buried in the earth.

An exploding knot in the firewood caused her to jolt, and as she did, something strange happened. Her form flickered for a brief moment as though a shadow had passed before her. I felt her body tense as she sprang to her feet and looked around the camp, eyes wild.

"What's wrong? I asked sitting up. My head felt heavy as though I was coming out of a deep sleep.

"Someone's here."

"What? I didn't hear nothing" I was alert now and all too aware that I'd left my gun behind. We were defenceless and I was sure that the jungle cat who'd been marking us earlier had followed us here. "It could be a jaguar, there was one following us earl-"

"Shhhh!" She quieted me as her eyes frantically searched the perimeter of the camp looking for the intruder she was sure was there. As I watched her crouch over in an almost feral stance a figure emerged from the trees in the direction of our camp.

Seeing who it was her eyes narrowed to condescending slits as she righted herself.

"Artho?" I looked at my friend whose expression was nothing short of triumphant rage.

"I see, so is you. I should have known." Maria's tone was as hostile as Artho's expression.

My friend made no remark, but faster than I was able to register, he lifted his gun and fired a shot directly at Maria.

With a wounded yelp and a stream of curses, she turned and sprinted off at an almost superhuman speed into the jungle, and within moments she disappeared from sight as the wall of darkness swallowed her whole.

I was up and after her before I even knew what I was doing. My instincts had taken over and I'd seen the spray of blood that had jetted out of her. She needed my help, and I, I needed to get away from the still armed and rapidly advancing Artho who was very clearly out of his mind. But my legs only managed to tangle themselves against each other and I fell forward with a huff. Panicked, I looked up to find Artho at my side with a look of sheer terror and concern etched onto his face. Looking around us, he nodded to himself as he stripped off his shirt and pressed it against the wound on the side of my neck, a wound I wasn't even aware was there.

"We have to go. Now."

"I...I don't understand...what...where's Maria? WHAT YUH SHOOTIN' AT MARIA FOR?!"

Dragging me to my feet, he cursed his luck that I seemed unable to function on any level, and as the snapping of branches approached us, Artho stood in front of me, lifted his gun, and fired off three rounds. I could see his shadow shaking as he struggled to reload his gun and that's when the creature appeared before us.

Hideous. That's the only word I can think of to describe it. Walking on elongated limbs that were clawed in the front and hoven in the back her stance mimicked that of an apex predator. The threads of saliva that dangled from her wide gaping maw revealed a massive toothy hole unlike anything I'd ever seen. Around its leopard spotted belly shreds of what was once Maria's skirts hung in bloody tatters, and around its neck, a thick jet black mane stood in spikes like that of an agitated cat.

"So you finally showing your true form, eh? No more pretty woman or jungle cat?"

The creature laughed. "There's no need for that anymore so what's the point? Besides, it will be easier to kill you both in this form."

I stared at it, at *her*, unable to wrap my head around what was standing before me. But there was no denying it, the voice that came out of this horrifying thing was certainly Maria's. This simply didn't seem possible.

The loud crashing that came from behind us distracted us all and as we turned to look both Theo and Akeem emerged with their guns drawn. Taking advantage of the moment, Artho unloaded all his shots at the Maria-beast, and in a stream of curses it charged at him. Slow to react to the absurd scene before them, Akeem was the first to raise the shotgun at the creature that was barrelling down on his friend.

The shots came in quick succession and blew the beast back but not before it lashed out with a ferocious intent and struck true. As he stumbled backwards, Artho held his bleeding face and turned towards Akeem and Theo.

"We have to go, NOW!" His command, slurred by his wounds, was enough to break our hazy disbelief.

Still unable to stand on my own, Akeem hurried over and picked me up. As he slung me over his back like a useless sack of rocks, we fled back to our camp all the while hearing the echoing laughter of the creature as it marked our passage from somewhere unseen.

Armed with torches and fully loaded guns Artho, Akeem, and Theo sat around the fire until morning, unmoving, unblinking, while Theo kept trying to reach the base camp on the radio. They never responded and I was later told that they'd left the camp once daylight broke and made their way to the base camp with an unconscious me in tow only to find it empty.

Fortunately the radio there worked and they were able to reach one of the nearby boatmen who was at another outpost. He came over at once and loaded us up and got us safely out of there.

I have no recollection of any of these events and came to days later in the sterile environment of the Linden Hospital. The last thing I actively remember was seeing a wounded jungle cat leaping at Artho's face, and even that is blurry in my mind. When they told me the story I couldn't believe it. There was simply no way that Maria, my Maria, had transformed into that demonic cat. But the half-eaten carcasses of both Yams and Mouse that had been recovered near to Maria's campsite, and the mottled mass of burning white scars that adorn the left side of my face and neck—scars that perfectly matched the rope-like slashes on Artho's face—stand as an eternal reminder of our harrowing escape from the powers of the bush dai dai's attack.

THE LEGEND OF GANG GANG SARAH

It was late one night in 1875
When Sarah heard the call of her kin.
A call that came from oceans away,
It was a call that permeated her soul and skin.

So the next morning she took flight
And she sailed across the skies.
Crossing land and ocean alike,
She followed the sound of her familiars' cries.

But a rogue northern wind
Sent poor Sarah flying sideways.
And her scheduled three day journey
Soon tripled into nine days.

When she finally landed in Les Corteaux, Tobago,
An exhausted Sarah made her way to Golden Lane.
And to the sugar plantation of Uncle Peter,
Where she found her kin free of their chains.

With a wide smile she greeted them all,
And they welcomed her with open arms.

Though there was one man in particular,
To whom she applied her feminine charms.

She knew this man quite well
For they'd been good friends in days gone by.
And as Sarah rekindled their friendship once again
She realized that it had been his call that'd made her fly.

Their wedding was a grand affair,
It was the talk of all the towns,
Officiated by none other than Uncle Peter,
Tom and Sarah were celebrated for miles around.

So lovely Sarah settled in
As the matron witch of Golden Lane.
And with her benign and beloved influence,
They soon added the mid-wife's title of "Gang Gang" to her name.

She comforted them and grieved over their losses,
And facilitated and celebrated in their births.
She provided them with potions for love and happiness,
And taught them how to reconnect with Mother Earth.

But then one day she felt the bitter sting of loss
When her beloved Tom passed away.
And when they buried him under the tallest Silk Cotton Tree
She lingered in Golden Lane for only one more day.

For when the sun rose the next morning,
She climbed to the top of the great Silk Cotton Tree.
And bid goodbye to the villagers who'd gathered
To support her in her time of need.

Standing on top of the tree's crown,
Sarah leapt with the intent to fly

Back to her home in Africa.
But Sarah never made it to the skies.

Instead poor Sarah plummeted to the ground
And suffered a tragic fate,
For she'd unknowingly lost all her powers
Because of all the salt she'd ate!

The villagers all wept and cried,
As they buried her beside her beloved's grave.
And there she lies to this very day,
Gang Gang Sarah, the African witch of Golden Lane.

Amber Drappier

TIPPING THE SCALES

Ah boy, times were hard! It seemed like the cost of everything was going up and up and up, while everybody's salary was going down. Imagine from last year to now the price of a loaf of Vita Loaf went up almost two whole dollars. And talk about layoffs. It was that time of the year again and everybody was feeling the heat. We were scruntin', plain and simple, and making a hustle was the only way to get by. Times were really hard, oui! And they didn't look like they were going to get any better...

***

The craggy chunk of concrete came sailing over the crowd, and though it was likely that it was only meant to stir up more bacchanal and create an even bigger uproar when it struck the little parlour's baby blue steel door, it instead struck Blue square on the side of his head.

It took a few moments for those nearest to him to realize what had happened, and like a ripple effect the mob fell silent with those to the front pushing backwards as all three hundred jiggling pounds of Blue came down. And when he landed, his head bounced against the hot concrete slab in the front of his shop with a sickening pop, and that was when the red began to spread like a river.

Like bulls, the crowd began to move, but instead of running

towards the thick, shimmering red fabric, they began climbing over each other to get away from it. Those who'd witnessed what happened began to scream, but none so loudly as Celia, Blue's devoted wife, who was already kneeling at her unresponsive husband's side, begging for someone to help her, begging for anyone to call for an ambulance, to do something, anything. But her cries went unanswered. It was every man for themselves.

When the ambulance arrived some forty minutes later, Blue was already turning cold despite the heat of the midday sun overhead, and by the time they loaded him up into the ambulance, a feat that took the three ambulance workers and a passer-by several minutes to achieve, Celia was inconsolable and could barely even lift her head as a few stray dogs wandered over and began lapping at the drying blood that was being baked into the concrete that hadn't been pressure washed since last year around Christmas time. It was a horrific scene, one that would mar the little village of Bamboo forever.

When the police began rounding people up for questioning, the investigation took an even darker than expected turn as the ugly truth began to emerge. The more people they spoke to, the more names and culprits were offered up, and it became apparent that the entire village seemed to have some part to play in Blue's death.

But why? Why had it happened in the first place? The answer to that was evident—Blue was an advantageous crook—but at the end of it all, no one they spoke to quite knew who or what it was that had brought it all to a head.

Those in the crowd all seemed to have a somewhat foggy memory of where they were and what they were doing moments before it all happened, yet everyone's stories began at exactly the same place, with people storming the shop and dragging Blue out into the front yard.

In the end, the police determined that in its own way, justice had been served. Besides, there simply wasn't enough resources to arrest or charge and entire village. And so it came to be that Blue's death went unpunished.

***

Blue had gained the majority of his great wealth thanks to his left thumb and his ruthlessness. He didn't care that the villagers had almost all fallen on hard times, that children and mothers were starving, that high class men had resorted to being day labourers if it meant getting work. No, Blue didn't care because he had it all figured out, and because of his business tactics he was able to thrive in a downed economy.

His little parlour served to supply many of the villagers with their meats and dried goods and if there was one thing that Blue knew how to do it was work the system. His prices were set at a rate that was just high enough for the villagers to not be able to justify taking a taxi to the next town over or to the big grocery store a few villages over. With little choice, they continued to patronize him until one day Madame LaCroix came out of the shop with a frown on her face. Holding her red and white striped crocus bag in her hand, she walked up the street until she arrived at the little wooden table that the fishermen had set up to sell their daily catch. With a pause she leaned over the table and whispered something to one of the men who nodded and picked up a sheet of newspaper. Holding out in his hands, he waited until she dipped into her bag and pulled out a plastic bag of dried lentils that she'd just bought at Blue's shop.

The fisherman placed the newspaper and the little bag of lentils onto the scale and together both he and Madame LaCroix watched as the little indicator tipped forward before spilling down and bouncing around under the weight. Finally it stood firmly between at one and a half pounds. Madame LaCroix's lips pinched together as she nodded and dipped into her bag for yet another little packet of peas.

With each weighed item her lips pulled in tighter and tighter until they'd all but disappeared. The old woman's face darkened a bit as she repacked her bag and returned to Blue's shop.

She approached the counter with the intent of giving him

the benefit of the doubt though she'd long since suspected Blue's unorthodox practices and had been watching him well as he weighed her goods. She'd seen him tip the scale with his thumb before quickly taking the packet off and setting it aside. But maybe it had been a mistake, maybe it was unintentional. She didn't think so.

Leaning over as far as the counter would allow she whispered to him that her goods felt a bit lighter than they should and asked him if he could kindly weigh them again and adjust as needed.

Blue straightened up and looked at her with a fire in his eyes. "Excuse me?" he began in an already defensive tone. There was no one else in the shop at the moment as he crossed his arms and unleashed his anger onto her. "You want to come here and accuse me of *what*? Robbing you of a handful of beans? You that greedy? Look, go on from here you ole quashie, before I run you down with my broom!"

With a small smile that made him nervous because of its unspoken promises Madame LaCroix gathered her bags and made her way out of the shop just as Ladoo, one of the regulars, sauntered in and asked, "What going on here?"

Blue shook his head in disgust. "Times hard for everybody and that ole *jagabat* coming here to make my life hell with a set of dotish ole talk!" The words shot from his lips like vitriol. Ladoo turned to look at the old woman who was already on the sidewalk and making her way home but said nothing as he turned back around to Blue and placed his order. He knew Madame LaCroix well enough to not interfere.

Night came, and with it a northern wind blew in, a wind that howled as it tried to force its way through the cracks and crevices of the homes, causing everyone to shutter themselves in for the night. As the streets stood empty save except for the periodic stray dog whose nails could be heard clicking along the asphalt, Madame LaCroix made her way down the sidewalk and came to a halt in front of the closed shop doors. Rooting around in her bag, she produced a small candle and a little satchel that she'd spent the evening preparing. Filled with a little prayer script, a ball of clay-textured grave dirt, a single white sensa fowl feather, and a pinch of dried herbs, she set it before the baby blue doors and lit her candle. The prayer was short, and as she ended it she allowed the breath of her final word to blow out the candle while holding the satchel over the curling tendrils of white smoke.

Taking both items she stashed them within the West Indian jasmine hedge that grew against the corner of the shop's exterior, then made her way home. Nothing and no one had seen her except for the fruit bats that streaked through the night sky and the night lizard whose coppery eye had spotted her coming and had scurried off to its dark corner. The only evidence of her presence had been a single drop of white tallow on the concrete floor in front of the shop.

Basking in the yolk of the orange streetlights, the craggy lines of her skin deepened even further as Madame LaCroix's face aged slightly as the obeah took hold and she made her way home. That was the price one paid for asking a favour of the gods, for nothing given was ever granted for free. Nonetheless, she knew that it had been done for the good of the village, and if Blue was really innocent then nothing terrible would befall him.

But as the days went by it became very evident that that wasn't the case, and as the Blue's patrons became more and more aware of his practices, things slowly began taking a turn for the worse.

His death had come as a surprise to her for it had never been her intention. All she'd wanted was justice and for Blue to do right by those who supported him and put the bread on his table with their hard earned money. If only he'd apologized and sought to make things right it would have all turned out differently. But instead he'd opted to come out from behind his counter and confront a few patrons who'd been commenting about his methods. The moment his wild gesticulations turned into a physical assault on Marilyn he'd signed his own death warrant as the mob had seemingly formed out of nowhere. And now look at what had happened.

With a sigh she went up to the bush and retrieved her items before they could be discovered by the police, or worse yet, by Celia. Slipping them into the folds of her dress, she picked a little bundle of the small four-petal orange flowers from the same hedge and made her way through the crowd to find and comfort poor Celia who remained inconsolable as the police launched into a series of rather blunt and brutal questioning.

That night the northern wind returned with a vengeance and Madam LaCroix awoke in a fright as the walls of her humble home shuddered and all her doors and windows shook in their frames. Sitting upright in her bed, she reached on the nightstand for her oil and quickly anointed herself. Some great evil was nearby and as the ground rumbled with the beast's approach, she crossed herself once more as the sound of dragging chains reached her ears. Could it be the Lagahoo? She wondered, but she knew that couldn't be the case. She knew his spirit well and he was not one to be filled with such hatred and malice.

Suddenly, a low howl rumbled across the rolling hills of Bamboo, and almost like a car alarm, the beast began to whoop and bellow loud enough to disturb Madam LaCroix's dinner as it sat in her belly. Pressing her hands against her ears she closed her eyes and began to pray. This was something else entirely, this beast was out for blood and she hoped that whatever it was, it wouldn't find it.

Hearing the almost muted sound of a scream, she was up and out of bed before she could register what she was doing.

As her bare feet thrummed across the still-warm asphalt she ran out to the roadway just in time to see the massive bull as it stood glowering over Leon. Though she had no idea why Leon was out and about at this ungodly hour, she knew if she didn't act now that the beast would surely kill him.

The beast was backed up slowly as it bobbed its head and snorted, scouring the roadway with its hoof. It was getting ready to charge and in the moment before it did, Madam LaCroix screamed out as she ran and stood between Leon and the beast whose flaming red eyes emanated the heat of its rage.

The beast gave pause and seemed to swell before her as a blast of heat enveloped her and seared her skin. Speaking in the old Patois, it addressed her.

"I should have known how much trouble a blasted quashie like you would have made, but mark my words, hag, vengeance will be mine. You and all the others have made your bed and now you will lie in it."

Black waves of seething hatred bellowed out of its nostrils, curling and wafting in the air around them as the beast grew and grew before their eyes.

Madam LaCroix shrank back in fright and closed her eyes as her lips silently moved, calling out to her father to deliver her home to his loving arms.

With a snort and a chuff the behemoth bull stamped his cloven feet against the roadway, and just as he was about to charge a loud snap rang out and the beast recoiled and reared up onto its hind legs. Standing at over ten feet tall from this position, a second crack issued forth and the beast screamed and retreated, leaving behind a trail of fire as it ran.

Her mouth agape, Madam LaCroix turned in relief to find Sunil standing a few feet behind her with a whip in his hand and a determined look on his face. When the beast was out of sight and the flames of its path burned down into nothing but scorches against the asphalt that resembled the skid marks of a tyre, he relaxed his stance and his body began to shake and tremble as he sank to his knees.

"What the jail was that?" he asked no one in particular.

Madam LaCroix shook her head. "Come on, let we make quick and go inside before it come back."

"It coming back?" Leon's voice squeaked in fright from behind her and without another word the three of them quickly and silently headed towards Madam LaCroix's little home.

Seated around her table, the silence was broken by Sunil. "I...I heard a bull calling and I thought mine had gotten loose so I came to see and chase it back home, but that...that wasn't no ordinary bull. I never see any bull like that." He looked at her and shuddered.

"No, it wasn't," she said finally as she threw a quick glance out the window, half expecting to see the beast staring back at her. "But we will be safe in here." Though she said the words she didn't quite believe them. Never before had she seen or dealt with such an evil power. Heaven only knew what it was capable of.

Turning to him she pointed at his whip with a twist of her lips. "Where you get that from?" she asked, curious as to how such a plain item was able to drive the beast away.

Sunil lifted the whip and looked at it as if seeing it for the first time. "This was Pa's whip. He used to use it to play mas. He was a jab-jab, you know, one of the best whip fighters around here. He did teach me before he died, but nowadays I does only use it to drive the cattle to and from the field."

She nodded in remembrance of his father, Errol. "Is a good thing you did come when you did, oui. That thing was probably going to kill we both." She looked towards Leon who was sitting in what she could only imagine was a daze.

"What was it?" Sunil finally asked.

She shook her head. "Not what, but *who*."

He frowned.

"He was a nasty man with a nasty spirit as rancid as the meat and eggs he used to sell we."

Sunil scrunched up his face as he thought for a moment before he shook his head. "Blue?" His guess was filled with doubt.

She nodded. "Blue."

The name settled in the silence between them.

"It said something to you, didn't it?" Leon's words were just a whisper. "I did hear it talking but it wasn't in no language I could understand."

Madam LaCroix nodded as she drew in her breath and once again gazed out the window.

"Well? What it say?" Leon pressed with a strange degree of urgency in his voice.

She lifted a hand to her head and sighed as a hard knot of

dread bore its way through her chest. Without looking at either of the men she cupped her head in her hands and felt her body grow weary as she related the words of the beast. And when she was done the silence that fell between them was as damning as the reappearance of Blue who would be come to be known as the Rolling Calf of Bamboo.

"He said that he'll keep coming back night after night until all of we here in this village ends up dead one way or the other…"

DRIVER

I leaned against the wooden porch railing and sighed. Rondell wasn't going to be able to pick me up tonight which meant that I had to make the walk all the way out to the main road to get a taxi. Stuffing my phone into my bag, I stared at the flutter of moths and flies that danced around the single hanging candescent bulb. I could feel the soft heat that came off of it and as the wind picked up I listened to the chatter of the coconut leaves as they shoo-shooed amongst themselves in competition with the screeching crickets.

It was going to be a long walk to the main road and the darkness of the night was nothing if not daunting. I was reluctant to leave the safety of the light but I needed to get to work. Taking a deep breath I stepped onto the roadway and began walking.

The skies were clear and cloudless, allowing the scatter of stars and the half-moon to partially illuminate my way. As the yellow glow of my porch grew smaller and smaller and then vanished behind me, I hugged my bag tighter and stared at the ground in front of me, once again telling myself that I needed to write that long-overdue and choicely worded letter to our local representative who'd promised us streetlights for longer than should have been legal.

As I walked my mind began to drift to what awaited me at the hospital. Most people tended to think it was the doctors who had it hard but that couldn't have been further away from the truth. The truth of the matter was that it was us nurses who worked our fingers to the bone.

We were expected to know everything about everyone and it was us who dealt with the worst situations while the doctors had the luxury of doing no more than paperwork, reviewing charts, and chatting with the patients for all of five minutes. Surgeons, of course, were different, those guys were really on a whole other level, but those cocky, fresh-out-of-school doctors who still had snot in their noses...

Running through the list of my patients in my mind, I mapped my plan of action for the night. There was Mrs. Monroe, she would likely need to be changed and cleaned up.

Flicker-flicker darkness.

Mr. Balkan needed to be checked on every hour to make sure he was responding to his new meds. I hoped beyond hope that Darlene had been doing it while I was gone. I doubted it though. Chances are if she saw a chance to slack off she would take it, and with Shirley away there was no one else to jump on her back and crack the whip.

Flicker-flicker darkness.

And then there was Mr. Sooksingh. I cringed. He had to be one of the most miserable people ever. He was abusive in everything he did and said. Just last week he'd sent one of my girls fleeing from the room after he exposed himself to her. That man was a real jackass in the truest sense of the word. But monkey knew what tree to climb and he never dared to pull any of his dotishness with me.

Flicker-flicker darkness.

And there was always a chance of new patients who would need looking after. Even if it was just for one night's observation I would still need to tend to them. Beds six, seven, twelve, seventeen, thirty-four and thirty-sex had been discharged yesterday so there was a guaranteed chance I'd have six new wards.

Flicker-flicker darkness.

Before I knew it I found myself veering off the asphalt and into the grass as I followed the glow of a lazily blinking green light that I'd unconsciously been following. I might have followed it into the bushes and kept on going had the light not stopped. Looking up, I found myself staring at the firefly as it crawled on the long blade of razor grass before it flew off and disappeared into the night.

I gathered my wits about me and cleared my mind. It was as if I'd been mesmerized by the light. I chided myself for not paying better attention to my surroundings, especially at this time of the night. Shaking off the incident, I moved back towards the road and stopped as I came to the edge. Something wasn't right. I felt a sudden wave of uneasiness wash over me as the gentle breeze that had been blowing turned cold.

Nervously I looked over my shoulder half-expecting to see someone, or worse yet, *something*, standing there waiting for me. But there was nothing there and I breathed a sigh of relief as I laughed at myself for being such a fool and allowing the night to get the better of my superstitions.

As I stepped back onto the road I smelled it in the air. Rain. But without a cloud in sight I wondered where it would come from. Before I could ponder on it too much I found myself stepping back as a flood of light washed over me. The soft hum of the car gradually grew louder and soon the lights became blinding enough for me to shield my eyes.

As the car approached it slowed down and stopped in front of me. I tensed and began preparing my escape route. I couldn't see the colour of the car, the plate, or the person driving. Perhaps I could run into the bushes where the firefly had been. Perhaps that had been a sign from my guardian angel…

"A-a! Is you family? How things? What you doing out here by yourself at this hour?"

The light inside the car came on and I looked up to see a familiar face but it was still one I couldn't quite place.

"Yuh don't remember me? I was in the hospital about three months ago. I did get into an accident with a van."

I vaguely remembered but there'd been countless people in and out of my ward in just the last month.

"Mark?" I asked, saying the only name that came to mind.

"Well yes! You have real good memory oui! Is me self. You want a ride? You going to the hospital?"

I hesitated, tempted by his offer but slightly disturbed by his sudden convenient appearance. "How you healing up?"

He lifted his arm and showed me the keloid scar that ran from his wrist to his elbow. "I still doing that physical-whatever twice a week but I better than ever man!"

I nodded. "If I could get a drop to the main road that would be nice."

"I could take you straight there if you want. I not going that way but really is no trouble. If it wasn't for you I wouldn't be here right now."

I nodded once more and glanced around. The feeling of dread was gone but I was still unsure. "If you sure it's not too much trouble…"

"Nah man! What kind of man I go be to drive off and leave a woman alone in the dark to walk when she going in the same direction as me? Come, come, let we go!"

I walked around the back of the car to the passenger side and as I did I glanced at the plate. Pulling out my phone I texted the plate number and Mark's name to Marleen before I got into the car.

PAL 4554 - Mark - former patient from 3mths ago, scar on right arm from wrist to elbow.

As I slid into the passenger seat the smell of incense enveloped me and I looked in the ashtray to see a few sticks of it poking out. The assortment of items that hung from his rearview mirror clattered as we drove off and he leaned back in his seat and laughed.

"Whey boy, what's the odds I go find you out here at this hour? You know I was only here visiting my buck-man family. They living Concord. I wasn't even going to take this road but something tell me to do it. You believe in that kind of thing?" he asked without ever once looking at me.

"I-"

Before I could finish he slammed on the brakes and brought the car to a sudden stop. I reached out to brace myself against the dashboard when I saw the tatu that was crossing in the middle of the road.

"Lord! Like he looking for death tonight!" Mark declared as he waited for it to get out of the way enough for him to go around it. "Anyways, I did never get to thank you and the doctors for saving me. I would of been a dead man if it wasn't for allyuh!" he laughed and his straight white teeth glistened in the darkness.

I smiled and nodded at him. "Well I glad to see you doing better. How's the pain?"

"Ah man, it was bad in the beginning but them pills allyuh give me sweet too bad, oui!"

He said something else but I didn't hear him because as he spoke I noticed a faint glimmer of light coming from the darkness that swirled around my legs. Leaning over I spotted the lazily blinking green light and as the firefly crawled up my leg and onto my knee I couldn't help but feel the unease wash over me again.

Mark stopped talking and turned to stare at me as I scooped up the lightning bug up into my hands and brought it to eye level.

"Put down your window and let it go." Mark said, his tone hard.

I turned to look at him and I could see the tension pulsing in his jaw as he looked ahead.

"You don't like them?" I asked.

He shook his head. "They're unnatural. Something about them makes me uneasy. I don't trust them."

"I think they're magical. I don't even know how they can make their body light up like that. It's fascinating. When I was small me and my brother use to collect them in jars and use them like lights. Our mother used to tell us they were fairies and she'd make us empty them out after an hour so they didn't die."

"My grandmother used to tell me they were the spirits of the dead and that we should never hold onto them but get away from them so they can go on their way or else they'll follow you."

The mood in the car changed in that moment and I could feel a slow boiling tension mounting. But it wasn't anger, it was something akin to fear and unease, or perhaps it was me who was projecting my own emotions. I cupped the bug in my hands and held it in my lap as we drove on in silence. I couldn't explain why, but I didn't want to part with it just yet.

We pulled up to the main road and as Mark turned his blinker on I shifted in my seat. "Right here would be fine, thanks."

I half-expected him to ask me if I was sure and to insist on dropping me off at the hospital, but he did neither. Instead he pulled off to the side and stopped the car.

"It was nice to see you again and I really just wanted to tell you thank you for everything you did for me."

I nodded as I got out. "I'm glad you're doing well. If you can, rub some aloe vera on the scar, or some cocoa butter if you have any, and it will make it go away. Thanks again and you take care of yourself." I closed the door and stood back as he turned the car around and drove back in the direction we came from. I could feel the bug crawling around in my palm and as I opened my hand, it flitted upwards and followed after the fading red taillights of Mark's car.

"I wonder why he turned around and went back?" I asked myself. Maybe he was going back to his family's place? Setting it out of my mind I moved to the corner and stopped the next taxi I saw.

I was halfway through my shift and just about to take a break when Marleen approached me. "Aye girl, I wanted to ask you something about that man who give you a drop." She held up her phone and showed me the text I'd sent her.

"What about him?" I asked as I set the stack of paperwork

down on my desk.

"I remembered him but I had to be sure." She said nothing more as she handed me a folder with a few sheets of papers dated from eight months ago. It was the hospital records for Mark Marshall confirming that he had indeed been a former patient but as I looked through the records I saw one thing that made my heart stop. I looked up at Marleen as I felt the room spin.

"You sure?"

She looked back at me and nodded. "I checked three times. It's right. He died shortly after being admitted from internal injuries."

"But I...I just..."

I stopped talking as bed nineteen's machinery began screaming for attention. Automatically everyone at the nurse's station, including myself and Marleen, turned and sprinted in the direction of the sound. I could hear the heart rate monitor flat lining and Marleen behind me screaming for someone to hurry up with the crash cart. I arrived first and pulled the curtain back just as a firefly lazily drifted past me. I turned and watched it circle the room while the others worked around me. Its path seemed random and it bobbed and weaved around the ward before disappearing through the open window.

Flicker-flicker darkness...

HOUSE OF CHIMES

[Author's Note: I wrote a similar story entitled "Keepers" that's been published in my short story collection, "The Shadow Things". However, even though it doesn't quite fit with any known Caribbean folklore, I really love this concept so I'm retelling it with a Caribbean twist.]

Growing up in Central and away from the city life fuelled my understanding and appreciation of the land, our people, and our culture. Hailing from the Amerindians, I held within me a certain pride for our way of life, and that was why I'd made the decision to abandon my studies at UWI and return home. The second I entered my hometown I felt relief spread over me. I was *home* and I knew that there was nowhere else in this world I'd rather be.

No one understood this better than my father who, needless to say, had had the same experience. So when he presented me with an opportunity of a lifetime I was helpless to say no. Like his father had done, and his father before him, I was granted my own plot of land to do with as I pleased. I chose the most logical choice; I would build a house and start my family.

The land was part of our people's heritage and its significance was something that we were taught to honour and respect from birth. We'd been taught to communicate with nature and how to give back for all that we took.

My house was a humble little board house that I'd built with my own two hands. It was labourious, but the end result was a picturesque, beautiful little home that sat in the middle of the lot, surrounded by forest on all sides. To the south there was a wide expanse of the massive pond could be seen from the back porch and to the north, a tiny sliver of the dirt road that led to and synced up with the rest of the village. To celebrate my new home my mother gifted me with one of her handmade wind chimes. Designed out of painted shells and long thin metal pipes, it was truly an amazing piece of art. I hung it in my drawing room with pride.

"The souls of our ancestors carry on the wind, and when you hear the chimes singing you will know that they are singing for you." She kissed my cheek and smoothed out my hair, looking into my eyes in a way that would often disarm even my foulest moods.

Outfitted with casement windows to the front and jalousie windows to the back, I found myself marvelling at how well ventilated the house was. Even on the hottest mid-April day, at the dry season's peak, the warm summer's breeze would flow through my home and keep the inside cool making the wind chime my constant singing companion.

At night I sit would on my back porch listening to the soothing croak of the frogs and crapauds in the pond and the incessant and rhythmic chirp of the crickets and cicadas, as they gathered around my home, attracted to the warm yellow glow of the oil lamps that I kept on the porch when I sat out there. These were the sounds that appeased my soul and reassured me of who I was and where I was. Plus, according to the legends, it was said that our people's history was preserved in the sounds of the nightlife. The elders in the village knew how to heed the noise of the insects and to understand the tales they told; tales we would have otherwise forgotten. The crickets, the frogs, the bats, even the fluttering wings of the night moths told their own story, and much like the wind through my wind chimes, the history of our people were all around us. One only needed to learn how to tune in…

When we visited the elders as overeager children, we used to sit with them outside under the moonlight and listen as they translated the stories for us. I'd tried on many occasions to learn but for whatever reason, I could never hear their words.

Still, the sounds of the night were sounds that brought me peace. They were sounds that I'd missed while away at university and it'd taken me weeks to realize that its absence was the root cause of my restlessness and near sleepless state. I just couldn't stand it. I was miserable. Spending time in university had only reinforced my love for my people's way of life as the urban sprawl and city life had damn near killed me; the noise, the loud, raucous people, the constant fast-paced lifestyle that got you nowhere, and the utter lack of appreciation for the environment were only a few of the things that deterred me from wanting to be a part of it. Everyone had their place in this world and while there were many who thrived in that environment, I just wasn't one of them.

My house was my idea of heaven. It was where I felt connected, where I felt my spirit at ease. Tonight, however, something was different. The air was colder as if the northern range had sent a rainy season cold front our way. Retreating from my porch in favour of the warmth of the inside, I shuttered myself away and was dismayed by the fact that I needed to wrap myself up just to keep warm. The weather had been a blistering and sweltering thirty-four degrees Celsius a few hours ago, so the sudden change was both alarming and unprecedented. I considered walking over to my parent's place for the night, but the wall of seemingly endless darkness intimidated me and kept me rooted to my home.

I'm not sure when it happened but at some point I fell asleep in my rocker, bundled up like a newborn baby. My dreams were troubled, and though I couldn't quite remember them, I awoke with a feeling of dread in my stomach. The world didn't feel right and my home suddenly felt like a cage. I looked around, trying to understand what was wrong with the picture when it hit me: it was the wind. It was howling and screeching like an animal in pain. One of the glass panes had somehow slipped downwards, creating a gap through which the wind was seeping in.

My lantern was almost out and I could feel the constant draft flowing through the room, chilling everything around me. Moving over to the window, I forced the pane back into place and secured the latch. I peered out into the night as far as the light of my lanterns would allow me to see. But there was nothing.

I spent the night huddled in my chair, alert to some unknown, and in the morning, the world seemed like it had the day before. The air was warm and humid and nature seemed at ease.

Going over to my parents proved to be even more troubling as they had not noticed any change in the weather nor any powerful gusts of winds. They advised me to visit the behique who made me recall the details of the night over and over again. When I finished he shook his head, troubled by my nervous disposition and my inability to recall my dreams. Using a spicy blend of herbs and tree barks, he bathed me and cleansed my energy, marking my body with a liquid that smelled suspiciously like the cassava beer my father drank when I was growing up.

As I was getting dressed again he produced a small handmade wind chime that was wrapped in a yellowing sheet of stiff cotton. Holding it out to me, he told me to hang it in the middle of my house. He said it would serve as protection and that the guidance of my ancestors would be heard in its musical chiming but as I nodded and told him that my mother had given me one that was larger and more intricate. He froze.

"You didn't mention the wind chime in your story," he said, his voice was cautious which set me on edge.

I thought back and shook my head. "Because I didn't hear it and didn't notice it. The wind was howling much too loudly."

He looked at me, his eyes dark with intensity. "Did you not

hear it or did it not chime?"

I scoffed. "Of course it chimed. I just wasn't paying attention to it. I was more focused on getting the window fixed to stop the wind from getting in." I could hear the defensiveness in my tone and I silently warned myself to tone it down, to not be so quick to temper as my university peers had been.

He went silent as he contemplated my words. Then as he looked up at me he asked once more, slowly this time as if I was some type of simpleton. "Are you sure the chimes sang?"

"Yes." I said it calmly and with great confidence, but the truth was that I wasn't quite sure anymore. In one line of questioning he'd planted a seed of doubt in my mind making me wonder if it was even possible for the freestanding wind chime to have not moved whilst the wind tore through my home.

Seemingly content, I saw some of the tension melt from his old body as it sagged forward and his shoulders dropped. "I think you'll be fine."

I thanked him and left, putting the ringing chimes matter out of my head as I scooted off home, eager to get some much deserved rest.

When night fell I found myself once more shuttered in my cabin, sitting before my lantern, I clutched my blanket against my chest because though the night was warm, my blood ran cold.

It was silent to the point that the hairs on my body all stood at attention. Outside, not a single sound could be heard. The insects had stopped telling the tales of our people and I dreaded to think what that meant.

It's now an hour later and I haven't heard a single chirrup or croak from outside, and though the trees remain eerily still, I can hear the screeching roar and howl of the winds as it tries to enter my cabin. It pushes against my doors and windows with such a force that I can hear the wood frame splintering and I can almost see the wood warping and buckling. And then I hear it, a crunching shatter as a back window breaks and my home is suddenly filled with a tornado of wind and a deafening moaning that makes my bones rattle and sets my teeth on edge.

As I lifted my hands to cover my ears and block out the mind-bending white noise I noticed it; hanging in the middle of the room, undisturbed and suspended in time, is my mother's wind chime. The same one that had sung to me so sweetly no more than a few hours ago.

The silence of the outside hadn't disturbed me as much as this did simply because it was so illogical. But I could feel it now. It was the same dread and emptiness that had filled me the night before. My ancestors were gone and there was nothing but me and the horrid cries of the wind that echoed out into the velvety darkness of the night.

Suddenly its intensity picked up. I could feel it surrounding me, crushing me and sweeping me away as it forced my own screams to ebb from my body like molasses while I struggled to retain my sanity. I would have given anything to hear the sweet, sweet sound of those chimes. Anything would have been better than this screaming. Anything.

BUCK-BUCK-GOOSE

The blue bottle made a round trip out to sea and back. Tucked into Goose's back pocket, it spent the day in his company observing him as he went about his routine. He'd pulled in his nets and sold his fish right there on the beach before going home just after lunch time with a greasy bag of doubles in his hand. Taking the bottle out of his pocket, he held it up to the sunlight that drifted in through the open jalousie windows and streamed past the tattered curtains. The rays bounced off the glass and sent a series of rainbows darting around the room.

Fascinated, Goose set his bag of doubles aside and shook the bottle's contents that sloshed and clinked within. The bottle felt heavier than he remembered and as he fished the knife out from under the cushions, he began to chip away at the cork cover until he was able to pry it out.

The moment the cork came free with a pressurized pop, a spicy smoky white mist hissed out of the top in an angry plume and Goose quickly dropped the bottle onto the floor and scampered away into the corner of the room.

The smoke continued to pour out of the bottle, creeping closer and closer towards Goose's bare feet. With a surprised yelp, Goose clambered up onto the couch and onto the barrel of clothes he kept in the corner as he wondered what fresh horror he had just released into his house.

Though he wasn't a superstitious man, he was no stranger to the tales his Gran used to tell him when he was little, and now that he thought about it, there was one story about a bottle that tickled the edges of his memories that he couldn't quite remember.

The smoke shimmered and seemed to sway in place as it gathered in the middle of the room and began to bloom upwards into a mushroom cloud, morphing into an almost humanoid shape as it went.

Goose remained frozen in place, only able to watch in terror as the smoke darkened and began to take the form of a small troll-like man whose face and body was covered in coarse, long, grey and black hair. With a pointed head and wild sunken eyes, his face showed his withered age. As he stood upright, revealing his emaciated body, he regarded a shaking Goose with an empty stare as his long fingered hands that bore nails akin to claws swung nonchalantly back and forth with just enough motion to make the tips graze lightly over the floor. He grunted and Goose felt his heart threaten to give out.

"Who…who are you?" Goose asked, in an attempt to gain and maintain some semblance of control over the situation. But the truth was that he desperately hoped that the thing would not answer for he didn't want to know what such a beast sounded like.

The creature made no reply.

"Who are you and what do you want?" Goose repeated, hoping that his voice wasn't shaking as much as he thought it was.

The creature's gaze came into focus as it observed the cowering man atop the large drum of clothes. "Thank you for freeing me." Its voice was deep and croaky. Ancient. Dead.

"What?" Goose could think of nothing else to say but he knew he very badly needed a drink. The whole situation reeked of vile and evil things, things that happened in the dead of night, in a cemetery, or under the branches of a silk cotton tree, not in his living room on a hot and blustering afternoon.

"In return for your...*kindness*...I can grant you whatever it is your heart desires as long as you feed me and let me live with you," the thing promised.

The thing's tone suggested that its statement was more of a command than a suggestion, and Goose, struck by its audacity, felt his temper flare up. Speaking in defiance without giving it any thought he scoffed. "Feed you and let you live with me? What you is, some kind of dog?" But the moment Goose asked, the answer popped into his mind. Before the creature could reply he amended his statement in a whisper as clouds of black spots bloomed before his eyes like yeast in sugary water. "No...not a dog, you is a *buck*..."

***

"What happened next?!" The question was hot on our lips.

The oily light of the kerosene lamp flickered within its glass prison and danced in Nana's eyes. He knew he had us right where he wanted. Reaching for a cigarette, he took his sweet time opening the box. As he took one out, he cradled the tube between his fingers and methodically rolled it back and forth. Once...twice...before he stuck the filtered end between his lips. Leaning sideways he fished his neon green plastic lighter out from his front pants pocket and ran his thumb over the metal cog-like mechanism.

Chk! Chk!

We could almost hear the tiny whoosh of lighter fluid eking out to feed the spark that flamed to life and set his worn and weary features alight. As he cupped the fragile fire, he touched the end of the cigarette to the open flame, drawing in as he did so.

Just like that the flame huffed out of existence, leaving behind the glowing orange end of the cigarette that winked on and off, flaring up like our fright and curiosity.

As he blew a long trail of smoke into the air like a dragon, he allowed the cigarette to settle between the loose pinch of his knuckles as he grunted softly. "That was when trouble really start," he said with a sagely knowledge.

Anna and I clung to each other with baited breaths as terrified children are prone to do. Nestled in the folds of the sagging hammock that hung from the pillars beneath our home, Nana reached up an arm and rocked us gently as he continued.

"Goose should have never touched that bottle. Better yet he should have cast the damned thing back into the depths of the ocean, but any man used to working day after day, tirelessly toiling to make ends meet knows better than to look a potential gift horse in the mouth. He might not have known what the bottled contained when he first picked it up but his senses told him there was something in it that he would need and use. And he was right…"

***

Akash opened his mouth in shock. "You mean he let that thing live with him?!"

I nodded solemnly, relaying the rest of Nana's tale to my friend as we pitched our marbles on the sandy portion of the school's field under the broiling heat of the mid-day sun. "And Nana say it worked too, because before long Goose started to see things turn around. He got a job working with the Ministry of Agriculture, he was able to buy himself a car, and he even get himself a nice red skin woman." We looked at each other and nodded as if we understood what that really meant. "And that was when the trouble start because before long she wanted to move in with him but he didn't want she to know about the buck."

"So he just let it go?" Akash sounded sceptical.

I shook my head. "Nah, you can't just let it go so. Instead he made a deal with it. Nana say he organized a fig patch for it and set up a little house and everything so it could live there. He say that every week Goose does take it some milk to keep it happy and keep it from raining stones down on he house."

"So it just there living by itself? For true?"

I nodded once more as if I were an expert on the matter.

"You know where the patch is?" The question was curious,

hopeful, bold-faced.

"I not sure but I think it I have a good idea where it might be…"

***

Dressed in our home clothes, we stood behind the wide berth of the samaan tree and nervously peered out at the wild outcrop of banana trees that stood sentry a distance away. Though the sun hadn't fully set yet, the sky was slowly melting into the pink and orange hues of dusk and the banana patch was beginning to take on a rather sinister and ominous look.

"You sure this is it?" Akash asked as he glanced around with wide eyes.

I nodded slowly, though truth be told, I wasn't quite sure myself. But according to Nana's very vivid description, this was the most likely place, a place the adults forbid us from ever setting foot in since it was said that a boy had died here some years back after being bitten by a mapepire. We were risking a sound licking, yet now here we stood, after tracking through the bush that often-time went well past the tops of our heads, past the boundaries that had been set by the adults, searching for a mythical creature who in all likelihood only existed in Nana's imagination. It was insane. It was stupid. But most importantly, it was thrilling. I'd never been this excited and terrified in all my life.

"I don't see it nowhere," Akash whispered still looking around.

"Obviously it not going to just be standing there. It probably sleeping in it house." My bravado was fuelled by Akash's obvious fear. Feeling my adrenaline rise, I looked at my friend and grinned. "I dare you to run to that tree and touch it and come back." I pointed to the first banana tree in the patch, a lone straggler that seemed half-dead.

"You mad or what?!" Akash almost yelped.

My grin widened. It was a lunatic's grin that betrayed my own budding fear and uncertainty. "Bok-bok-bok!" I crowed in the best imitation of a chicken's call that I could manage as I tauntingly flapped my arms at him.

"SHHHHH!" Akash's eyes were ready to pop out. "I not chicken, but since you so brave, you go."

"Alright," I said as I puffed up my eleven-year-old chest. "Watch."

I stepped out from behind the samaan and strolled brazenly up to the first of the banana trees. Touching it, I turned to face Akash and shrugged to show that this was no big deal. I walked back slowly, deliberately, feeling the fear building with each step but I refused to let it show.

I got back and Akash's attitude seemed to have changed. Suddenly he didn't seem so afraid anymore as he stepped around me and walked towards the second banana tree with purpose. Touching it, he turned around and came right back in a series of quick hot-footed steps.

We stood regarding each other with the mischief that only exists within young boys with insatiable appetites for trouble.

Akash looked around the ground until he spotted a smooth white piece of gravel that was perfectly pebble-shaped. Cocking his arm back, he unleashed the stone and we watched as it sailed into the banana patch and landed with a soft thump.

He turned to look at me and didn't even need to say the words. The challenge was written all over his face and I set out since I was not one to ever back down from any challenge.

With the stone in hand, I rushed back to the safety of the samaan tree and showed Akash my prize. He twisted his mouth in a show of unimpressed apathy, but underneath I could see the fear of knowing what was about to come next.

My throw landed further in than his and without caring to make a show of it, he sprinted after it and came back as quickly as he could.

And so we took turns, chucking the white pebble as hard as we could, playing our own lop-sided version of fetch while the bleeding sun slowly sank lower and lower on the horizon.

It was to be the last throw and Akash hurled the stone as far and as hard as he could. Throwing all his might behind the pebble I watched as it skipped and bounced, kicking up little puffs of dirt before it disappeared further into the bushes than either of us had managed to throw before. The triumphantly smug look on his face called out to my stubborn side and I set off after it before my rational side could catch up.

It wasn't until I was midway there that my bravado began to splinter without cause. Yet still I refused to back down. Standing amid the banana trees whose broad shiny leaves fluttered and wiggled in the breeze, I felt the hair on the back of my neck stand on end.

Plunging through the trees I batted several of the shiny leaves aside as my eyes searched the ground for the stone. I was sure I'd seen it fall right where I stood yet there was nothing but the dry earth and a brittle layer of dead leaves. Hunting around, I shuffled back and forth, weaving through the trees as if I were playing in and out the dusty windows, paying no mind to the several rusted Klim pans that were stacked to my far right.

As that pin-prickly sensation radiated through me once more I noticed how quiet the place had gotten. Looking back towards Akash, I was dismayed to see that he wasn't there anymore. Standing up straight I could feel my heartbeat quicken. I'd scarcely turned to head back to the samaan tree when a slow movement in my peripheral drew my attention towards it. Turning, I found myself face to face with the creature. It was slowly circling me on all fours, looking more like a hideously disfigured ape than anything else. With a pinched head and eyes that were as deep as a chasm, it stared at me with a hatred I will never be able to describe. As it openly stalked me, I found myself rooted to the spot and unable to think or react.

The moment it reared up and stood upright I was able to see that it stood at no taller than three or four feet, and when it leaped towards me, my reflexive backwards jerk was only just enough to get me moving. I stumbled backwards as the creature reached out with incredible speed and grappled me. The skin on its fingers were cold and wet, while the hair that brushed against me felt as though I was being rubbed by a steel brush. With a scream I batted at it with enough force to make it unleash a harrowing snarl as it dug its nails even deeper into my soft flesh. Locked together, we scrambled through the dirt, disturbing the crop of banana trees and tearing their pliable leaves apart as we went. Finally, by some stroke of dumb luck I managed to loosen its grip on me, but as I made to escape, it took the opportunity to bare its blackened cat-like teeth and sink them into my arm. I immediately felt a sharp, searing heat flood my body and a stinging sensation like that of a jack spania's sting rang out. With a scream I recoiled and my efforts to free myself intensified.

It all happened within seconds, and I'm not even sure how, but at one point I felt it release its grip on me and with that opening I was off running through the brush and back out to track that would take me to the main road. As I fled home I realized that there'd been no sign of Akash anywhere and for a fleeting moment I feared that the beast had gotten him, but on the heels of that dismaying thought I knew better. The coward had seen the thing before I had and instead of warning me or staying to help me he'd simply run away in an attempt to save his own skin.

I was out of breath by the time I got home and as I entered the yard I could hear my mother's voice trailing out from underneath the house.

"I fed up tell him when he see it getting dark that is time to come home. I ent have time to deal with his dotishness tonight, you know!"

I rounded the colourful flare of the croton hedge and Anna, standing at my mother's side, tugged at the hem of mother's lily white nurse uniform and pointed towards me. Following her direction my mother let out one long steups as she set her sights on me. With three quick steps she closed the gap and had me in her grasp. "Where you was?" she demanded as her open hand connected with the back of my head. I felt my head rock forward and fixed my gaze on the ground. I knew better than to try and answer. Making myself as small as possible she looked me over in horror. "How you scratch up so? Like you get into a fight or what? Look how you bleeding! Boy, what the hell happen to you?"

I'd caught a glimpse of Nana who was standing with my sister. His eyes were narrowed and his lips were drawn tight.

"You and that Akash boy running racket again!" she declared. "I better not get any call from any of the neighbours about you, you hear me? Where you was?" she asked again as she scrutinized my wounds. "Like you gone and interfere with some blasted cat or something and it get you good. It damn good for you. I going to work, I go deal with you in the morning."

Looking back at her father she nodded. "Make sure he do he homework and then is straight to bed. No TV, no games, no computer or phone, no nothing, you hear?"

With a quick nod Nana shooed Anna inside and walked towards me. Together we stood and watched as my mother hailed a PH taxi and was off. Then he turned to me and examined me without saying a word. With a disappointed sigh he shook his head. "Go on inside and take a quick rinse and wait for me in the bathroom. I go be back in a few minutes."

When he appeared in the doorway of the bathroom I looked up with him as tears stung my eyes. With the scratches and the bite lancing, I was both afraid and embarrassed and ashamed of what had happened. Holding the mortar and pestle in his hand he called me over to him and scooped up a handful of bushy, bitter smelling materials that he'd crushed together into a poultice. Placing it against my bite wound I winced in pain as its juices seeped into my open flesh and burned unlike anything I'd ever felt.

"Ent you is a big man? Stop complaining and hold still," he commanded as he began rubbing the rest of the mash over all my scrapes and bruises. "I suppose is my fault for telling you the story in the first place." He sighed. "Mayhap I should have told you the story of how trouble make monkey eat pepper because I never thought you would be so dotish to go seeking it out. You lucky you alive, you know."

"Nana…" the words burned in my chest as he shook his

head and laughed wickedly.

"Just you wait though, it not done with you yet." And with that he left me standing there smelling like a bush with a terrified expression on my face.

Hours later as I lay in bed deep asleep and utterly exhausted from the events of the day I had dreams of *it*. Dreams that were fuelled by the lingering bushy smell on my skin, and in those dreams I fought the creature who was now twice as big and whose nails were claws that shredded me to bits. Suddenly from above a hail of stones rained down on me and as I looked around I saw that the stones were all white pebbles, much like the one Akash and I had been throwing into the banana patch.

I sat up in bed with a jolt, covered in sweat as the sound of the falling stones echoed in my mind. It took me a few moments to realize that the sound wasn't going away and as the hail of what I could only assume were stones rained down on our house I found that I could hardly even hear myself screaming.

Nana was there with Anna in his arms, and as I threw myself onto him and cowered, he seemed both calm and unsurprised.

"What happening?" I screamed as fistful after fistful of rocks rained down on the roof and chinked off the outer walls and windows.

"It's the buck come back to take revenge on you for bothering it."

Fear seized me in that moment at the knowledge that this *thing* knew where I lived. Minutes later, the barrage of stones stopped and Nana crept up to the window and peered through the slit in the curtains before turning back to us with a nod. Hugging a crying Anna, I looked up at him on the verge of tears myself.

"We'll sort this out tomorrow. Go back to sleep. It's over for now."

Anna hugged me tighter and refused to let go so with a nod he left the room with a final word. "Take care of your sister."

As we settled down on the bed, I found that I could not go

back to sleep. Was this what my life was going to be like? Tormented by the buck each night? Or perhaps it was only a matter of time until he came to take me away for good. Nana said we would sort it out in the morning, what did that mean? I fought the urge to tremble for fear of waking Anna up, and though I thought I would never fall back asleep I must have at some point because soon enough Nana was gently shaking me awake.

As my heavy and gritty eyelids fluttered open and the memories of the previous evening flooded back into my mind I started. Laying a hand on my shoulder to still me, Nana signalled for me to not disturb Anna and motioned for me to change my clothes and follow him. Once outside, he handed me a heavy brown paper bag. "We have to be quick and hurry up before your mother gets home."

"Where we going?" I asked as I hurried to catch up to him. But the answer soon became evident as we left the outskirts of the village and reached the track that led to where the dreaded buck lived. I balked. There was no way I was going back there.

"You have to," Nana said. "It's the only way to make it stop. And remember, you brought this on yourself by doing whatever it is you and the Mohammed boy did to bother it."

Reaching the edge of the banana patch, I stood shaking as Nana whistled low. Soon enough the buck emerged looking even more terrifying in the low early morning light. The beast snarled and Nana held his palms up and open towards it as he bowed low and motioned for me to do the same.

By the time we righted ourselves the buck had ceased his snarling and stood upright, regarding us both with mistrust. Nana spoke to it in patois, and I, unable to understand the conversation, stood behind him trying my best to not scream or run away though every fibre of my being urged me to do both.

After a moment the beast spoke in a horrible breathy croak, addressing Nana in what I could only assume was the same Patois though it now sounded even more alien. Nana nodded and bowed once more and placed his hand on my shoulder, pushing me forward and towards the thing. A blinding panic unlike anything I'd ever felt enveloped me as my initial reaction was that he was sacrificing me to the beast. I tried to turn away, to run away, but Nana's breath was hot against my ear. "Bow before him and offer him the bag," he whispered.

Stumbling forward on legs that felt numb, I bowed low and spoke though I'd had no intention of doing any such thing. "I-I-I am very s-s-s-sorry for yesterday. P-p-p-please forgive me, Mr. Buck...Sir..."

I held out the bag to the beast and closed my eyes, grimacing in anticipation of another attack. But the creature merely reached out and plucked the bag from my hands.

Opening the top he peered inside and grunted. With a guttural snort he retreated through the trees, leaving us standing there alone.

As we made our way back I had a thousand burning questions but Nana remained silent and seemed in no mood for dealing with me or my queries. Nonetheless, there was one thing I simply had to know.

"Nana, how did you know what to do and say to it?"

At first I thought he was never going to answer but then he spoke and though his answer wasn't really an answer, I took his meaning well.

"The story of the buck has been around for generations though few who ever go looking for it ever finds it and some who do find it never survive their encounter. But it seems like dumb luck and dotishness continues to run in our family."

When we got back home I was about to go inside when he stopped me. "Nuh-uh, you not going nowhere. Go and get the cocoyea broom and sweep up the yard and brush away every last little stone you see before you mother come home. I not explaining nothing to she, so if she catch you, you on your own." His voice was stern and laced with annoyance, yet still there was a spark in his eyes, one akin to the look he had when he'd relayed the buck's story to Anna and I. It would be years before I understood that that glint was one of pride, for much like himself, I had faced and stood against the buck, a supernatural being, and I had survived. Though my survival was due to sheer luck and mercy on the buck's part, it still counted for something in Nana's eyes.

"Oh, and by the way," he added, "it goes without saying that you are not to utter a word of this to anyone, *ever*, you hear me? And if I were you I would be extra nice to your sister after the fright your nonsense put her through, because if she goes and tells your mother anything..." He let the threat hang in the air.

"And Akash? Will he be okay?" I finally asked realizing that I hadn't heard a word from my friend since yesterday. Not even a phone call or a text or anything. A small part of me hoped the coward was okay.

Nana waved his hand dismissively in the air. "If his mother didn't show up here last night asking questions he is most likely safe. If he's smart he'll keep quiet. If not...well that's his mother's problem, not mine." He narrowed his eyes at me and I shrank away from his gaze.

Though I knew I was pushing my luck and trying his patience I asked one more question. One that I needed to know the answer to. "Nana? Will it leave us alone now?"

With a mischievous sideways glance and a twist of his mouth, he shrugged. "We'll see."

UNTIL DEATH DO US PART

Norris found himself standing in front of the display of herbicides in the gardening section of the local Walmart in an almost trance-like state. His mind was a whirlpool of emotions, and as the background chatter of the other patrons faded to near silence, he felt his despondency bubble up in a series of screams and accusations, the same ones that had haunted him for almost seven years now and had fuelled his insomnia.

"Norris? Are you ok?" Heather's soft voiced reached him from deep within the void, and he turned to face her with a smile.

"Yeah. Just trying to decide if we need this or not. I've been seeing dandelions sprouting up in the backyard again." His lie was smooth and natural.

Heather wrinkled her nose and nodded. "Come summer we'll see how bad it really is. For now I say we let it be. I really don't want to be one of those grass people who always makes a fuss about their lawns and grass height and all that nonsense."

Norris couldn't help but laugh. "You're right, as always." He planted a tender kiss on her milk-white cheek and together they continued pushing their shopping cart down the aisle.

He was a man with a past, one that he'd been only partially truthful about. Heather knew where he was from, knew he'd been married before, but that was where her knowing ended. Norris planned to keep it that way. He'd left his Caribbean home for that exact reason, to put the terrible tragedy behind him. But every so often he'd get a reminder, a whiff of some woman's perfume that smelled like her, or the sight of some brand she loved would dredge up sudden memories that threatened to overwhelm him. But he was determined to put it all behind him and move on. Trouble was, that was easier said than done…

It was almost as though his guilty conscience was manifesting itself since that day in Walmart. Something about that whole afternoon had felt off, and now, a few days later, Heather was acting strange and her behaviour was getting stranger by the hour.

It began the same evening they'd come back from the store. It was early but Heather complained about being tired and went to bed. Not too long after, while Norris was still in the living room watching TV, a loud mournful wailing began coming from upstairs. Rushing to Heather's side, Norris found her sitting up in bed sobbing with such grief he was sure she was dying. Then as he wrapped his arms around her she stilled and quieted. Before her eyes slowly fluttered open and focused on him.

"Norris? Norris, what's wrong?" she asked, her voice sluggish with sleep.

Leaning back he examined her and found himself speechless. "You were crying…bawling down the place, I thought something was wrong with you!"

Her eyebrows knitted together in a frown. "Was I? That's strange. I must have been having a dream. I don't remember what it was though." She yawned and stretched, slow and deliberately like a cat, as she settled back into her nest of sheets. "Come to bed and cuddle with me." Heather cooed and Norris, unable to help himself smiled at her as he nodded.

"Let me go turn off the TV and check the doors and set the alarm. Wait for me, I'll be right up."

He left her then but his mind and heart were heavy. Never

before had he heard his wife make such a haunting noise, and the more the sound replayed itself in his mind, the less and less human it became.

In the days after that Heather seemed...unlike herself. Her usually positive and pleasant disposition seemed to waver in oscillating and sporadic bursts of anger, sadness, joy and even paranoia.

The worst of these states would come at night, when she would awaken suddenly in near hysterics over dreams she couldn't remember. And during the day, when Norris was away at the office, she would find herself being driven to her knees as her stomach would wring itself into a hard knot that would drive all the air out of her lungs. She kept this to herself. Something was wrong but she didn't know what and the last thing she wanted was to worry Norris. But Norris was already worried for he had been having some lucid fever dreams of his own, dreams in which his ex-wife's accusations would bombard his restful sleep and cast him into a restless and agitated state.

The breaking point came six days later, when, in the middle of the night and during Norris' first night of restful sleep in years, Heather suddenly sat upright in bed and began babbling that someone was stalking her and following her every movement, and that they'd wanted to hurt her, that they *were* going to hurt here. They were just waiting for the right moment...

Norris was at her side, trying to calm her down, to ask her to tell him what was wrong, but all she did was screech and howl as though she was being attacked.

As Norris tried to soothe her, she turned and began clawing at him and beating on him with her fists. And Norris, unable to get her to stop, did the only thing that came to his mind. He cocked his arm back to slap her out of her hysterics, and in the moment he swung his arm back she stopped and looked at him through eyes that weren't quite hers.

"I've spoken to her, you know. She's told me *everything*. You think it's right to hit a woman? You think that makes you a man? And to think she was pregnant! Norris, I never thought I would ever be so ashamed to call you my husband. And the lies, you've been lying to me this whole time. Lying to yourself…I don't even know which is worse!"

Norris was speechless. There was simply no way Heather could have known any such thing. His wife before her was dead, she'd committed suicide and she had indeed been pregnant when she'd done it. Norris' mouth opened and closed multiples times like a fish as he struggled to come up with an excuse or some sort of explanation. Yes, he'd hit her, but she had been acting out, she was being unreasonable, she wasn't listening to him and that was the only way he could get her to just shut up and let him talk.

It was a piss poor excuse, he knew that, but in the moment, in his anger and his desperation to silence her for just a moment, it was all he could think to do. Never in his life did he imagine that she would have walked away from him then and done what she'd done to herself and to their child.

"I just wanted us to be a family," she said in a mournful voice that Norris never thought he'd hear again.

And there in the bed next to him was *her*. Opening his mouth to speak, the only sound that came out was a screeching howl of fear as Norris tried to get away from the bhoot that was his first wife.

"Norris! Norris, wake up!"

His eyes flew open in a panic as he sat up in bed. Heather sat at his side, her eyes wild, hair dishevelled with sleep and her arm tightly wrapped around Norris' bicep as she tried to calm him down.

"It was just a dream. Whatever it was, let it go, you're safe, I'm here."

He let her voice bring him back down to earth before he sank back onto his pillow. Turning to face her, he examined her silhouette in the semi-darkness of their bedroom and let out a long sigh of relief.

"I had a dream, a bad dream that something happened to you. I don't know what I would ever do without you."

He could hear the smile in her voice and in his mind could almost see the corners of her eyes crinkle in that familiar way.

"Don't worry, nothing will happen to me. I'm here, you're here and everything is fine. Better than fine actually."

With a distracted chuckle Norris nodded and was about to roll away from her but the sight of her hand cradling her lower abdomen made him pause. Looking up at him with a smile that seemed almost borrowed, a smile that didn't quite touch her clear blue eyes like it usually did, she tilted her head to the side and sighed. "I wanted it to be a surprise, but there's no point in hiding it anymore. You're finally going to be a daddy, Noni. I'm so happy and excited!" Her laughter was genuine but Norris' blood had run cold as he looked at his wife as though he didn't recognize her anymore.

"What...? What did you call me?" It was the nickname his deceased ex-wife used to call him. A name he'd never told Heather about. A name she would have never come to on her own. Nori, maybe, but never...

She looked up at him again mid-laugh and shook her head like he was crazy. "What's the matter, Noni? Like you losing your mind or what? They say too much happiness does do that you know!" The Caribbean accent poured from between Heather's naturally plump and red lips like sour wine. It didn't suit her, it didn't match, and it was a voice he'd spent all this time trying to forget.

As the bhoot sidled up to a frozen Norris it sighed in contentment. "There will never be anyone else. It will always be Noni, me, and baby makes three, one happy forever family."

Norris squeezed his eyes shut, willing it all to be nothing more than a dream...a nightmare. As he opened his eyes he found Heather smiling at him, the corners of her eyes crinkling in that reassuringly familiar way, but Norris knew better. This was his cross to bear for life, and in nine months' time he knew that the child they would have together would bear little resemblance to Heather and would instead resemble *her*.

Fairy Garden

Kalinda slipped out into the garden
In the middle of the night,
To gaze upon the fireflies
As they floated and flickered their lights.

Lost in their hypnotic dance
She stared out into space,
Until the brightest little firefly
Flew up towards her face!

With a smile she held out her glass jar
And swung the lid down tight.
Trapping the firefly within,
She giggled in childish delight.

On and on she went,
Collecting them all until
Her garden stood dark and empty,
While her jar was completely filled.

But before she could go inside
A final flicker caught her eye.

And as she turned towards it
It dipped, it dove, it darted on by!

So Kalinda gave chase,
And followed it with glee,
And the closer she got to it,
The faster it seemed to flee!

"I just need one more," she thought,
 "And my collection will be complete!
Then straight to bed is where I'll go
To get some well-deserved sleep!"

But the final firefly drifted onwards
Into the forested darkness of the night.
And a determined Kalinda gave chase,
Only to be led astray by the mischievous sprite!

COUNCIL OF ELDERS

Ellie stood gazing in amazement as the balls of fire streaked across the night sky. It was one a.m. and almost everyone was asleep. The only other person who lay witness to this event, this phenomenon, was the homeless drunkard who lay only semi-conscious on the side of the road. And with each streak he muttered a wish as though they were shooting stars.

Ellie's hands hung limply at her side as she debated what she should do. Never in her life had she seen such a thing and it truly was a sight to behold, one that became even more spectacular once you recognized the balls of fire for what they truly were. It was a once in a lifetime event and though she was still young, a mere eighty-three years old, she made up her mind in that moment that nothing would keep her from experiencing the event that had been whispered about by great-great-great-great grandmothers for centuries.

But first she needed to change out of her nightie.

Turning around, she disappeared into the neat little one bedroom concrete house that she'd slowly built herself over the years with help from some of the villagers. She moved with a speed she reserved for the cover of the night-time. Going into her bedroom, she felt around her dresser for the box of matches. Striking one of them against the muddy brown hexagon-patterned side, she held its wavering flame to the candle until its wick caught. The flame grew three times the size and illuminated the bare bones room. On the dresser next to the matches was a tortoise shell comb, a large tub of Vaseline, a sealed amber-coloured bottle of bay rum, and two half-filled dark brown glass bottles. One was filled with homemade coconut oil and the other with a clear, viscous, foul-smelling oil that she'd attained thanks to the recently deceased Madam Tilda.

Moving to the open window, Ellie peered out into the night just as another flaming ball lit up the sky and disappeared eastwards into the dense forest of Guayaguayare. Drawing the curtains shut, she untied her head scarf and slipped off her blue nightgown. She smoothed out the white lace collar and neatly folded her head scarf as she placed each on the edge of the bed just below the gold-framed picture of Christ. Then she opened both bottles of oil and poured a generous amount of both into her cupped palm. Mixing them together with her finger, she began methodically rubbing it over her loose, wrinkled skin starting from her feet and working her way up to her scalp. When she was oiled from head to toe, she rolled her neck and shoulders to loosen herself up as she walked over to the darkest corner of the room and rolled back the carpet to reveal a hole she'd chipped out of the foundation years ago. Though she couldn't see it she knew that the dark, well-worn mortar lay nestled inside.

Stepping back, she reached up into her hair and slowly worked her scalp back and forth before she peeled off her skin and stepped out of it like a coat. Standing there with her oiled skin in her skinless hands, she methodically folded it like one would fold a onesie. When she was sure that every nick of flesh was in its place and set just right to preserve its shape, she placed it into the mortar and rolled the carpet back into its rightful spot. With quick strides she moved to the window and transformed herself into the dark translucent mist she used when she needed to get into someone's house. Squeezing herself through the slat in the louvres, she moved out of the house so quickly that the candle's flame huffed out of existence.

Up into the air she flew until she was trailing high. It was only then that she would allow her true form—a flaming ball of fire—to take hold. To anyone watching it would look as though the night sky had suddenly burst into flames and then shot away like a balloon that had been blown up and released. Ellie would never be caught flying out of her house in her true form. Oh no! She was smarter than that! In these times one had to be very careful to protect themselves.

Joining the phenomenon above, she flew over the village and as she flew over the drunkard in the gutter he looked up and mumbled a semi-coherent wish. Ellie laughed to herself as she raced over the trees and along the Guayaguayare-Mayaro Road until she got to the edge of her little village of St. Margaret.

But before she could head to the gathering, she first needed to sup. Going two villages over, she slipped in through the vent block of Brother Austin's house she perched over him looking for a soft spot. The back of the arm was her favourite place and it usually caused the bruising to remain unseen. After she'd drunk her fill, she once more slipped through the vent block and left a still sleeping Brother Austin behind. He would be none the wiser, and the only effect he'd suffer was a groggy feeling in the morning as if he'd slept too deeply. She made three similar stops in the nearby houses before she veered west into the dense forest.

Even though she'd never been to the location where they were gathering, she knew the way. The power emitted by the massive tree would guide her there. And even if her senses were dulled, she would still be able to follow the streaks that raced to its place from all directions. This would be her first meeting and she was as nervous as she was excited. Very few realized that even the world of the supernatural had ranks to it and she'd only just recently worked her way up.

The tree was legendary, and though they had flown from all corners of the island, only a few of them had the ability to harness its power. To protect itself, the tree kept its location hidden in a perpetually dense cloud cover to ensure that it was not only impossible to see from above, but to shroud it in an unsettling degree of darkness that would deter and intimidate any mortal who happened to wander too near.

In the centuries they'd been gathering there, a large circle of land had been cleared at the base of the tree, and though it was still early it seemed as though everyone was already there. Ellie began descending through the clouds and came to form at the very edge of the circle which was illuminated by a series of brightly burning flambeaux. She knew no one here but based on the chatter around her it seemed as though most of the others were familiar with each other.

The minutes slipped by and suddenly a form appeared before her. "Yuh make yuh contribution?" The voice was cold and stern but it did not frighten Ellie.

"No, mama," Ellie responded to the elder.

The form nodded and stood aside for Ellie to move up. Standing in front of the massive Silk Cotton Tree was quite an experience. She could feel its power throbbing below its rough, hard, wooden exterior. Giving up the blood offering up to the tree, she chanted under her breath the request to Brazil, asking him to grant her the power to do as he bid. She'd made these types of offerings before when she'd been an obeah woman, but this time it was different. This time she could feel the true power as it flowed into her. Standing back, she gazed up at the branches in awe.

"Out ah mih way I ent have all night!" A voice screeched as she was elbowed aside and another woman stood before the tree for her offering.

Ellie once more drifted to the back for the crowd and no sooner had she done that did a voice speak out. The voice spoke in patois, a language Ellie knew well.

"Settle down my children. Let us be done with this well before the dawn since many of you have far to fly."

The chatter and cackling of the women all simmered down as everyone looked to the voice of the oldest one amongst them.

"Now that we're all here we'll do a quick headcount and those of you who haven't yet made your offerings should do so now. If you negated to bring your offering with you, I advise that you fly fast and retrieve it. This will be your only chance for the next seventy-five years."

A murmur spread through the crowd as a few shifted and moved forward while others took flight.

"Times are getting harder for us," the voice continued. "This new generation is significantly larger and are more advanced than the last. Moreover they still have their elders to warn them and caution them and advise them. Elders who can easily recognize the signs of our presence. It's a transitional time, a time of satellites, and cameras and solid concrete houses with sealed doors and keyless entries. It is a time of transition from old to new and many of us will soon find ourselves struggling.

"Last month one of our sisters in Penal found herself at their mercy. After being unable to feed for many nights she took too much and it alerted the community to her presence, and the next night they lay awake in wait. Last year in Filette some of you would have heard of the fate of Tamari. It is not known how she was captured but I'm sure we are all aware that she was tied down, covered in boiling pitch and sealed into a barrel that was then cast into the sea. A horrible end for anyone.

"But it doesn't even end there. There has been rumours that in some cases it is the obeah men who are alerting communities of our presence in an attempt to have us destroyed so they can garner our skins. Brazil himself has warned me of these occurrences and so our numbers dwindle.

"It is why I want to encourage you to help each other. Back-a-day only one of our kind were allowed per village and we've all drawn these lines of territory from years of settlement but with the growing population that is no longer necessary so welcome your sisters into your region if needed, and should trouble arise you may report to one of the seven elders to address the matter. Our numbers are declining and as I look around I see less of you than ever before and though we have quite a few new members, things are still not in our favour and I fear the end of us might be near."

"That's not really true," Ellie had been so caught up in the moment that she spoke as she often did to her TV set without regard of her status or who she was addressing or where she was. Everyone turned to look at her and as the elder spoke and demanded she be brought forward, Ellie found herself being pushed and elbowed as the crowd forcefully delivered her to the base of the tree before they backed away in fear.

Ellie could hear the whispers and the edge of excitement in their voices and she feared her fate would be grim. The elder stood over her, her body bent and crooked with age.

"What in hell would you know? You is only a child! Not even a hundred years and you want to talk to me about what I know for centuries?!" The elder's form flared and sputtered as she tried to contain her anger. "If is one thing I can't stand is insolence and rudeness. I does have to take it from them blasted village chirren and I can't do nothin' about it, but to have this coming from you…"

Another one of the elders came beside her and reached out. "Sister. She is young, this is her first meeting and I'm sure she meant no disrespect. Spare her only for the sake of hearing her out and seeing if her disruption is justifiable."

The elder turned on her comrade and screeched, "You willing to allow this? And on top of that you want to grant her the privilege of addressing us all? Who the hell is she to know anything?"

The other elder nodded as she spoke once more. "Like you said, times are hard and it's getting more and more difficult for us. She's the youngest so she might have some knowledge to impart that can help us all." She turned to face Ellie. "Tell us what it is you disagree about and why it is you disagree."

Ellie sat on her knees shaking and cursing herself for her big mouth. Of all the times to speak up this had to have been the worst.

"Kill her!" someone behind her shouted and the crowd erupted in agreement. They'd been stirred up and now they wanted blood only for the sake of excitement.

Ellie cringed. She could feel their excitement mounting to a potential lynching of sorts, and she feared being lashed to a tree and left for morning, a fate she sensed would soon be upon her if she couldn't do something. Maybe she could take flight and try to disappear over the sea, but then she would leave her skin behind and perish, or maybe she could try to make it home first, but then she'd be easily hunted... That left one option, she needed to speak. As she tried to summon the courage she felt it, a power that came from in front of her, but it wasn't from the elders, it was from the tree.

Rise.

And so she rose.

Speak.

And so she spoke.

The power of Brazil commanded her and in their wake there was nothing greater. The Elders both stepped aside having heard the voice but it seemed that none of the others had heard it.

Ellie rose with confidence and turned to face her sisters who had been asking for her end only moments before.

"While it is true that this new generation is significantly larger that is to our advantage. Now we can sup from a range of them without leaving a trace if we only take a little at a time. And though there are more, they believe in our existence less and less. The mention of the word 'soucouyant' no longer sends chills down anyone spines but instead garners a laugh, a scoff, a sideways glance or a couyah mouth. This bodes in our favour as it enables us to go relatively unnoticed and be dismissed as 'Nansi stories but..." She trailed off and looked around. "It is also true that this new generation is more advanced than the last, but if we adapt to them we can remain as we are. The times are changing and we need to change with it. Their elders know the signs of what to look for because it has remained the same. We remain old women who live alone on the edge of town in dilapidated old shacks. We stand out, and to make matters worse, they only have to look to our house in the night to see us take form to confirm their suspicions.

"If we do little things we can assimilate. I live in a concrete house in the middle of the village. My mortar is kept hidden in the floor, when I transform I leave my house as a mist and take form once I'm away and in the air. The villagers know my name and come to me for counsel. I keep my door open and I keep a garden in my front yard. My house is adorned with pictures of Jesus and children who aren't mine but I say they are anyways and that they live in England. I make treats for those who visit me, I shop in their stores, I buy pills for ailments I do not need, I interact with them and so suspicion is never on me. To them I am just a lonely old woman and nothing more. Though I lie about my age in thirty years' time I will leave that village for another one. If I go to the cemetery I go to the third closest one before midnight and wait until the time is right and I never fly there in my true form. If anything I go as an animal. Yes, it is more taxing on me and it is more difficult but I know I will likely never be caught.

"Cameras cannot catch us in our mist form. And if we fly high enough they mistake us for shooting stars and wish upon us. And even concrete houses have gaps below the doors, and if not, there are many others to choose from. We are no longer being hunted unless we give ourselves away, and in that case we only have ourselves to blame. We have abilities beyond their wildest imagination and we are more than able to blend in if we let go of some of our old ways and adapt to these changing times."

The silence carried on after she spoke and Ellie turned to look at the elders as she bowed her head in respect.

"Whey you learn all this from, girl?"

"From my days as an obeah woman. The more Brazil granted me power, the more I realized I needed to learn to hide them to keep myself safe. It started when I almost got caught one night as I left my house to go to the nearest silk cotton tree to pay my dues, and when I got there I found a man waiting with a cutlass in his hands. He didn't see me but I knew he had to have known somehow. From then on I vowed to be more careful and to keep my affairs to myself."

All seven elders gathered together to confer about her fate and from their whispers Ellie could tell they were conflicted. Never before had anyone been granted the ability to address the council, but never before had there been a need. The true purpose of these meetings were to touch base, exchange stories, take a headcount, and most importantly to pay homage to the demon who'd bestowed them their powers. But now it seemed that that demon had spoken up on her behalf, something that seemed almost impossible.

The elders pondered amongst themselves as to what made Ellie so special but there was no denying how useful her information had been. And if they were to harm her, there was no telling what the demon might do.

"Should we ask him?" one of them said.

"Better not, he is not one to be disturbed about such matters."

"And he already spoke in her favour."

"But she had no right. She must be punished."

"Maybe we should punish her and if Brazil wants he can save her."

"What if our actions anger him? Was speaking out on her behalf not enough?"

And so the conversation went until the council turned to address Ellie and inform her of her fate.

The meeting was at its end, the next one would be held in seventy-five years' time. A lifetime for a mortal but a mere passing for a soucouyant, and as Ellie flew through the night sky towards her quaint little home she silently thanked Brazil for granting her the power and ultimately for saving her life. Never had she been so foolish, but perhaps it was for the best and some of her sisters had learned something that would allow them to continue existing among the people, unknown and unseen for many more centuries to come.

WAYWARD CHILDREN

There's a local superstition that warns that traveling at night with food attracts hungry spirits. To keep them from following or entering your home put a hot pepper into the pot or dish with the food and be sure to cross your home's threshold backwards so that any jumbies who have been following you will know you're aware of their presence and leave. Failing to do so invites them in…

The black car pulled up to the house and Kimraj peered through his dusty windshield at the group of children who were running around the poles upon which the little wooden house stood. There were at least a dozen of them and none of them seemed to be wearing any clothes that he could see.

Their laughter and voices danced in the overcast midday air as they continued to run their racket as children are prone to do. Kimraj's eyes scanned the area looking for any sign of an adult but saw none. With a grunt he consulted his clipboard and read over the report.

The call had been put in by a neighbour who had apparently had enough of sheer number of children which she stated fluctuated between twenty to sometimes fifty at a time. The children, she'd said, were always dirty, naked, unsupervised, and forever making noise even at odd hours of the night. As far as she knew, none of them ever went to school, and her attempts to talk to the woman who owned the house, a Miss Beverly Vega, was met with a lethargic response and a dismissive brush off.

A frown crossed his face as he looked up once more and examined the sight before him. Two of the children were chasing a chicken while another two were squatting down in the dirt enjoying a game of marble pitch. The rest flitted around the yard, locked in their own imaginary play world that he wasn't privy to. They all seemed to be between the ages of seven and nine, and despite him sitting there parked in the front of their yard, none of the children even looked his way. In fact, as they ran around, none of them even gave any sign they'd noticed him. Kimraj grunted again as he snapped a picture through his windshield for his report. What an absolutely bizarre situation, but it was one he was determined to sort out before the day was over.

The call from the neighbour had stated child abuse, but at first glance this really seemed more like negligence. Either way, Kimraj had zero tolerance for such matters. As he opened his car door the silence fell so suddenly he looked up in surprise. The yard stood empty.

Getting out slowly, he made his way up the slight dirt slope that was the front yard and heard a series of stifled giggles and whispers. Abuse or not, the children at least seemed to be happy and healthy in their games. Coming up to a little hopscotch grid that had been traced into the dirt, Kimraj hopped into the first box on one leg. One, two, three, four-five, six, seven, eight-nine, ten. He did it quickly and smoothly and paused, waiting to hear what they would do. Someone laughed and the others quickly silenced them with a "Shhhh!" He smiled.

His soft spot for children stemmed way back to his early childhood. He was the oldest of eight children and with a father who travelled for work and was gone most of the time, his mother had come to rely on him to help her with the others. Even in school he'd assumed a fatherly role with his peers, and when he'd gotten his passes—five ones—he'd gone straight to teaching college and became a teacher's aide before taking a role as a teacher and eventually the principal of the Primary School he'd attended as a child.

When the opportunity to work for the Children's Authority had arisen he hadn't hesitated to step up. This was what he'd been made to do, to make sure that children had a good environment to grow and thrive in. After all, they were our future.

Reaching the side of the house, he looked up the front steps into the verandah that was stacked with an assortment of plants, and then to the faded red-painted stairway that stood on the side of the house and led to the opened backdoor. The smell of boiling split peas was heavy in the air.

"Morning!" he called out and waited for a response, his sharp eyes flitting between the both doorways.

Getting no response he called again, slightly louder this time. "Morning-morning! Anybody home?"

A head popped out of the backdoor and the woman's eyes regarded him with mild curiosity.

Lifting his hand in greeting he waited for her to acknowledge him but she only stared at him in wait.

"Um! Hello! Morning! I looking for Miss Vega?" She lifted her chin in a semi-nod but said nothing. He continued, "Ummm...I was wondering if I could talk to you for a minute?"

She looked him up and down and then looked past him at the car that he'd parked in front her house. "What you want?" her tone was brisk.

The question was sudden and he felt a mild annoyance flare up within him. Standing his ground, his initial approach of being slightly awkward and friendly fell away. If she wanted business she would get business. "My name is Kimraj Seepersad. I'm with the Children's Authority. We got a report about a situation regarding the number of children who live here and I was assigned to come look into the matter."

Her eyes flickered to the house next door and a small smile

played on her lips. Following her gaze, he turned to look at the neighbouring house and saw the curtain quickly fall back into place. Clearing his throat, he spoke up once more. "If it's alright with you I'd like to take a look around and have you answer a few questions."

"I don't have time for that," she said as she met his challenging gaze but her tone didn't hold the hostility her words implied. She seemed to almost be enjoying the interaction as if it amused her.

"It won't take long. If it's too much trouble I can always come back with a police escort." He let the threat linger in the air and she cackled.

"Oh-god-oye! Allyuh real serious! Alright, come on up. I have to mind my pot before it burn so you could fix up with whatever it is you need."

He climbed the steps and stood just outside the door. As he made to take off his shoes she waved her hand. "It ent have no need for that. Leave them on, mister."

A chorus of laughter came from both inside as well as downstairs, and though he couldn't see them he was taken aback by how many voices there seemed to be.

"That woman next door too damn macocious. Ah go do for she and she go learn to mind she damn business. Calling the authorities on me." The woman snorted as she rested her hands on her hips while a massive pot of soup bubbled on the stove next to her.

Kimraj stepped into the house and the wooden floor creaked below his weight. "All due respect, madam, this is a very serious matter."

"Hrumph!" She rolled her eyes. "Serious my ass."

"Whose children live here? Surely they're not all yours? My records show you don't have any children of your own and never adopted—"

"Mister, let me stop you there." She raised her massive arm and he fell silent. "I don't know who they are, where they come from, or what they doing here. All I know is they always bothering up my head and no matter what I do they don't leave me alone."

He frowned as he contemplated how best to approach the situation. "How many children live here with you?"

She shrugged and made no reply and he felt his impatience growing but he'd dealt with more than his fair share of stubborn and even crazy adults in his life.

"So you don't know whose children these are, but they're not yours. They never leave, and you don't know their parents…but you're cooking for them?" He motioned towards the pot with a jut of his chin.

"I have to. If I don't feed them they start to bawl and cry and mash up my place and then is headache for days."

The sound of running footsteps echoed through the house from one of the other rooms and Kimraj peered through the kitchen door and into the living room just in time to see a muddy, naked child run past.

He drew in a breath and asked the next set of questions he needed answers to. "How come none of them wearing any clothes?"

She shrugged once more. "What you asking me for? I is not their mother."

"Why aren't any of them in school?"

"Mister, like you not getting it? These blasted children have nothing to do with me. If you care so much go ahead and take them all away nah! I really want to see you try."

"Lady, I warning you to watch your tone with me, you hear? I here on authority of the government and this is a serious matter."

She let out a loud steups and turned her attention back to her pot. "Suit yourself, do what you have to."

Realizing that she had no interest in answering his questions to any satisfactory level, he pulled out his phone and moved off into the living room. Turning on his camera, he began recording his walkthrough. He needed to determine if there was sufficient bedding and comfortable housing for the children, but he already knew the answer was no based on just the size of the house and the sheer number of voices he could once more hear running around in the yard below. At this point, all the evidence would simply go towards building a case against this hapless woman, and chances were strong she'd end up going away for a long time on child endangerment, negligence, and a host of other charges depending on what he found in the other rooms.

As he walked through the house, the situation began to make less and less sense. The house was a neat one bedroom, one bathroom, with a large enough living room, dining room and kitchen. But there was no sign of where the children were kept or where they stayed when night came. Returning to the kitchen he looked at her and wished he didn't have to ask her anything else.

"Ma'am, where do they sleep?"

She scoffed dramatically. "Sleep? They don't sleep. All night long they does be up and down the place. Making noise, making mischief, and nothing I say or do does ever make them sleep." She turned to face him with a long drawn expression. "Honestly, if I could kill them all I would."

He felt the anger in him flare up like it never had before. Biting his tongue, he stared at her as she turned back to the stove and began to dish out little Styrofoam cups of soup and set them on the vinyl covered table that also housed her bottle of oil and tins of what was likely flour, rice, and sugar. He watched as the little chunks of flour dumplings bobbed and floated in the richly salted coconut flavoured broth while the curls of steam flowed upwards and dissipated into the air. Unable to help himself he inhaled and called forth memories of his own boyhood days in his grandmother's kitchen. Those had been some of the best memories of his childhood.

Having heard enough from this crass woman, he lifted the phone in front of him he dialled 9-9-9 and held it to his ear. It rang once, twice, and on the third ring she knocked the metal pot spoon against the rim of the pot, a sound he would later learn was her version of ringing the lunch bell.

The answering officer was a man he knew well. Officer Ramdass had been with the force for as long as he could remember.

"Ram, this is Kim...raj..." his voice trailed off as one of the children ran past him from the living room and collected a cup of soup.

The woman turned to face him, her expression softer now though a flicker of amusement danced in her eyes.

The faceless child grabbed a plastic spoon from the chipped enamel cup on the table and moved forward on bowed legs to sit on the back stairs to where Kimraj could see just its naked back.

"Not all of them have backwards feet," she said quietly. "I never really figured out why that is. And sometimes they does have a face and you does think is a real child, but is never the same face. It does always change."

"Kimraj? Is you? You there?" the worried voice on the other end of the line asked.

"Yeah, umm is me...lemme uhhh... lemme call you back." Kimraj hung up the phone without listening for a reply as he moved towards the back door and stood behind the child who was slurping his soup.

"You, boy, look at me."

The child stopped eating and turned around slowly and peered up at Kimraj, seeing him without any eyes.

The child had no nose but it did have a mouth, that was nothing more than a lipless, toothless hole, and when he closed it there was nothing more than a thin, barely discernible line.

Kimraj stepped back in horror and bumped into yet another child who quickly moved his cup of soup out of the way to avoid his lunch from being spilled. This child, like the one sitting on the step, had no face, but unlike the other boy, this one's legs were turned backwards.

The woman continued dishing out cups of soup, and as Kimraj struggled to find the words, he heard a group of them making their way up the steps. Their chatter and laughter sounded so much like children but as they entered the kitchen their grotesque forms made Kimraj shudder as he crossed himself and began to pray. Surely this had to be a test from

God.

Seeing him praying, the children giggled amongst themselves as they nudged each other and whispered.

"You want to sit down, Mister?" The woman's voice was a mixture of concern and victory.

He had so many questions, so many doubts. Were they douenes? Couldn't be, those things didn't exist. Some looked like douenes, others didn't. So what did that make them then? Were they sick children? Possibly. But how did they breathe with no noses? How did they see without eyes? What was he to do now?

He looked up into the impassive gaze of the woman who tilted her head and patted an itch on the side of her scarf-wrapped head. "I don't...I don't understand..." his words trailed off into the air.

The last of the children took their cups and filed out of the kitchen leaving the two adults alone.

"*You* think *you* don't understand!" She laughed. "I was coming home one night after going to a fete down the road. See me walking all by myself coming home with a box of food in one hand and a cup in the other. Next thing I know, I come in the house, open the fridge to put my food in and when I turn around one of them damn things standing behind me!" She shook her head and sucked her teeth. "Man you shoulda hear me bawl! Then the thing ask me for some food. Tell me it smell the box food and follow me home. I could only stand up in the corner of the kitchen shaking like a leaf as it walk over to the fridge and take out the food and start eating."

Kimraj listened to her tale with a feeling akin to disbelief. This had to be some nonsense 'Nansi story. Surely this was a set up. The children were wearing masks to hide their faces and some of them must have been double jointed... He knew it was wishful thinking and that the reality was far worse than the fantasy.

Thunder rolled across the darkening skies as the midday rain began to fall. Hearing shrieks of glee, he looked out through the backdoor and down into the now muddy yard to where the *children* were running around and playing.

"They look sweet, ent?" she said and he turned to look at her once again. "Is not so. I stand up in the corner all night long, too frighten to move. By the time the sun started to come up the thing open my backdoor and whistle low, low, and from the bush about ten others come out and climb up the step. They tell me I invite them in so now I have to take care of them. I try everything I could think of to get rid of them, all kind of ombudsman and priest and obeah man try to get rid of them, but no matter what they try, all them things does do is laugh. And the next day, more of them does show up."

"And what will happen if you don't take care of them?"

"They go kill me." She said it so simply as though the answer was obvious. "I used to always think I wasn't afraid of death, but now that it waiting for me I 'fraid bad." Her face looked like she was on the verge of tears. "So tell me, Mister, you come to protect the *chirren,* but tell me, Mister, you think could protect me too?"

"I...Look I...um" Kimraj scrunched his face up as he found his mind blank. He simply refused to accept what he'd been told, but the situation was more than he was able to handle.

"Ah thought so." She turned away from him as he fought to come up with some reassurance. Some promise. Some...something.

But nothing came.

"I think is time for you to leave."

He looked up at her face and felt himself turning as rosy as a ripe pomerac. "Well...um...yes. Thank you for your time," he mumbled as he stepped out into the rain.

She made no reply as he went down the steps under a hail of rain and small pebbles that the *children* were throwing at him as they cackled and hid themselves around the yard.

Kimraj got into his car and drove off, sparing only a singular glance back at the house through his rear view mirror. Much to his dismay, he saw that a small army of *them* had lined up in the front yard, sightlessly glaring at him as he drove away.

He shuddered as his foot pressed down on the gas pedal, encouraging the car to move along as quickly as was possible.

Back at the office he sat down at his desk and stared blankly at the report he was expected to hand in. Unlocking his phone he looked at the pictures he'd taken and scrolled through them from last to first. As he got to the first picture he'd taken, the one he'd snapped before he'd even gotten out of his car, he felt his mind finally break. The picture showed an empty front yard with the house positioned on the right. There was not a single trace of any *children*.

Setting the report aside he opened up a blank Word document and began to type. The letter of resignation was brief and only stated that his resignation was effective immediately and that he was using up his remaining vacation days in lieu of his two week notice. Placing the note on his boss' desk, Kimraj gathered his belongings and drove himself to the nearest bar, looking over his shoulder every step of the way.

THE SCULPTOR

Alexander was both an artist and a philanthropist. There was no one on the planet that would debate that. It was a simple and easily acceptable fact. His chosen artistic medium was meticulously warped wire that he then covered in hand-churned concrete. Working with only hand tools and his hands themselves, he would shape and mould the piece until it not only took form but appeared to come to life with the level and extent of details he would put into it.

If there was an event anywhere in the world he would sculpt out the icons or persons associated with it, and like hotcakes, his pieces would sell. From the working class to celebrities and politicians, his works had been bought by all walks of people. The wealthy would pay pretty pennies for his commissions to sculpt the busts of their husbands and wives and children, each seeking to be immortalized by the man who, despite his connections and his expanse of life experiences, remained humble and affable to everyone around him. And for those who couldn't afford his work, all they needed to do was ask and Alexander would likely create their desires for nothing more than a bag of mangoes or a nice round breadfruit. He was loved and admired by all and it seemed as though his generosity and good nature knew no limits.

Little did the people know that just underneath the surface a dark force was culminating within him and it all began the day he'd been nominated and then overlooked for an award he'd been told he was a shoo-in to win. But instead he'd received an "honourable mention" and later learned that as an unspoken requirement to qualify as a winner, a handsome donation had been required. It seemed like all the nominated winners had gotten that memo, but not Alexander. The real kicker came when a newspaper article about the event denounced him as "tired" and "outdated" and even went so far as to call him a has-been. That was when the veil slowly began to slip and he began to see what the newer generation really thought about him.

By then he was well into his sixties, and as the years went by his bitterness and resentment grew. Suddenly he was no longer as sought after as he'd once been, and like the memories of an Alzheimer's patient, his friends came and went until they slowly faded away for good.

Jilted by those who'd once put him up on a pedestal for his skill and his work, and reeling from the loss of his wife of almost forty years, Alexander retreated into his home and continued to work, this time for himself. Night and day he would work his finger to the bone, carving out intricate details of the people and characters of the Caribbean. Soon his works began to spill out into his yard. Like an army of misfit stone soldiers, they all stood their ground around their creator's home as though it were some grand gathering.

When the people came calling he would pretend he wasn't home, when they knocked on his door he would hide out of sight. If they caught him outside he would pretend he hadn't seen them and rush off inside, closing the door with a soft but firm push that would allow the lock to engage and snap into place.

In his mind the visits weren't genuine. They were either pity visits (and he was no charity case) or it was someone who only wanted something from him, usually someone seeking some donation for their cause. These people had lost their respect for him and as the years wore on he slowly disappeared from their memories, and his works, even the ones featured in public places like the town hall or on the corner of Cipero Street, slowly began to age and fade away from their former glory. The plaques that bore his name at the base of each of his works had been weathered to the point of non-existence, and so the people completely forgot who Alexander Ronwald was.

Until the day a social worker came knocking. For the second month in a row Alexander hadn't been by to collect his pension check and at almost ninety-five years of age these visits were almost always a bad sign.

The army of weathered guards stood their ground as she slipped around them and knocked on the door but the moment she did, she heard it; the swarm of flies that were congregated on the other side of the door. The smell hit her next. Created by either her mind or by a change in the wind at that particular moment, she knew why he hadn't been by to collect his check.

As the body was removed and the van drove away, the team of three cleaners descended on the house. The smell had been atrocious. Two weeks of decomposition in the humid and sweltering home that had been lashed by the Caribbean heat was to blame. And as they worked to disinfect, sanitize, and deodorize the home, they found themselves both marvelling at and creeped out by the thousands of statues and figurines that adorned almost every surface of the home. The ones in the yard seemed...benign. They were recognizable as the characters they were meant to be. From Bob Marley to Marcus Garvey to Ronald Reagan and even the great Lord Kitchener himself, the yard army was a collectively famous lot, but it was the ones that were inside the home that gave them pause. Hundreds and hundreds of creatures and demonic looking beasts stood, their expressions locked in eternal hand-carved rage. And at the centre of it all, right where his body had been discovered, the massive floor to ceiling statue of the black horse stood reared back with its teeth bared. The horse's front right leg was still just a shaped wire frame but it seemed as though the rest of the beast had been completed and painted including a harrowing set of eyes so realistic that Surresh found himself glancing up at the statue every few seconds with distrust. There was something not quite right about it...

"You know, they say he was old and crazy. Possessed by the devil himself! And I never would have believed it but looking at all these evil creatures he made...I don't know nah..."

Melissa was running her mouth again as usual instead of just working. As Surresh looked up at her she nodded all-knowingly and leaned against the body of the horse statue. Curling her lips over her teeth, she snorted. "They say he was a nasty man who used to pelt stones at the people who used to come calling, and at night they say he used to peel off his skin like a soucouyant and..."

"Please shut up." The words were out Surresh's mouth before he could stop himself.

"Excuse me?" Melissa's words were sharp enough to cut, and as her eyes narrowed she stared down at Surresh who only shook his head and continued to scrub the floor. "Mr. Man, I don't know who you feel you is, but don't you ever make the mistake of talking to me like that again, you hear me? I is not-" Her words ended in a short and sharp yelp.

His head snapped upwards just in time to see her hand recoil. Nursing her somehow bleeding finger she held it in front of her face and examined it with a scowl.

"See what you make me do? I cut my blasted finger on this nasty old man's dotish statue because of you! Look, you see me, I don't need this today. I go see allyuh tomorrow."

With a huff and a stomp, she left the crowded home, leaving Surresh and Karim looking at each other with blank stares that soon dissolved into apathy as they went back to doing their work in silence.

"It's not true you know," Karim said softly after a few minutes had gone by.

"What's not true?" Surresh asked as he continued to scrub.

"That he was crazy or possessed by the devil."

Surresh sat up and smiled. "Oh, I know that. His name was Alex Ronwald and he was a great artist. My grandmother knew him and she used to tell us about him."

Karim nodded and smiled. "He was also a great man. He did a lot of charity work. Because of him my grandfather went to school and got a good education. It's kind of sad how things turned out for him. I hope I don't end up alone when I'm old."

A steely silence fell between them and Surresh felt compelled to add one final thought to their conversation. "You know, they say he'd completely lost his sight some twenty years ago but would create his pieces by touch alone."

Karim's eyebrows shot up. "Yuh lie! For real? That is some real talent and skill, yes. Maybe that's why he stopped making famous people and made these things." He motioned to the figures that surrounded them both from all sides. "You think that he made what he saw or felt after he lost his sight?"

Surresh contemplated his co-worker's words and shrugged. "Maybe."

The silence melted into a quiet state of contemplation, and as both men continued their work they thought about the man who had been known as Alexander Ronwald and pondered upon what his life had been and what it had become in the end.

As they finished their cigarettes, Surresh stretched until his back cracked. Exhaling with satisfaction, he dropped the cigarette butt onto the ground at the base of JFK's concrete clad feet and crushed it with the toe of his boot. "I think I'm done for the day. I've done all I can for now and I want to go home and eat before it gets too dark. Tomorrow we'll finish up. I might step out early though as I planning to go visit my bird down Cedros side." He smiled slyly.

Stubbing out his own cigarette Karim nodded. "Yeah, man. No worries, you go on home, I still have some things to finish up and then I will leave."

Surresh didn't need to ask anything more. With a nod he stuck his hands in his pockets and strolled off towards his car. Another day, another dollar, he sighed as he drove away.

Morning came in a blur and a groggy Surresh pulled up and parked his van on the side of the road and made his way through the front yard army, with his head bent in drowsy contemplation. As he approached the front door that was set on the side of the building, he stepped over a chunk of concrete without giving it any thought. It was only when the little edge of wire snagged against the hem of his pants and tripped him up that he was drawn back to reality.

With a frown his eyes followed the trail of random concrete chunks all the way to the front door which stood wide open. No, not open, it had been torn clean off its hinges as though it had been the victim of an explosion. As he cautiously stepped through the doorframe and into the home he found the inside in ruins. Though the yard army stood untouched, all of the figurines inside the home had been destroyed and pulverized. Chunks of concrete littered the floor, punctuated by snaggles of twisted wire that jutted out every which way.

As the question of what had happened touched his lips, he found himself feeling uneasy.

"What happen here?! Like allyuh didn't lock up this place last night or what?" Melissa asked from behind him having seemingly appeared out of thin air. Her tone and phrasing was a loaded gun that made it clear she was already looking to remove herself from having any blame in this situation and Surresh was sure she'd gotten here long before him.

"I left, but Karim stayed behind to finish up some things. But what does it matter?" Surresh asked. "The door isn't even here anymore. Locked or not ent make no difference."

"We have to call the boss first and then the police." Melissa said as she pulled her phone out of her bag and began dialling. "This is beyond me."

As she wandered off and disappeared between the statues Surresh turned to examine the extent of the damage. Just what had happened here? A break in? Maybe just vandals? No, this was a lot of damage for some vandals. They'd completely destroyed the place but didn't touch anything outside? This amount of damage seemed personal.

Though the entire floor had been covered in destroyed statues there was one spot that was clear and free of any debris and that had been where the massive horse statue had been standing. That statue was no longer there so it had either been destroyed and had joined in the rest of the mess, though Surresh hadn't seen any traces of the black paint on any of the pieces on the floor, or perhaps someone had taken it for some reason, though how they'd managed to move that heavy thing he would never know. Or...no, the alternative made no logical sense and wasn't possible. Surresh shook his head and scoffed to himself. There he went again, letting his imagination get the better of him.

The moment he heard the scream his legs were in motion, guiding him between the silent and untouched statues in the yard. Melissa was there in the back corner of the lot backing away from something as quickly as she could. As he reached her she turned with a horrified expression but it was as though she didn't even see him.

As she ran past him he rushed forward to see what had caused her to come so unhinged, and the moment he moved around the last statue he saw the trampled body lying face down on the still dew covered earth. Though the clothes were soaked in either mud or blood he felt sure that it was Karim.

His mind and body went numb as he slowly approached the form, almost as though he was afraid it was going to pop up and attack him. There was a little voice in his head that assured him that this was all just an orchestrated joke, but the closer he got the more the illusion of that hope fell away as the putrid smell of death wafted through the air around him.

Surresh looked around in wide-eyed mortification as the morning's sun illuminated the land. A soft whoosh, almost like that of a snort, came from the trees to his right, and though there seemed to be nothing there that he could see, Surresh was positive that he heard a soft neighing followed by the slightly irregular clatter of retreating hooves against the soft earth.

Mother Knows Best

The thump of soca music filled the air. Three different tunes coming from three different directions had somehow managed to blend their beats together in one harmonious rhythm that was further complimented by an orchestra of other sounds; the children's high pitched wails of delight as they darted around the grounds, the splash of water from those taking a dip in the river, the clang of pot spoons against the rim of the massive iron pots bubbling with stew chicken, cow tongue dumplings, or pelau, the crackle of the stoked fires below those pots, and jingle of the ice cubes as the drinks sloshed around in their Styrofoam cups. The river lime was in full swing and there was nothing sweeter.

Inshan was sound asleep in his hammock. His fat, rounded belly protruded into the air with a stiffness that had been attained over decades of beer and indulgent home-cooked meals, and as Patricia looked at her husband she grinned and moved to join him.

As morning slipped into afternoon, the children continued playing their endless games with seemingly renewed energy, and by the time the adults had packed up and put everything away the sun had already began to settle into the evening sky.

As they piled into the car Patricia looked around for her

youngest.

"Where Inicia?"

The children all shook their heads and shrugged from their places in the backseat. Patricia looked around at the now empty river bank and she felt a hollow pit form in her stomach.

"Inicia?" She called but there was no answer. "Inicia?!" Her voice rose, tinted with panic.

"What happen?" Inshan opened the door and regarded his wife.

"Inicia's missing," she replied already moving towards the far end of the river bank where she'd seen them playing *in the river, on the bank* earlier. Getting halfway there, she hesitated and her pace slowed. Torn between rushing back to the car and rushing into the forest, she turned and sprinted towards her children who were now standing beside their father.

"When last you see her? Where she was?"

The three children paused for thought.

"About an hour ago?"

"No, it was when we was playing marble pitch and she was out."

"Yeah, she went off over there to play hide and seek with some of the others."

"And none of you went with her? What happen to allyuh? Allyuh is the bigger ones, she's only four years old!" Her open hand connected with the back of her oldest daughter's skull, and a hollow sound echoed forth as the daughter recoiled from her coco-tap.

Suddenly the reality of the situation settled on her. *Her child was missing.* All manner of terrible thoughts ran through her mind but only one stood at the forefront. *Kidnapping.*

She was sure of it. Someone had kidnapped her child. Holding her head she bent over at the hips and began to wail. "Oh gawd! Somebody take she! What I go do?!"

"Alright, alright." Inshan's tone was firm as he comforted his wife. "Stop crying and let we look for she." He looked up at the sky and calculated that they had at least thirty minutes of daylight left. If they didn't find her by then, they'd drive to the Tunapuna police station and file a report, then he would come back armed with torchlights, or maybe even a flambeaux, and his cutlass and search all night if he had to. All of this flashed through his mind as they walked towards where the children had been playing and called out to Inicia.

As Patricia plunged headfirst into the surrounding greenery she called out and stopped, listening for a reply, but the only thing that could be heard was the screech of the cicadas and the whisper and groans of the surrounding bamboo.

Anger, guilt, and remorse wracked her and she felt a sense of desperation swarm. As she opened her mouth to call out one more time, she heard the sweetest words of her life.

"AH FIND SHE!"

It was Inshan, and as she ran towards his voice she found him standing near the car with Inicia in his arms. The child was dressed in her bathing suit and was silently clinging to his neck but she seemed unharmed.

Taking her from him she cradled her child and examined her for any signs of injury, chiding her as she went, but her relief soon extinguished into anger. "Baby, you okay? Where you was? You didn't hear me calling you? You must answer when you hear me calling you! I thought something bad had happened to you. You know better than to wander away. Next time I go put a solid licking on you!"

Inicia said nothing and watched her mother wordlessly with an unreadable expression as the last traces of daylight disappeared behind the trees.

"Let we go," Patricia said as they all loaded into the car and made their way home. Inicia remained silent the entire trip home while the other three children sat talking and laughing in the backseat, and that silence continued on through the night and into the next day.

As the four children sat on the floor of the living room methodically breaking off bits of bake and dipping it into their morning cup of tea, Inicia finished her entire bake in record time and held out her plate and empty cup to her mother as a means of asking for more.

Patricia was concerned, but as she broke off a piece of own bake and handed it to the child she watched her carefully, observing her movements and actions. She'd never seen Inicia eat so much. When the child finished and turned around to ask for yet another piece Patricia shook her head. "You've had enough. Save your appetite for lunch time."

She braced herself for the cries of protest, but Inicia simply turned around and went back to join her siblings with an air of indifference.

As the day wore on, Patricia found her youngest sitting on the back step watching out into the wooded area beyond the fence while her other three children were busy running around the yard playing.

"Inicia?" she called, and in the second that her child turned to look at her she sensed that something wasn't quite right. Patricia's maternal instinct kicked in and a fear once more welled up inside her that something had happened to Inicia when she'd been lost in the forest.

Sitting down next to her daughter she pulled her into her arms and cradled the girl. "Doux-doux, you feeling ok?"

Inicia stared at her without saying a word.

"Listen, yesterday when you were gone, did you see anyone? Did anyone…any stranger…talk to you? Did anyone try to touch you?"

The words were hard to say and her eyes roamed over the child's face, trying to read any expression, but Inicia remained unreadable. Then she slowly shook her head, slid out of her mother's grasp, and ran off to play.

Two days later and Inicia still hadn't said a word to anyone, and worse yet she'd developed a fondness for suddenly appearing out of nowhere and standing behind her unsuspecting family members then grinning wickedly and running off when they screamed in fright. The times that she wasn't scaring the life out of everyone she spent it alone, glowering at the skies or at the surrounding trees, or eating whatever she could get her hands on. Twice already Patricia had the cause to send Ian, her second eldest, to the shop to buy more cheese, and though she was tempted to snap at Inicia something held her back. This behaviour was more than acting out, it was like her child was a completely different person.

"Like she have worms!" Inshan had laughed.

But Inicia's attitude was changing as well. She was restless and seemed prone to violent outbursts that consisted of her slapping or pushing at anyone who tried to force her to do anything from coming inside to taking a bath.

Though she couldn't quite place her finger on it, Patricia was sure her daughter was physically different at well. It was subtle and could only be seen from certain angles but the child's arms seemed slightly longer than they should have been and her jawline seemed a bit rougher and less smooth, and her skin…her skin seemed uneven somehow. The changes were almost indiscernible but Patricia was sure something was off. Maybe she'd picked up something from one of the other children, or maybe she did indeed have some parasite. Patricia was seriously concerned and had made a resolve to take her daughter to see a doctor or even the local counsellor the very next day in the hopes of getting to the bottom of her strange behaviour, but that night something happened that changed everything.

Patricia and Inshan were sound asleep in their bed when the sound of heavy breathing drew Patricia out of the terrible dream she'd been having. As her eyes fluttered open she saw the creature standing at the side of her bed just inches away from her sleeping form. It was hideously disfigured and it's murderous and angry gaze bore into her. Moving as quickly as she could Patricia recoiled with a gasp and reached out for the lamp next to her bed, and without taking her eyes off the creature she turned on the light.

Her sudden movement awoke Inshan who sat up, alert to any danger, but as he saw Inicia standing next to her mother's side of her bed he relaxed a little. Patricia on the other hand was still rattled. She'd been sure of what she'd seen…or had it been a dream? Her confidence faltered and she looked at her daughter and scrutinized her every detail.

"What's wrong?" Inshan asked. "You had a bad dream?"

Inicia nodded and looked at her father with eyes that seemed darker than usual.

"You want to sleep with mummy and daddy tonight?"

Inicia's face broke into a grin and she moved towards the bed but Patricia held out her hand and stopped her. "No. Stay there."

Inicia froze and cocked her head before she took another step.

"I said stay there. You not sleeping in my bed."

She could sense that Inshan was about to question her gruff tone and actions, but her focus was on the child before her. She was suddenly sure that this thing was not her child and she was prepared to do whatever was needed to get her child back to normal.

A silence settled on the room, broken only by the loud, shrill screeching of the insects outside and by her own laboured breathing.

Inicia grinned just before she launched herself into the bed and began clawing and biting at her mother who, unprepared for such an attack, let out a shriek.

Inshan sprang into action as he forced himself between his wife and daughter, and as he pushed Inicia off she screamed and bellowed in an impossibly deep tone and inhuman tone before she bolted from the room and disappeared into the darkness of the house.

"You okay?" Inshan asked his wife.

Patricia was bleeding from several of her bites and scratches and her eyes were wild. "That thing is not my daughter," she screamed as she stared at the doorway, terrified that whatever it was it would come back.

Inshan was at a loss for words and had no idea what to make of the situation.

"We need to go get the pastor. That child possessed by a demon or something. Something happen at the river. I sure of it." Patricia was hysterical and Inshan placed his arms around her without replying as he tried to figure out what to do. The house was eerily silent and that concerned him. There was no way that none of the other children hadn't heard the commotion, they should have come to see what was going on. Unless…

Letting go of his wife, he got up off the bed and looked around for a weapon or something to at least defend himself with. The very thought of needing a weapon or even having to use one against his own child pained him but he needed to protect the rest of his family.

"What you doing?" Patricia asked, and Inshan put his fingers to his lips to silence her. He wanted to hear everything that was going on and he didn't want to be distracted for even a second. He needed to get to his other children. Once they were safe then he could figure out what to do about it all.

Opening the wardrobe as quietly as he could he reached in and felt around in the back for the cricket bat without taking his eyes off the doorway. Finding it, he drew it out and readjusted his grip on it. "Hand me the torchlight," he said to his wife, and she reached over to her side of the nightstand and handed him the heavy metal flashlight. "Stay here," he instructed her.

As he flicked the button and a beam of light flooded the bedroom, he ventured out into the hallway, shining the light around as he looked for Inicia.

Patricia wasn't about to sit idly by. Keeping an eye on the doorway, she called her mother and hoped that her call would be answered. Even if her mother didn't know what was happening there was a good chance she'd know someone who would.

Her mother picked up on the third ring and Patricia could hear the sluggishness in her voice as she answered.

"Mammee? Is me, I need your help." Patricia was whispering into the phone.

"What happen? The children okay?"

"Is Inicia…something wrong with she. The girl just trip off and attack me for no reason. If you see she pelting bite and scratching me. And you should of hear she, just before she run off she make this noise…I don't even know how to describe it, it sound like some animal!"

Patricia could hear her mother sit up and her breathing on the phone changed. "How long this going on?" her mother asked.

"Since we come back from the river lime on Saturday she wasn't the same. She not talking at all and she hungry, hungry all the time. And I don't know…she just…something not right. I ask she over and over if something happened, if someone…do anything to she, but she always shaking she head no."

The silence on the other end was worrying and Patricia's fear and impatience was growing. "Mammee?"

"I here, child. Give me a minute, let me think." After a moment she asked, "You take she to the doctor?"

"I was going to take she in the morning but then she trip off…"

"Where Inshan?"

"He gone to get the other children and make sure they okay."

"And where Inicia?" Her tone was guarded now.

"I don't know. She run out the room after Inshan pull she off me."

"You have your bible with you? Start praying and don't let she out of the house or out of your sight. This sound like some kind of possession but I not sure. I go call on Papa Abayomi. He might know what to do. Give me about ten minutes and we will be there."

Before Patricia could say anything more her mother was gone and she went to the door, bible in hand, to wait for Inshan to return.

***

This wasn't no horror movie and he wasn't going to spend a second in the dark if he didn't have to. Making his way to the end of the hallway, he shone his light into the first bedroom, the one where Inicia and Patsy slept. Both beds were empty and Inshan felt his unease grow. Reaching out his hand, he flicked on the light before moving onto the boys' room. Their beds were also empty but as he stepped into the room he heard a small sound coming from the wardrobe.

Gripping the bat tighter in his hand Inshan glanced over his shoulder before he silently padded across the vinyl-covered floor. With the flashlight in his hand, he reached out and grasped the handle of the wardrobe and as he pulled it open and shone the light inside he drew the bat back just in case.

His three children screamed in fear and relief flooded over him as he shushed them and helped them out of the small space. Turning around, he glanced about the room for any sign of Inicia, but the room stood empty.

"What happened?" he asked them, and it was Patsy who spoke.

"Inicia wake me up. She was standing next to my bed and acting weird and her face looked funny. Then she growled and turned and ran from the room like a dog. I got up to follow her but I heard Mummy scream so I ran in here to hide."

Inshan gathered them up and ushered them out of the room. Out in the hallway they all bolted towards the bedroom where Patricia was nervously waiting in the doorway.

"You see she anywhere?" she asked and Inshan shook his head as he wondered what they would do now. It was three o'clock in the morning, no one would be up or around and this wasn't exactly a situation that came with a clear answer. His daughter had tripped off, that much was clear, but Patricia seemed to believe it was something far more sinister.

"I call Mama. She gone to get Papa Abayomi. They go be here soon but we should find Inicia."

"Papa Abayomi?" Inshan asked. "The obeah man?" He almost spat the word. Getting a pastor, or better yet, a pundit, was one thing, but an obeah man? He thought that was going too far.

"Let we go find she."

Inshan knew it was pointless to argue so he held his tongue, nodded, and moved forward through the house, turning on every light possible. But in the end it wasn't necessary as they found Inicia calmly sitting in front of the open fridge gorging on a block of cheese and drinking from a bottle of pepper sauce.

Inicia turned around to look at them for a brief moment, looking perfectly normal despite her actions. Then, without a care in the world, she turned back to the fridge and continued eating.

Patricia met her mother and hunched over figure with the carpet of white hair that dusted his balding, mottled scalp at the front door. As she greeted them both she turned to thank Papa Abayomi for coming over at such a late hour. Looking up at her with unexpected tenderness, he reached out towards her. His arthritic hands were slow and stiff in their movements, but as he clasped her hands in his, she found an odd sense of reassurance in the cool, dry feeling of his crepe paper skin. Nodding in equal parts of understanding and sympathy, he let her hands go as he walked past her and into the house as if he knew where he was going. Suddenly, he stopped just short of the kitchen and sniffed the air as his eyes came alive.

"Ah! Is so!" he exclaimed as he dug into his bag and pulled out a short black metal rod.

The group made their way towards the kitchen and though Patricia had a thousand burning questions she forced herself to remain silent.

As Papa Abayomi approached the child she stopped eating and looked up at his smiling face and seemed to shrink.

"It's alright little one. I'm not going to hurt you," he spoke in a language that only he and the child seemed to understand. "I just need to be sure of something. Can you hold out your hand for me?"

The girl reluctantly nodded and held out her palm and Papa Abayomi lightly touched the rod to it.

The moment it made contact, Inicia screamed and pulled her hand away while her body twisted and her form retreated. As everyone watched on in horror, the creature that looked like Inicia screamed inhumanly and spat at them as it skittered across the floor and cowered in the corner.

Papa Abayomi nodded to himself as he turned to face Inshan and Patricia, who were holding their three terrified children.

"It's in good shape. You haven't beaten it or mistreated it like most people tend to do. There is hope yet."

"What are you talking about? Of course not. I wouldn't beat my daughter. Old man you playing up here tonight!" Inshan's anger flared up and he felt his face flush. He knew he was being irrational but his mind refused to believe what his eyes had just witnessed.

"This is not your daughter, nor is she possessed by anything. This is an *ogbanje*. I think in English places they call it a *Changeling*. They live deep in the forest and can assume the shape of human children in the hopes of taking the human child's place.

"Long ago the solution was to beat the creature and mistreat it but I find that unnecessary and does more harm than good because if its mother senses its offspring being beaten, it will return the favour to your own child. Kill it and you will be killing your own child. But I'm sure if we take the creature back to where it came from it will lead us to your daughter providing that it hasn't gotten too used to human luxuries."

The questions burned in Patricia's mind but it was Inshan who spoke.

"How come I never hear about this before? This seems like some kind of go-bar old people talk."

Papa Abayomi nodded and smiled. "It is true that this being is not typical and very few people know of them. It's been decades since I've had to deal with them. The truth is they exist all over the world though they carry different names. At any rate, let me make it clear, this thing you've brought home isn't your daughter. Your real daughter is somewhere out there, locked into a slumber and is being watched over by another of its kind. She can only be awakened if we return the creature to its rightful place. The choice is yours."

"By the river. That was the day she started acting strangely." Patricia suddenly had an image of her daughter sleeping on the forest floor somewhere and she was sure that as crazy as it sounded, that thing in the corner was not her child. Inshan hadn't seen what she'd seen when she'd awoken to find it at the side of her bed, nor had he noticed the changes over the last few days, but she had.

"Let we go to the river," she said in a whisper and Papa Abayomi nodded.

"You can't be serious!" Inshan exclaimed. "The girl need a doctor. She need professional, medical help."

"Scepticism is one thing, son. But listen to me, do it this way first and if it turns out we're wrong we'll take her straight to Port-of-Spain General." His mother-in-law's voice was stern and Inshan felt his defiance growing. Surrounding herself with her other three grandchildren, she led them upstairs and without looking back she called out. "I will stay here with them, you two go and get your daughter back."

Papa Abayomi seemed unaffected as he dipped into his dirty, old bag and produced a small bottled and a length of rope that seemed almost impossible to come from such a small pouch. "I need to keep it tied up, and as much as I wish I could chain it, iron will kill the creature."

He opened the bottle and tilted it upside down, allowing its contents to spill out onto his finger before he stepped up to Patricia and used the liquid to draw a thin line from her third eye down to the tip of her nose and two other lines that ran from her temples to her cheekbones. The liquid was floral smelling, and as if he could read her mind he smiled. "It's concentrated morning glory with buttercup, nutmeg, and sweet broom. It calms the creatures and identifies us as friends."

As he tilted the bottle against his fingertip once more and moved to Inshan Inshan held up his hand and shook his head firmly. "You not touching me with that."

Papa Abayomi chuckled and shrugged as he anointed himself. Moving over to Inicia he squatted before her and began chanting and whispering under his breath. Inicia sat enthralled by his words and without question she stood up and held her wrists out, allowing the old man to tie the rope around them and to loop it around her waist and into a makeshift harness.

Inicia grabbed the car keys and stood watching her husband. "You coming?"

Though he wanted to scream no, he saw the look of determination in his wife's eyes and knew that he was not about to let his wife and ill daughter go off into the forest with whoever this man was.

Inicia cooed and reached her arms out towards her father and he instinctively reached down to pick her up.

He expected Papa Abayomi to stop him but he didn't. Cradling his rope-leashed child against his body, he followed his wife out to the car.

The drive to the riverside was uninterrupted, and as they parked and got out Papa Abayomi once more dipped into his bag and this time produced a kerosene lantern. As he lit the wick and adjusted the flame, he held it up to examine the child who was still clinging to her father's neck.

"You might want to put her down," he said to Inshan but Inshan shook his head firmly. Papa Abayomi shrugged before he grinned. "Suit yourself."

He once more called to the girl in that strange language and as she turned her head to look at him she smiled as his words began to pour out faster.

The language sounded tribal, and Inicia began rhythmically swaying back and forth in her father's arms, and as she did her shape and form wavered as she began to revert to her original state.

Inshan felt his world turn upside down as every logical thought and belief he had departed him as he set his gaze upon the creature in his arms.

Its eyes, which sat above its deformed nose that looked like it had been chopped off, were a cloudy, dark yellow and bulged out of its head. Its skin held a bluish tinge like that of a corpse and it looked as though it had been stitched together with many parts and pieces.

Inshan fought the instinct to fling the creature as far away from him as possible. Hearing his wife's gasp, he looked at her and her horrified expression only served to confirm what he was so reluctant to believe. The creature squirmed in his arms and he felt his blood pressure plummet as his world threatened to go dark.

But Papa Abayomi was there and as he placed a firm hand on Inshan's shoulder he steadied him and spoke. "It will not harm you, now set it down carefully."

Following instructions since he was clearly in over his head, he set the gurgling creature, who was no breathing like a bulldog, down and stepped back into the arms of his wife.

"You might want some of the morning glory elixir now, otherwise you might be better off staying here." Papa Abayomi's voice was low as he addressed Inshan, and though the man remained rooted to the spot, he allowed himself to be anointed by the liquid.

Speaking to the small, ugly, child-like being, Papa Abayomi unwound a few coils of the rope and the creature turned and began walking into the forest. Holding his lantern out at arm's length, the three adults followed behind the changeling and soon they disappeared into the darkness of the riverside forest.

As they walked on Papa Abayomi was clearly keeping up communications with the being, and while they held their unintelligible discourse, Inshan began to experience the hair-raising sensation of being watched. As he looked around, he saw the occasional glow of yellow eyes trailing them as they trudged deeper and deeper into the forest.

Feeling hysteria bubble up, and he fought back the urge to scream and take off running through the bushes. To calm himself he began to recite a mantra meant to drive away evil and negative spirits.

"*Om dum durgayei namaha.*" Over and over he said it under his breath as he forced himself to look away from the growing number of eyes that surrounded them.

Though they could still hear the roar of the river, they were far from where they'd parked and as they approached a large immortelle tree the leashed creature stopped and chattered as it pointed towards the base of the tree.

Papa Abayomi untied the creature, and the moment it was free it dashed out of sight and disappeared into the forest.

Patricia screamed after it, calling out, beseeching the creatures to return her daughter, but Papa Abayomi remained unmoved as he looped the rope and put it away. Then, seemingly out of thin air, the small form of a child appeared at the base of the tree before them. As Papa Abayomi thrust the lantern's light in the child's direction and examined the frail form before them. The child lifted an arm to shield herself against the assault of light and whined in protest.

"Inicia?" Patricia's voice was laced with scepticism.

"Mummy?" the child's voice sounded drugged with sleep.

Patricia rushed forward to sweep the child into her arms but Inshan was uncertain.

"Don't worry, we will make sure it's really your daughter."

As Patricia approached, Papa Abayomi once more pulled out the metal rod and took the girl's hand. Running it across her open palm, he carefully scrutinized her reaction but the girl didn't flinch or cry out. Instead, she giggled.

"Tickles!" she declared.

Satisfied, he turned and led the way back to the car, though Inshan noticed that he kept the rod firmly gripped in his hand as they walked back.

The eyes followed them all the way back to their car but their deformed silhouettes lingered within the forest and came no closer much to his relief.

As Inshan drove them home he felt both mentally and physically exhausted. Nothing made sense anymore, and though he had more questions than he had answers, he refused to ask any of them since he was sure he would be better off not knowing.

"Drop me here," Papa Abayomi said, and as Inshan pulled over and the old man climbed out and paused as he seemed to consider his words. When he spoke his voice was soft and reverent. "There are things in this world that neither you nor I will ever understand. Things that have been around before we were and things that will be around long after we're gone. It's not our job to understand them or to ever seek them out since they fortunately prefer to keep to themselves, but every once in a while, when our worlds mix things can go very wrong. You were lucky. That ogbanje was young and relatively tame. Trust me that you don't want to know what those things can truly do when they're unhappy. I once knew one who would skitter across the walls and ceiling like one of those twenty-four hour lizards." He flitted his hand through the air in an erratic motion and laughed. "You are good people which is probably what drew it to you in the first place, but I think that goodness is really what saved you."

"Saved us?" Patricia considered the implication but the old man simply nodded as he closed the door and slowly hobbled his way into the street.

Looking then at their child who was faithfully sucking on her thumb, and then at each other they exchanged worried looks.

"Mummy?" Inicia called as she pulled her thumb from her mouth and rubbed her eyes with the back of her hand. "I hungry. We have any bread and cheese?"

THE OFFERING

Dressed in her garden boots,
Arleene stood before the small shrine.
Armed with her offering,
But things were slightly different this time.

As she unpacked the brown paper bag,
She placed each item down with care.
And as she lit the deya she asked
For Dee Baba to hear her prayers.

"Dee Baba, I offer you this satwick
To thank you for this past year.
And I'd like to ask for you
To treat us with continued care."

And with a pause she stopped
And dipped into the bag once more.
And produced a fish fresh from the market
That she added to the score.

"But please, Dee Baba, I beg of you
For a little extra blessing this time around."

And with a smile, she added to the pile,
An image of her three month ultrasound.

The Plea

Over time we've gotten quite a bad reputation. We're known as a creatures that should be avoided at all costs. As a plague on society. Unnatural and supernatural. Magical fiends. Witches and practitioners of obeah. We've been scorned and looked down upon. They whisper behind our backs thinking we don't hear, they roll their eyes and turn up their noses thinking that we don't see. They think we don't know how they cringe when they go past us, or how they subconsciously avoid us in public. But it never used to be like that. Back in the day things used to be so much different and I remember that time well.

It might be shocking to know that there is one of us in every village. You might know who it is without even realizing that you do. Back then we were the ones who people used to come to, who they confided in, who they sought solace and comfort from. We were the unofficial ombudsmen of the times. We were more than a novelty, we were an embodiment of the mindset of the village.

People came to us for more than just spells and charms. We were midwives made into godmothers time and time over. We looked over the people of the village and assumed a matriarchal role. We were respected and admired.

But then things changed. People started whispering out of

boredom and out of a need to make bacchanal. Soon the rumours became too juicy to ignore, and like a game of telephone, each time it was told and retold, muttered in the dark depths of rum shops and whispered from hairdryer to hairdryer, someone added in one extra detail, one additional element of flair to make the story not just juicy but believable. And in order for it to be believable, a personal element was needed. Soon whole villages had collected tales and crafted their own 'Nansi stories, and shared events, and like the Emperor's new clothes syndrome, no one wanted to admit the truth of the situation.

And so it snowballed, rendering us into the decrepit and unwanted members of society that we are today. Our families and villages were steeped from us, and the looks of respect and admiration turned to cold, hard stares of mistrust.

We ate the babies. We hexed the people. We served the dark master named Lucifer who granted us powers we used for our own benefit, powers we used for malicious reasons as we did the bidding of the villagers for high prices. Our herbs came from the damp, rotted corners of the cemetery, our fingers grew knobbed from clawing at graves for bones, our pots were filled with foul broths and our fires stoked with wood chopped from the silk cotton tree. Our cups flowed over with blood, and those who sought us out only did so in dark desperation. That was what they made us into. That was who we had become in their minds.

Instead of walking up and knocking on our doors they slinked around at dawn or dusk, watching and waiting until no one was around before sneaking around and softly rapping on the side window, nervously whispering for us to let them in. And once help was given, once their needs were fixed, they reverted to looking down on us in the presence of others—though when they thought no one was looking their gazes would soften in gratitude, their heads nodding ever-so-slightly in our direction. But if they ever spoke in our favour, if they ever uttered a word of reassurance on our behalf, they would be scorned like we were. And so we forgave them and let them be.

Now it seemed that no man, woman, child, or animal was safe around us. And if we refused to carry out their malicious requests the damaging rumours continued to spread as they sought revenge. You'd be surprised at how many people want each other dead, I've even had a few people appear at my window whispering *your* name. But don't worry, I never have and never will entertain such requests. Love we can do, if it's true and genuine our interjection will only help it along, and if it wasn't true it will unravel on its own and that's on their head, not mine. But death...death is different.

Death is a nasty business, and meddling in its affairs often leads to blowback for everyone involved. Oh no papa-yo, death is one thing we steer clear of. We have knowledge and abilities, we can see things most people can't, but we are not God and we don't try to play God. However, what we *can* do is help ease pain and suffering and make the inevitably approaching death slightly better. That is something we certainly could and would do for you if you asked it of us. We care. Don't you see it? We love you all, we see you as our children, but instead of embracing us you've cast us into darkness and condemned us and though you may think your words don't matter they do hurt us.

That is the reality we face and I really wish it wasn't so. I wish I could hold the babies on my hip again. I wish my open gallery could be filled with the raucous laughter of the village women who used to pass by at all hours of the day and who would leave at late hours of the night. I wish I could teach the young ones about which herbs in their gardens can be used to remedy what ailments. I wish I could give my counsel without shame and that I could openly help those in need instead of sitting in the shadows, hoping things never got bad enough to warrant them a visit to my doorstep.

But that is not our reality and I fear it never will be. I am the old woman who lives in the dilapidated wooden house on the hill. I am the one they whisper about and the one who is famed for things I've never done. I am the village witch—

though some think I am the soucouyant. They are only partially wrong on that account. I do attain my abilities though a supernatural means but only few amongst us ever become those vile creatures of darkness—and though you may never know me or even see me in your lifetime, I see you and I know you. Oh yes, I know you well, and I'd like to caution you about your ways. Mind your actions and heed my words or else one day, at dusk, you'll find yourself nervously knocking on my window hoping for a solution to your problems.

WHO DON'T HEAR GO FEEL

I couldn't believe it. She was lecturing *me*. After I'd given her all these years of my life, after almost twenty hours of labour, after being alive donkey years on this earth and seeing and experiencing more than she likely ever would, she had the nerve to lecture *me*!

"Don't fill the child head with that back-a-day nonsense," she said clearly forgetting her roots and where it was she'd come from. "You go scare she."

"Well she should be scared! If she doesn't know she will end up like…"

"Like who? Auntie Mavis?" Her face twisted into a scold that showed not only disrespect but disbelief.

"Yes, just like Mavis. You know, Mavis was her age when she disappeared, and whether you like it or not, that child is Mavis in print."

"Mammee…" Her voice was softer but still patronizing. "I know those stories like the back of my hand. I hear them a million times already, and while I had no choice in hearing them, I not going to let you fill up she head with it. You know last week you gone and tell she about that flickin' lagahoo and she come home and couldn't sleep. You know how long it take me to get she to settle down only for she to wake up in the middle of the night bawling how she hearing chain draggin' on the road outside! No, not again. You not going to fill she head with them 'Nansi stories and that is final!"

"Oh-ho. That is final, eh? We go see, child."

"Yes we will!" She raised her voice. "If you can't control yourself then I not going to bring she over here anymore."

Listening to her I felt my anger swell. "Catch yourself eh, little girl! Who you feel you talking to? You feel because you is a big 'oman you can talk to me however you want? Don't forget it was me who teach you everything you know, it was me who was working my finger to the bone to make sure you had what I didn't. Show some respect, yuh hear me? I raise you better than that!"

She shrank back at my words and I could see the fear in her eyes. She knew she had crossed the line and I secretly relished that my cut-eye and sharp tongue still had its power.

"Mammee, I'm sorry. I didn't mean to be disrespectful but Lani is my child and I get to decide how to raise her."

I shook my head and gave in for now. "At least you doing right well enough. She smart and doing good in school. She have good broughtupsy and know how to respect her elders, she says her nightly prayers but you know…" I hedged my words carefully because I knew this was a sensitive matter for her because of her husband. "I only wish you would let me organize a little baptism for she and I wish you would let her come to church with me more…"

"Mammee…" There was that tone again.

"Alright, alright, calm yourself," I said no longer in the mood to argue. For now I would let the matter go. But I needed get that child baptized as soon as possible. She was coming up on that age where it was crucial. But for now I really needed to figure out a way to warn my little choonkoloonks about those unseen and unknown dangers in this world without scaring her too much. It was better to know so you could fight if the time came than to be a total dunce about things when faced with it—and we all prayed and hoped we would never be faced with *that*. But that child…she really was Mavis in print and that worried me deeply.

The months rolled past and I still hadn't figured out a way in which to educate my gran' about the dangers of the world. The best I'd managed to do was warn her to not talk to strangers. And as much as that line had been said, it had no real impact or bearing. It instilled no real fear in the child and with her quick mouth and curious ways I knew it was nagging advice that would fall on deaf ears.

Sunday came and I found myself walking down the street towards Sari's house. With my purse on my arm and my hand on my hat to keep the wind from blowing it away, I walked along the pavement, nodding a quick hello to the pepper sauce vendor who sat on an upside down crate fanning himself with a rumpled up copy of Awake.

"Miss Mabel, you looking real nice today! You going to church?" the young man said with a grin as he peered up from between the yellow and red bottles filled with chunky pepper sauce that was sure to set your mouth and backside on fire.

"Yes, yes! Thank you, Darlin'. How your Mammy doing? She good? You must pass by to collect some pommecythere for she sometime."

He nodded and I continued on my way down the street.

When I arrived at Sari's house I found her sitting in the hammock outside, rocking herself back and forth against the smooth brown leg that was thrown over the side.

As I got closer I noticed some black marks on my daughter's skin.

"What happen to your foot? How it have so much bo-bo?"

Sari jumped a mile into the air and stared at me in surprise. "Mammee! What you doing here?"

"Sorry girl, I didn't mean to scare you. But like your mind far? You ent hear me open the gate and walk up? What if was a bandit or something? Anyways, I come to see if Mama want to go to church with me," I said as I looked around for my little grandchild.

Sari's face dropped. "She not feeling too well today. I don't want she out and about in this hot sun."

"What happen? She catch the virus? I hear it have something passing around."

Sari looked at me and shook her head. "She say she couldn't sleep last night."

I shook my head and readied myself for the accusation that was most likely to come. It was Sunday, the Lord's day and I wasn't in the mood for any ole talk. "It wasn't me. I didn't tell she nothing to keep she up."

Sari smiled a tired smile and nodded. "I know, Mammee."

"Well, I gone then. It might rain later on today. If not, I might pass by. I make curry conchs last night and I go bring some and I go make some pommecythere chow for Mama to make she feel better."

Sari nodded and I made my way out towards the main road to hold up a PH taxi.

By noon the skies opened up and it rained long and hard all the way into the evening, marooning me in my house. With the doors and windows locked up tight, I lit my oil lamp and sat down to read my bible. The mood of the evening had me on edge and the cold wind that came with the rains set into my bones making me feel drowsy and lethargic. Without knowing when, I dozed off and dreamed about Mavis.

The scream that pierced through the night woke me up in a near blind panic. It was Mavis' voice calling my name. Screaming for help. Something wasn't right and I felt it in my heart.

Acting on instinct I jumped up and fled the house not caring that I was dressed only in my nightie.

I sprinted down the road in the rain two streets over to Sari's house. Once there I wasted no time in running into the yard and towards the front door. I pounded against it as hard as I could until Sari's husband, Ram, opened the door.

"Mama what hap-?"

"Where she?" I demanded. "Where Lani?"

Sari stood there in her tank top and pyjama pants looking at me with a bewildered expression. "Calm down, look how you soaking wet. Let me get a towel for you."

"WHERE LANI?" My voice was shrill and Sari turned back to look at me.

"She sleeping in her room."

"I want to see she."

Sari stepped in my way as I moved towards Lani's bedroom. "Mammee, keep your voice down. What happen to you? Like you going mad?"

"Something wrong. I feel it in my heart. Something happen to the child."

Ram let out a loud steups. "You wake me up at his ungodly hour with a set of nonsense talk? Sari, show she the child so she could go back home and leave we alone. I have to work in the morning. I going back to bed."

Sari moved towards Lani's room and I followed closely behind.

She opened the door and stepped in. "You see, Mammee, she right...Lani?"

The bed stood empty and the sheets were tossed aside.

The moments passed by in shocked silence before Sari said, "She must be in the bathroom." But I could hear the anxiety in her voice. "Lani?" she called out again, louder this time.

Ram called from the doorway. "What happen?"

"Lani not here, I going to check the bathroom."

"I now come from there and no one was in there but me," he replied and I could hear the hint of worry in his voice as well.

And so the hunt for Lani began with Sari's voice growing more and more shrill as she called her daughter's name over and over as they moved through the house.

But I didn't move from the room because as Sari called out I heard the mocking reply of a child followed by a giggle coming from outside, but it sounded much louder and closer than it should have.

"Sari?" I called out to my daughter and both she and Ram entered the room with wide eyes.

"You find she?"

I pointed to the window next to Lani's bed and it was at

that moment that the curtain gently bellied outwards like a fat man's breathing, allowing the chilly night wind to gently waft into the room.

It was then that we all heard a giggle followed by someone saying, "Shhhh! They know!"

Sari and I rushed to the window just in time to see several short, stocky, pale skinned figures retreating into the bushes. It was the same sight I'd seen years ago as I stood at the backdoor of my childhood home, the only difference being that it had been Mavis who'd been lured away.

Sari remained frozen to the spot, but I knew I had to go after her. Lani wasn't baptized which meant that they could keep her. Her soul would be bound to this earth like theirs and she wouldn't be sent back to reside with her maker when her time came. But maybe if we moved quickly she would still have a fighting chance.

I and Ram looked at each other for a brief moment and then we were off. Ram went left and I went right towards the backdoor. As I swung the top and bottom of the half-door open I heard a shower of what sounded like small stones hitting the galvanized roof. The sound echoed throughout the house and the laughter outside amplified as I darted across the yard and into the bushes beyond. I had no light but the rustling sounds ahead of me and the mischievous trail of laughter served as my guide.

I heard a loud crashing movement and heavy breathing coming from directly behind me and as I looked back I found myself blinded by a bright orb of orange light as Ram ran up to me.

"Which way they gone?"

The laughter around us brought us both to a halt. We were surrounded and Ram held up his cutlass and shook it at the darkness, shining his light around in a wide arcing circle that revealed no signs of anyone or anything. The dismembered voices snickered.

"You want to fight?" He challenged them. "Give me back my daughter or else I go kill every last one of you!"

A shower of stones and twigs rained down on us as they taunted us. "Lani! Lani! Sweet as frangipani! Stuffed her into every nook and cranny!"

"Daddy!" Lani's voice called out, and before I could tell him to stop, before I could tell him that that wasn't really Lani, that it was a trap, that it was deceit, Ram took off and fled in the direction of the call leaving me in the darkness of the forest.

I watched as the light bounced up and down before disappearing completely, and it was then that their whispers and giggles turned into a loud whooping sound. I could hear them moving away from me now though, they were no longer concerned with the likes of me, they had what they wanted but I refused to give up. If only Sari had listened to me things might have been different but alas it was a matter of *coulda, woulda, shoulda, but didn'ta* as the saying went.

I could no longer hear Ram or the douenes, and without a choice, I turned back and began to make my way towards the house.

The situation and the sheer blackness of the night pressed against me from all sides and fostered my sense of claustrophobia. The heady smell of the loam in the earth and the mildewed wetness of the rotting leaves and wood on the forest floor brought forth images of being trapped in a coffin, piled with dirt six feet under. I knew all too well how easy it was to get turned around and to lose your way indefinitely.

Never before had silence been so loud. From the screeching of the insects to the rustling of my movements to the distant call of some animal, I could no longer hear Ram or the douenes which meant that I was, for all intents and purposes, all alone. Forcing myself to remain calm, I focused on my breathing as I stumbled through the dark. Luck was on my side because a few minutes later, just as my anxiety told me I was heading in the wrong direction, I spotted the lights of my daughter's home. Nearing, the backdoor Sari rushed out. Her pallor was deathly pale and her eyes had taken on a dark, sunken look.

"Mammee! You find she? Where Ram?"

I shook my head. "She gone, and Ram chasing after jumbie."

"How you could be so damn cool and calm? That is my child out there!"

I moved inside towards the phone. The best thing I could do at this point in time was report the child missing. If I claimed it was a kidnapping, which it was, then maybe they could get some men out here to search for her. Maybe they would have dogs that could track her.

As I neared the phone in the kitchen a wave of overwhelming warmth filled my heart. Something had happened. Maybe Ram had found her. As I turned to look at Sari a movement under the kitchen window caught my eye. As I moved towards it I could see the small child standing below the window peering up at me with eyes it didn't have. It's small round mouth twisted into what I could only believe was meant to be a grin as it pointed at me and laughed.

"Granny!" the thing called and I immediately knew that it was too late.

With the phone still in my hand I reached out and touched the too-cold glass as I stared at the pale gangly creature with its sexless form and backwards turned feet, but as I leaned forward I noticed that the thing wasn't alone. Stooping down just below the window and just out of sight was another creature who stood up and slid its hand into Lani's. The second creature fixed me with its sightless gaze and I bit back my tears. Even though it didn't speak I knew beyond a shadow of a doubt that it was Mavis. Mavis had come back after all these years and she'd found herself a playmate. Both she and Lani would remain as they were, bound to the earth for all eternity as playful forever children.

A series of whooping shattered my revelation and toppled our connection and the two creatures looked away from me and towards the sounds of their comrades, and without another glance or word they hobbled away into the darkness of the night. I knew in my heart that I would be seeing them again at some point, but it was still a bittersweet goodbye. I had failed to protect them both and in the end there was nothing that I or anyone could do.

Sari rushed into the kitchen with a bruised and battered Ram in tow.

"Oh, gawd! Call the ambulance! They almost kill him!" she wailed.

I turned to look at Ram and I shook my head. "Them wounds superficial. He'll live."

"And what about my child?" Sari demanded.

"She gone," I said simply. "Just like Mavis."

Sari looked at me and though I expected her to retaliate and deny the situation she did neither. Instead she crumpled to the ground and bawled like a baby. I wanted to be angry with her. She was too harden. But she was my child and so I went and stooped down next to her and held her and comforted her.

"Is alright, she with family. She go be fine."

Sari pushed me away and reached out for Ram but he wasn't there.

That was the last time we saw Ram. He left everything behind that night and moved back to his mother's house in Tabaquite.

Mavis and Lani come to visit me every night when they can, and though I never see them I always hear them whooping in the bushes outside at two in the morning. There's a river that runs about a quarter mile in from the back of my house, and every day I make the journey there to leave them food, and on special occasions, toys, after all, they are children. As for Sari, the doctors say she will one day be released from St Ann's, but for now, it's imperative that she be there. That child was harden too bad, yes. I tried to warn she, I tried to intervene, but she thought she was a big 'oman. Too big to listen to she mother. But you know what they say: *Who don't hear go feel.*

Endless Cycle

To me, being a journalist means putting yourself in a position to report on things that can oftentimes be unsavoury. It means risking your own life and reputation to get to the root of a story or to chase that tip, that lead, like a mythical dragon, in the hopes of pushing boundaries and capturing the next big headline. For me, I can tell you it's like an addiction, so when my editor challenged me to go out there and get a story outside the norm, I couldn't help but allow myself to really seek out something unbelievable...something unexplainable. And I think once you're in that frame of mind, it really doesn't take long for trouble to find you.

The police have questioned me almost to the point of abuse and charges will very likely be laid against me for "obstruction of justice" but the first rule of being a journalist, an honourable one at any rate, is to never reveal your sources. Anonymity is understood, it's embraced and encouraged, and much like your doctor or lawyer or psychologist is held to that ethical standard, I firmly believe that I too am so bound. And so I present to you this interview with a murderer. One who is still at large, one who has granted me the strange...dare I call it *honour*...of telling me who he is, what he is, and why he does what he does.

I would like to state that I do not condone any of his actions, quite the opposite actually, but for the sake of my integrity I believe I am bound by my own governing ethic to preserve his identity and to remain relatively objective so that you can draw your own conclusions and opinions.

[We stand in the small musty room its too-low ceiling. A room beneath someone's house that he calls home for now. The windows are closed and a series of mismatched furniture is scattered around. The walls are unpainted and their plain orange-ribbed bricks with rivets of dried concrete that oozed out from between them serves as the backdrop to his abode. There is a small radio on the equally small wooden table and an old enamel pot on and rusted stove-top. Next to the sink, a dish rack holding a single plate, a single cup, and a single spoon stands with a droplet of water dangling off the edge. Yet still despite the sparse and arguably uninviting setting, the place seems relatively clean. The floors are covered with a sheet of green patterned linoleum and the smell of some detergent—most likely lavender scented Fabuloso—softly wafts up. His bed, a twin size, is neatly made up with a blue and white Candlewick bedspread draped over it. He looks me up and down, regarding me like he would a mangy dog on the street. I'm honestly surprised he's even allowed me into his home given that I've just accosted him on the street in an overexcited manner, asking him—begging him—to talk to me. With a sneer on his clean shaven face and a narrowing of his eyes which are alert and vibrant, he tilts his head to the side and speaks and I can't help but detect the slightest twang of a British accent in his words.]

So you went through all this trouble to try and talk to me? You feel I didn't see you in the market tailing me around? Or that I didn't see you cashing at the other register same time as me in the grocery? Or that I didn't notice you getting into the same taxi as me? You not good at playing detective you know. But I have to ask why. Why me? I'm not interesting. I'm just a normal man like anyone else. Struggling to make ends meet. I'm not…

[I interrupt him with an overeager interjection as I reveal the reason why

I'm here in parts. I hope my voice does not betray my fear, my excitement, my complete nervousness. My mind's eye is wholly focused on getting 'the scoop'. I tell him I've been following him for days now after receiving a tip from an anonymous source, that I've seen what it is that he does and I merely want to talk. He allows his pause to be brief as he takes in my words and when next he speaks, there is a hint of amusement in his voice.]

Ah! Ah, ok...I see now. So you saw that, did you? Is that why you're here then? Looking for justice? Was it your child? No? Then I don't get it. Why are you here? An interview?! You want to interview me? Who you working for? The police? Oh! Is for school. I see, I see! Oh-ho, so top mark go get you a feature headline in the newspapers! Really? Which one? No lie! I does read that every day! Ok, ok, fine, maybe I'll answer some of your questions. Why not.

[I remain standing close to the doorway, its brass knob poking into my hip, but I dip into my bag and pull out my notepad, hoping he will not suspect that I have been and will be recording this entire conversation on my digital recorder. He sits down in a chair and leans back. His posture is lax, legs splayed before him, one elbow propped on the table he leans his head against it and looks at the wall on the other side of the room. I ask him my burning questions.]

My name is irrelevant because it changes almost daily. My age you wouldn't believe if I told you so I won't even bother. Look, why don't we skip the small talk? It's boring, don't you think? You're here because you saw me do something and you want to know the why and how and when and what, not so? So let's deal with that.

[I can almost appreciate his brisk answer though my teachings tell me I need to establish some connection and ascertain some sort of control over the interview to guide it to where I need it to go. I'm not sure my theoretical teachings can apply here. However, he seems more than willing to talk, and before I can search through my list of questions, he begins of his own accord and honestly, I'm just happy he's willing to talk to me.]

Look, I'll be honest with you. Truth is, I don't enjoy it. That's the first thing I'm sure you want to know. It's not something I take pleasure in, it's not fun, it's not something I look forward to. It's nasty work, but I do it because I have to, because it's addictive, because it's survival. Because if I don't, I'll die.

You see what you have to understand is that killing is a natural event. Everything must eventually die and sometimes taking a life is necessary be it for food, fun, defence, or merely survival. Animals understand this concept better than anyone, but the thing of it is, we humans are animals too. Imagine you could stop your own death. Wouldn't you jump at that chance? I would and I do. But it's nasty work. No one would ever want to be in my shoes for that...but when you learn about my life, the things I've seen, the things I've experienced, the historical inaccuracies I could correct because I *was* there, because I lived through it, then you might think differently.

And don't get me wrong, I believe in karma too, oui, oh yes, I believe in it too bad, and that is why I do my best to help people, to give back in any way I can. That is why I live like a vagabond, a nomad, well that is one of the reasons anyway. The other reason is kind of obvious, you know? But it's why I have no home, why I have no material riches. I'm full of remorse but not regret, never regret, and I think if you had the same opportunity I do, even if you might not give in and take it in the end, you will at least sit and consider it for a moment. I wonder if I tell you it gets easier each time if that would make a difference. I think it might, that it makes it a bit more alluring because of what you stand to gain. People are all self-serving, but you already know that. If you didn't you wouldn't be here…

[He says all this without once looking at me. I think it makes it easier for the both of us and as a small smile crosses his face he turns to look at me only once at the end, a daring expression of challenge lurking in his upraised eyebrows. I do not want to answer him because I'm not sure what the right answer, if there is such a thing, is. Flipping through my notepad,

I ask him if it always has to be children and if so why. His expression falls and a slight look of disappointment crosses his face, but as he draws in a breath and resumes looking at the wall once more, he answers.]

Why children? Ah man, that is a hard question to answer, and not because of the reasons but because you want me to talk about the act itself. Well, if you insist you simply *must* know... For me it *has* to be children. Others disagree, others go after criminals and the like, real life Superman thing I tell you. But me, I go after children because they're easier to lure away, because they don't fight much, because they're trusting. But mostly it's because they offer longer lives. It's a plus that they are easier to...*handle*, their flesh softer to cut into, and their bodies easier to move and dispose of.

The only real disadvantage is their rib cages are smaller so it's harder to get your hand up into their chest to get their heart. Of course I could crack them open and just rip it out but that real messy, and the sound...*ugh*! I don't like that. Going up through a cut made just below the ribcage and the diaphragm is easiest. But you have to know where you're going when you stick your hand up there and hope they don't wake up...

[I will never be able to describe the feeling of revulsion that wells up inside me at hearing him talk about it so openly, so casually. This is not a man, this is a demon, plain and simple, and in listening to him talk, even if he's just pulling my leg and having a laugh, is a stark reminder of the evil that resides in this world. It takes everything in me to remain standing before him and to keep on with my interview but I push myself onwards, trying to swallow the vile clot of reflux and hatred that's building in my chest.]

They may have their lives ahead of them but in a sense they don't really have any real life yet, you know? It also means I have to do it less because they last longer. When you do an adult or an old person their lives are almost over, then you have to do it more to keep on going, with a child it's just one and done for the better part of a lifetime so to speak. You get what it is I saying, boy?

[I nod in mock understanding as my pen scribbles at my notepad. Gibberish. I'm writing gibberish, just hollow loops of nonsense because my mind cannot focus enough to write his words down and because I know (and hope) my recorder is capturing this all. My stomach is uneasy, my back wet with sweat. I feel like I might be coming down with something but I don't want to let him know. I clear my throat, an obvious sign of nervousness and potential weakness—I know—but I need to find my voice to continue. He speaks of it with such ease, as though it's just business to him, which I suppose it is, but how can one talk about taking a child's life so easily I will never understand. But now that I have him talking I have to know more, the prospect of that A on my final assignment dangles in front my eyes.]

What do I do with them? Ah chut man, you sure you really want to know? Is real nasty business you know! Fine, fine, if you insist. You really is a curious one, oui!

[He throws back his head and laughs. Then there is a brief pause as he considers his words, with nod he begins talking but his voice is lower now, almost reverent.]

Children are dumb, really trusting you see. It doesn't take much to convince them to come away with me. Sometimes I wonder if I was that dumb when I was a child, but I don't think so. Times were much harder for us, life too good now, there's little to fear, it's much too safe, and so they think they all know better, they think they don't have to listen to when their parents tell them not to talk to strangers. And you see me, I don't look threatening, my voice soft, my face and clothes clean, my hands unmarked. They don't feel a-how when they around me, it's easy for them to trust me, to believe in me. So when I give them some sweet drink laced with something to make them sleep they does drink it down real easy and I does see their nose wrinkle at the slight bitter taste but they never say anything, they does just go to sleep.

And that is when I does take them to the tree. No, is not

one special tree, they're all over, it just have to be the *right* kind. And I does lay them down gentle, gentle at the base and then, while they're still sleeping, I quickly cut them open and take out their hearts. But understand, they doesn't feel no pain or nothing, they does just stay asleep. I is not no monster, or even if you think I is, know there is worse than me out there. Anyways, then I place the heart at the base of the tree, or better yet within the roots, and call to my master. And he bubbles up from the earth, and takes my offering, a heart and soul in exchange for their lifetime to be tacked on to mine. And that is all there is to it really. It is the law of the universe, what you take you have to give back. There has to be balance, you know.

[He shrugs as if it's no big deal, as if he's just passing the time with small talk but my knees feel like Jell-O and bile is slowly building up in my throat. I badly want to go to the bathroom, to wash my face, to have a drink of water but I dare not because I know if I do there will be nothing in the chair but a potential puff of smoke when I come back. I swallow and try to match his easy nature whilst reminding myself that this man before me just revealed that he frequently strikes deals with the devil himself.]

How many times? Ah, I really don't know nah, I don't usually wait until the lifetime up to get another one, that would be reckless, I does…top-up…like a phone card…if I see the opportunity present itself. To tell you the truth I don't really know how much years I have left. Might be fifty, might be a hundred.

[He laughs at his own joke and looks up at me with wickedness in his eyes, intentionally trying to scare me, to derail me, to test my limits and my inner stubbornness responds with more confidence than I thought I had. I wanted this story so bad I was willing to come down to his level. I wanted to walk over and sit on the chair across from him, to conduct this interview the proper way, but my instinct didn't allow for that. And so I continued it from across the room.]

How did it come to be that I know to do this? Well, that's a long story really, one I don't care to get into, but I'll say this much, I was presented with the opportunity and I took it. Simple as that. If I tell you anything more you might want to go looking for it yourself, or worse yet, you might tell others and they go looking for it. This world have enough *me's* in it, it don't need no more.

[I stop scribbling my nonsense looping and look up at him astonished. Asking a question that goes slightly off script. "Does that mean there are others who are...like you?" I'm not sure why the thought has never occurred to me before now and in his answer he admonishes me and I feel as though I've disappointed him as he shakes his head at me. It's like I've let him down and proven I'm not worthy of the job of interviewing him. Though he doesn't say it, his attitude towards me changes ever so slightly.]

Well of course there are others, I thought I made that clear earlier, like you not paying attention or-what? But we are few and far in-between, many of the others migrated decades ago, but I...I could never entertain the idea of leaving my beloved country. I born and grow up here you know! First generation Bajan, ah man, this country's grit runs hot in my veins.

[Never before have I understood something without really understanding it. I ask him if he knows that there is a bounty on his head, that the police want to get their hands on the notorious child killer, that there are people out there actively looking for him. I ask him if he's not worried, if it doesn't concern him especially since I was able to find him as easily as I was.]

Bounty? There's been a bounty on my head for centuries, young blood, and they have yet to catch me, and if they ever do...well to tell the truth I wouldn't even be mad at them. To say I look for it is an understatement, but I slippery like a snake and I have certain...protections guarding me. The fact that you were able to find me is no big deal to me. If I wanted to get away and disappear right now I could. Besides…

[He bares his teeth at me in an almost horrifying grin that is surely designed to intimidate and is rather effective in doing just that.]

…don't think that I will not or cannot do away with an adult, I'm not limited, I just have my preferences.

[Maintaining my composure is somehow becoming easier despite his obvious taunts and threats. I go back to a statement he made and ask for clarification as to what his 'protections' are.]

Ah, never you mind that! All that matters is that you don't have to worry about me. I stopped walking in the light centuries ago and it's something I've long since learned to live with. Whether you kill one or a thousand, you're still as damned so there's no point in stressing about it anymore, I just do what I have to do to survive.

[He stands up and stretches, a passive and polite way of telling me to wrap it up, that he's now bored of me and my questions, and as I look at him I find that he almost seems taller, that his features seem different somehow, or perhaps in my terror I was the one who shrank? Running a hand over his crop of short hair he scrubs his jaw with his open palm and yawns. He seems so ordinary yet at the same time not. So I ask him my final question, one I already know the answer to but it's best to hear it directly from him.]

Stop? Why would I stop? I have the world at my feet. I have been going on like this for a long time now, boy, and things have been nothing if not interesting and rewarding. Think about it, I get to indulge in immortality, I've seen this country build itself from the ground go up, seen it change hands countless times, seen it become what it is today, I've been everywhere and done everything but there are still more things to come.

I've seen people come and go and the endless cycle repeats

itself over and over, yet I remain here stronger than ever, wiser than ever. So tell me, why would I stop? I've already come this far. Besides, I doubt I could stop even if I wanted to. This to me is the best and only way to live life, to the end of time itself and to the fullest. So no, boy, I wouldn't stop. And if you were in my position I doubt you would either. *Would you?*

Dark Angel

"Knock-knock."
"Who's there?"
"The dark angel."
"What for?"
"Colours."
"Name them..."

It was a game as old as time itself and my grandmother knew it was my favourite one to play in the evening time. We sat outside under the red flamboyant, Granny on her bench knitting a onesie for my newborn cousin, whilst I sat cross-legged at her feet with a small bowl of freshly boiled peewah in my lap.

The sounds all around us were the sounds I will always associate with my childhood, from the soft musical tinkling of the wind chimes that forever swayed in the ever-blowing breeze to the near constant stream of cars and foot traffic that came from the main road. Even the barking of the neighbour's dogs and the quarrelsome arguments of the kiskadees and blue jays was familiar and welcome. To some the sounds would be considered noise but they never bothered us, they were like background music, we barely even noticed them. Our little world was thriving and vibrant and that was just how I liked it.

Licking the salt crust off of the skin of my first peewah, I methodically peeled it with my teeth, spitting the peel back into the bowl. The dry almost crumbly texture of the stringy palm fruit was heavenly to me, and as I set aside the round black seed for later Granny looked around before making her first guess.

"Green?"

"No."

"Blue?"

"No."

She looked at the peewah in my hand and smiled. "Orange."

"Yes!" I beamed brightly as she shook her head and laughed.

We continued playing the game taking turns to guess the other's colour of choice until my bowl was empty. Handing me her little hammer, she watched as I placed the seed on the concrete and pinched it between my fingers before lightly tapping on it until the shell cracked. Once it split, I fished out the white inside and popped it into my mouth, relishing in the coconuttiness of it.

"Make sure you don't swallow it," she warned, and I nodded as I chewed and sucked out all the flavour before spitting the mealy leftover back into the bowl. As I picked up another seed the smell of someone's evening meal drifted through the air and as I inhaled it my stomach greedily growled with want.

"You ever hear the story of stone soup?" Granny asked in a somewhat gossipy tone.

She had my rapt attention. "No. Tell me!" I leaned towards her and she nodded as though it was serious business. And so, with the smell that was surely someone's bake crisping on the tawah wafting through the air she began her tale.

***

It was late at night and the weary traveller had walked for miles and miles along the lonely road. He was tired and hungry and very much wanted to stop for the night. But he couldn't, not yet. He needed to find some place safe. There were just too many jumbies out and about tonight and they would never let him sleep in peace.

Finally, after what felt like forever, the traveller spotted the light of a flambeaux in the near distance and with a renewed stride he marched on towards it until he came to the doorway of an old house. Knocking on the door, a woman answered.

"Good evening," said the traveller as the smell of food floated through the doorway in greeting. "I am very tired and I was wondering if you would be so kind as to let me lay my head down for the night."

The woman eyed the traveller warily and was about to close the door when the traveller reached into his pocket and held out three silver coins.

"Please," the traveller said, "this is all the money I have. I promise I will leave as soon as the sun comes up."

Snatching the money, the woman reluctantly held the door open and the grateful traveller entered into the house.

Sitting in the corner, he saw that the woman was making fried bake. She made four large bakes, and without offering him any she sat down at her table and silently ate one.

"Can I please have one of your bakes?" the traveller asked.

The woman looked at him and frowned. "Oh no," she said. "You don't want these."

"Why not?" the traveller asked as the woman rose from her seat.

"Well, this one is too soft," she said as she wrapped it up and put it on the top shelf of her cupboard. "And this one is too golden," she said as she wrapped that one up and put it away as well. "And this one, it's too round and perfect, I couldn't possibly give it to you!" And with that she put the third bake with the others and slammed the cupboard shut.

"Do you have any other food to spare me?" he asked, already sure of the answer that was to come.

The woman snorted and looked down her nose at the

haggardly traveller. "My food is far too good for the likes of you. If you didn't have any money I would have never let you in here in the first place!" she declared.

The man, realizing that the woman was selfish and greedy, decided to trick her. With a sigh he reached into his pocket and produced three smooth black stones. The man had tripped over these stones as he walked along a river and thought they were too pretty to leave behind.

"Well then, I suppose I will need to use these once more," he said looking at the stones in his hand.

"What are those?" The woman frowned.

"These are magical stones. All you have to do is add it to a pot of boiling water and it makes the most delicious soup anyone has ever had. I did a favour for the Queen of England and she gave these to me as a gift."

The woman was curious about these magical stones and without a word she filled her round bottom cast-iron pot with water and set it on the stove to boil. The man nodded his thanks and walked over to the pot.

"For it to work, you have to drop them in as soon as the first bubble hits the surface."

As soon as a tiny bubble rose to the surface the man dropped the three stones in and smiled. "This pot will be the best one yet!"

The pot bubbled and boiled for twenty minutes before the man dipped a spoon in and took a cautious sip.

Stepping back he grinned. "Oh lord! This soup is delicious! But you know, the only thing that can make it even better is half a carrot and a potato and maybe an onion, just like the Queen likes it."

The foolish woman, eager to taste the soup that pleased the Queen herself, reached into her wicker produce basket in the corner and emerged with a carrot, and onion, and a potato. "Will these work?"

The man took them from her and examined them. "Yes. The stones will transform them into something amazing but I'll need a bit of salt and pepper and some spices and maybe a little bit of meat to make the magic really work."

The woman eagerly brought the other ingredients and handed them to the man who added it to the pot with care before waving his hand over the bubbling stew in a grand and magical gesture that allowed the wafting smell to fill the little kitchen. Then they waited until the woman, unable to contain her curiosity any longer, demanded to taste the stone soup.

The man shook his head. "Look into the pot, see how the stones are dancing? The magic is working but it's not ready yet. You have to have patience."

When it was ready, the man dished out the soup for the two of them.

"Stone soup fit for her majesty!" he declared with a note of sarcasm that went undetected as the woman slurped at the hot soup.

"This is the best tasting soup I ever had!" she professed.

"Better than any I've made for the Queen!" he agreed.

With the pot empty, the man fell asleep in his corner while the woman went to bed, happy and full of stone soup.

In the morning, the man washed the pot and pocketed the three black stones. As he picked up his bag and opened the door, the woman called out from behind him. "Traveller, would it be possible for me to have one of those stones?"

The man shook his head. "These stones only work if you have all three and I simply cannot bear to part with them. After all, they were a gift from her Majesty." He reminded her.

The woman turned her pockets out and offered him all the money she had. "What about if we make a trade?" she asked.

The man considered her proposal and finally shook his head. "I don't want all your money. You have been very kind to me so how about this, I will give you my magical stones in exchange for my three silver coins back and, three of your fried bakes."

Astounded at the man's generosity, the woman rushed to her cupboard and took out the three fried bakes.

The man placed the bakes into his bag and handed the woman the stones. "Remember that you must drop them in as soon as the first bubble reaches the surface and you must wait and give the stones time to work their magic."

The greedy woman eagerly closed the door in the man's face and retreated to her cast-iron pot to make another batch of the magical stone soup as the thought of how famous she would be because of it drifted through her mind. The traveller shook his head as he turned away and continued down the road on his journey, laughing to himself at the stupidity of the greedy woman.

***

"Crick-crack," Granny said as she drew her tale to an end.

"Monkey break he back…"

"For a piece of pomerac."

"Wire bends…"

"Story ends."

"Monkey dead." I added slyly with a giggle.

Granny furrowed her brows at my childishness but a small smile danced on her lips. "I wonder what…" Granny's words trailed off as she looked around. Following suit, I glanced from left to right wondering what we were looking at.

"It quiet," she mused as she set her knitting needles down. "Time to go inside."

"Why?" I asked, I could sense her unease and it scared me.

"You hear that silence…? No cars, no people, no birds, no nothing? Look around, see how nothing moving?"

I nodded.

"That is a dark spirit passing over the land. It's a warning. It telling us that the Lagahoo go be out tonight. Time to go inside," she repeated.

She didn't need to tell me a third time, I was inside before she could collect her yarn into a ball.

Wasting no time, we secured the house and made sure every door and window was shuttered tightly. When it came time for bed, Granny knelt by my bedside with me and together we said our prayers but for me it wasn't enough and when Granny tucked me in and left the room I slipped out of bed and made my way across the room to unhook the wooden crucifix that was hanging on the wall. Clutching it against my chest, I fell asleep to the sounds of *his* clanking chains and dragging coffin penetrated my dreams and fuelled the nightmares of my already agitated sleep. Nightmares that to this day, some twenty-something years later, still makes my blood run cold every time I hear a silence settled upon my surroundings.

*The story of "Stone Soup" has been adopted into many cultures based on an ages old folktale to which the author is unknown.

WHITEY DON'T KNOW NO BETTER

Frank looked up at the woman who had brazenly taken an uninvited seat across from him and raised his eyebrows in question.

"Can I help you?"

She smiled and revealed a set of near perfect teeth that stood out against the bright red smear of lipstick, and Frank immediately felt a sense of déjà vu as she placed the still closed, dark green beer bottle onto the table in front of him.

"I don't know, honey, maybe you can. I'm looking for a little company tonight."

Looking around at the other men seated at the bar and the patrons who were seated in the booths having dinner, he turned to face her once more, sure of her game now. He'd been warned of these kinds of women by bosses and co-workers alike before his company deployed him to Trinidad.

"I don't think I can help you. I'm not very good company."

"Why don't you let me decide that for myself?" She smiled and leaned forward in her seat, staring at him with a smouldering intensity that he had to admit was beginning to work. "I'm just looking for a good time."

"I don't have any money." His words were blunt and cut through the mood she was building like a knife, but musical laughter escaped her lips as she tilted her head back and his eyes were at once drawn to the smooth curve of her caramel-coloured neck.

"Honey, I'm not interested in your money and I don't recall asking you for any. I have plenty of my own, thank you very much."

He snorted as a small smile played on his lips. There was no denying her beauty, and maybe a little company wouldn't be such a bad thing after all. Cutting into the dry and overcooked chicken he'd been served, he shovelled it into his mouth and chewed without even tasting. As his fingers reached for the beer she'd placed before him she produced an opener seemingly out of nowhere. The meaning was clear, he was to open his own beer so he'd know she hadn't done anything to it. It seemed as though this wasn't her first time doing this.

As he popped the top, a small tendril of frost drifted up through the bottle's neck. Handing the opener back to her, he lifted the bottle towards her in thanks before taking a long draw from its mild contents. He was more of a dark brew sort of man but he never turned down a free drink.

"So where are you from?" she asked as she brought the straw within her own dark green bottle to her lips.

"I'm from the UK."

She nodded and the long ringlets of her soft mulatto hair spilled over her shoulder. "Do you like it here?"

He shook his head. "It's too hot. And the air conditioning never seems to work right anywhere."

She snorted softly and once again nodded. "It's not really the heat though, is it? It's the humidity that really gets you. It makes you all...sweaty and sticky." She drew out the words low and slow as her fingers reached out to caress the pendant of the necklace that hung low in her ample cleavage.

His eyes followed her movements and her smile deepened as his Adam's apple bobbed with the desire that hadn't yet caught up to his brain. He was like all other men and she knew well how to work him over and soften him up. Much like a governor plum she only needed to slowly roll his willpower between her hands, using just enough pressure to make him sweet and pliable enough to be eaten up, and this man was already close to being ready.

"So, what's your name?"

"Frank," he replied as he took another bland bite of food. "Yours?"

"I'm Sanaa. This your first time here?"

Swallowing, he shook his head. "Third. We get sent to work with and train Trinmar's offshore workers on safety procedures."

"Are you married?" Her eyes flitted to his hands in search of a ring.

He knew she could see the untanned white mark on his ring finger so he shook his head. "Divorced." It was a lie of course, but that was irrelevant.

"Why don't you finish your dinner so we can get out of here?" she suggested as she bit her lip and ran a leg up the seam of his pants. Frank was more than happy to oblige.

With dinner finished, the bill paid, and a few more beers in him, Frank and Sanaa stepped out into the night and walked towards the gated entrance of the restaurant. Motioning to the guesthouse across the street that his company had rented out for the workers, he cocked his head. "Shall we?"

She glanced up at the darkened windows and shook her head. "I know the owner. She's not the type to allow unregistered guests up there, and if you're here for work you could get into trouble."

She had most certainly done this before. He chortled softly to himself. "So what do you propose?" His voice was guarded as he studied her delicate and exotic features under the glare of the security lights.

"We can always go back to my place…"

"Where do you live?"

"Oh, not too far from here along the South Central road."

"Where's that?" he asked his tone growing more and more suspicious.

"You know where Cap-de-Ville is?" Frank nodded. "Right

around there." She could sense his hesitation and shrugged. "Either ways, I think I'm going home, it's getting late. You're more than welcome to come with me, Frank of the UK, or if not, it was nice to have met you and perhaps we will be able to meet again sometime soon…"

She flashed her winning smile as she cinched her skirt around her and shifted from side to side, drawing attention to her shapely hips. As she moved, the sweet floral smell of her perfume wafted off of her in waves while the chain she wore around her neck jingled softly, its pendant shifting between her bosom. Turning away from him, she didn't need to look back to know that Frank was following. Keeping the rhythm in her stride she led the way to the main road and then veered right.

Hypnotized by the overwhelming power of her femininity and dreaming of the things they would do and the life they could have, Frank walked on in a daze, intent on following her to wherever she was leading him.

From a great distance away he heard someone shout, but the sound was muffled and sounded like it was being relayed through a pool filled with wet cotton. Ignoring the sound because it wasn't his concern, Frank carried on, but much to his annoyance the call became persistent enough for him to register that it was calling out to him.

"Pay him no mind, doux-doux," Sanaa cooed, "it getting late and we need to go home, right?"

Frank nodded and forced the voice out of his mind as he reset his focus on her once again, but the hand that landed on his shoulder drew him out of his stupor, and as he turned around, partly in anger at being distracted from his prize and partly in confusion at being accosted, he found himself staring into the grinning face of his co-worker, Berkley.

"You didn't hear me calling you? Where you going this hour of the night?"

"I was going home with my lady-friend," Frank said, dismayed that his words were coming out in an almost drunken slur. How many beers had he had? He couldn't quite remember but he was usually a man who could hold his alcohol well.

"Home? Ent you staying in the guesthouse on the hill? And friend? What friend?" Berkley glanced around and noticed the woman who was walking away from them both. "That old nasty smelling hag is your *friend*?" He burst out laughing. "Nah-man, I know is not that old beat-out woman you was going home with!"

Turning away from his co-worker's mocking cackles, Frank searched for the lovely Creole lady but instead only saw an unsightly old woman hobbling away from them in a series of uneven strides that sounded as though she were only wearing one high heel. The lingering smell of wet mould hung in the air, and under the glow of the streetlight, her once shapely form was now a series of lumps and bumps clad in dirty old rags that dragged along the floor.

"That's not the woman I was just talking to…" Frank said and Berkley stopped laughing long enough to wipe the tears away from his eyes.

"Well it ain't have nobody else here, just me, you, and the hag."

"She didn't look like that a minute ago."

"Whey-boy! Like she chain up yuh head good. You bazodee on the woman."

"No…I don't know what that means, but she didn't look like that, she was…younger, prettier…"

Berkley's laughter fell away as he examined Frank. "Whey yuh say?" He turned to stare after the woman. "Nah dread, it can't be…" he murmured as he crossed himself.

"What can't be?" Frank asked following his gaze.

Berkley shook his head and made to move towards the old woman who was suddenly much further away than should have been possible given the amount of time they'd been standing there. As he took a step in her direction, he reconsidered and turned to look at Frank. "Nah, you serious? She looked young and pretty you say? Like a red woman?"

"A red woman?" Frank's confusion was obvious, he could hear Berkley's words but he was having trouble making sense of them.

Berkley rolled his eyes. "A red 'oman, a red-skin woman, a creole, a mix-blood..." He looked at Frank with impatience.

Frank nodded slowly. "Yes, she was mixed, she had long, brown, curly hair and smooth skin and full red lips..." He could feel his longing for her bloom once more, and as a delicious warmth swarmed his mind he thought if he left now he could race to catch up with her and they could continue on their journey...

"Was she the nicest woman you ever see?"

Frank's face scrunched up as he considered the question. "Yes, I suppose she was."

"Frank, you ent easy, nah!" Berkley playfully clapped him on the shoulder and Frank felt himself jerk back to reality as though he'd somehow fallen asleep. The feeling was surreal. "You ent even realize what just gone on here. Look at you standing there like a cunumunu." Berkley carried on blissfully unaware of just how out of it Frank felt, but as Berkley laughed, Frank could tell that his typically raucous demeanour held a note of unease as he once more glanced in the direction the old woman, who was now completely out of sight, had gone in.

"Well brother-man, I just saved your life."

Frank frowned. "Saved my life? From what?"

"From a La Diablesse." Berkley's voice dropped as he said it and his eyes once more flitted to where they'd last seen the old woman. Before Frank could ask, he turned towards the nearby bar and began walking away. "Let we go inside and I will tell you all about the Devil woman, and since I just save your life, drinks are on you. Lord knows I need one, oui!"

Frank followed after him unsure of what was happening, but with each step he felt his mental fog receding much to his relief.

Berkley was waiting for him by the door, beaming with pride. "Wait until the boys hear about this!"

Making their way up to the counter of the bar, Berkley called out to the bartender and declared that drinks were on

Frank, and as the men all cheered loudly, another co-worker, this one a foreman if Frank remembered correctly, scoffed at Berkley, "Like you get dressed in the dark or-what? How your clothes turn up inside out so?"

Looking at the inside seam that ran down the arm of his shirt Berkley's eyes popped wide in understanding. "Well look thing! Aye fellas, hear this nah, I have a story to give allyuh, serious talk eh, allyuh not going to believe this…!"

I Heard a Cry…

Someone was crying
Outside my front door;
Someone was crying;
I'm sure-sure-sure;
I listened, and peered out,
Into the darkness of the night,
And something was stirring
Something that gave me a fright;
Her hair was dishevelled,
Her white dress torn,
Her raised arm pointing,
Expression vitriolic with scorn,
Accusing me as if I'd caused the death
Of her and her stillborn,
Then suddenly into the night we both vanished, forever,
Gone. Gone. Gone.

*Inspired by and based off of the poem "*Some One*" by Walter de la Mare.

HIDDEN TREASURES

Eboh ran through the fields, oblivious to the whips of razor grass that tore into the exposed flesh of his arms and back and legs. As adrenaline surged through his body he was only vaguely aware of the three other slaves who were fleeing through the field and bushes beside him. As he pulled ahead of the others, heading towards the tree line, he could hear the vicious snarling of the plantation dogs giving chase behind them.

There were six dogs, and though he'd fed them many times he knew they wouldn't hesitate to launch themselves at his throat as they'd been trained to do.

Eboh's sinuous body tensed and his muscles flexed as he transitioned from the fields into the dense undergrowth of the surrounding forest. Hearing a triumphant yell behind him, his mind had only a fleeting second to register that someone hadn't made it. That the dogs had caught up, and if that were the case then the beasts were hot on his heels.

Moving deeper and deeper into the undergrowth, he clutched the bag tightly in his hand and forced himself to focus on the path ahead and ignore what was happening behind him. There was no time to worry now, it would only slow him down. They'd known that the chance of making an escape was going to be slim, but it was a risk they'd all been willing to take.

The canopy above blotted out the daylight, making the surrounding air significantly colder. He wanted to push on, to keep running as fast as he could, but the roots that snarled themselves around his feet, and the slowly closing gaps between the trees halted his progress. With a rush of blood swirling in his head and his breath coming out in ragged gasps, he came to a stop and leaned against the massive trunk of a Brazil nut tree and listened.

A chorus of insects carried about their lives around him though nothing moved. There was no sight or sound of the dogs, the plantation owners, the curabans, or of his friends. Eboh was all alone. For a fleeting moment he was overcome with his predicament. In their plan, their dreams, they'd all made it safely to the other side of the forest that was said to house the remains of a plantation that had been abandoned after a massive fire destroyed the main house, killing the owner's wife and child in the process. There they planned to set up their own base, and in time, return to rescue as many of their brethren as they could until they had enough to overthrow the whole system one plantation at a time and take their revenge on the wicked men and women who had enslaved them. Though he knew it was a possibility that one or none of them would make it, that possibility had seemed like nothing more than a wisp of smoke, a figment of a long forgotten nightmare. Yet here he stood, alone and unsure of how to continue.

Stick to the plan.

The voice was clear in his mind. It was the voice of his grandfather, the same voice that had always guided him through life.

Drawing in a breath of fresh air, he fell to his knees and placed his hands on the ground. Closing his eyes he called upon his ancestors to help him evade the curabans and their dogs, he asked for their protection, and as he traced the symbol his grandfather had taught him into the dirt—the same one that the Whites had beaten and berated him for, had called him a heathen over, had demoted his life and value as a human being to being worth less than livestock simply because it didn't match their Christian ways—he could feel his senses heightening and he knew his ancestors were with him.

Though they were much too far away to be heard under normal circumstances, Eboh found that he could now hear the faint voices of the curabans and the frantic tracking of their hounds. Giving himself a few more moments to ensure that it was safe, he stood up and began to move through the brush as quietly as he could, pushing deeper and deeper into the forest. He knew how determined the curabans were and that they would keep up their search until the sun went down, so until then, he needed to be alert and aware.

To make matters worse, there had been rumours and whispers that the surrounding forest for miles out was rigged with traps to prevent any escaped slaves from going too far. With that in mind, each step felt like death was peering over his shoulder, but he needed to keep going and he hoped beyond all hope that the others had somehow managed to get away.

The going was slow and arduous, and as Eboh slowed to a stop to rest against a nearby tree he found himself feeling worn down to the point of debilitation. He had no idea if he would be able to keep going. Though he'd encountered no set traps he was still weary of their existence. Perhaps luck had been on his side and he'd somehow manage to evade them all, but with no way of knowing for sure, he needed to tread carefully.

The curious thing was that he was no longer being followed from what he could tell. It seemed that the curabans had either given up or had been called off by the Massa. Regardless of the reason, Eboh felt his strength renew and he pushed on, determined to get as close to the meet point as he could.

As the kilometres rolled on, the sound of rushing water reached his ears and a feeling akin to relief flooded his system. This was all part of the rumour; the river needed to be followed south and crossed at the point where a large silk cotton tree stood sentry. There the dilapidated old bridge would take him across and into the plantation.

Focusing his attention once more, Eboh tried to listen for his friends hoping for any hint of sound that would indicate that they were alive and well, but the forest whispered a sad response to him that he was still alone and would remain so, at least for now.

The moment the first overgrown building came into view Eboh sprinted towards it. Much like the buildings he was accustomed to, the slaves' quarters held the same layout and much of the tools and utensils had been left behind.

Well done my son.

The voice in his head was rich with warmth and love, and as Eboh picked a bunk that would have matched the same one he'd been assigned at his former quarters, he set the bag he'd been carrying down under his head and fell asleep out of sheer exhaustion almost immediately despite the fact that the sun was still looming low on the horizon.

***

"Eboh!"

The jovial voice snapped him out of his dream-state reverie in which he was back with his family in his native land. Jolting upright, he found himself staring into the grinning and relieved face of Tomori through the filter of the early morning light. Their reunion was loud and uproarious as they embraced each other, and when Eboh stepped back he looked his friend over and noticed the almost bruise-like circles under his eyes and the bloodied and scratched state of his body. "What happened to you?" he asked, "and where are the others?" He spoke in his native tongue, feeling at ease to do so for the first time in years.

Tomori shook his head. "The other two have been captured. I saw Yele being dragged back to the estate and I saw the dogs leaping towards Oba. I hid in the forest under a rotted out tree and stayed there all night, too terrified to even breathe. They were out all night long searching for us. I thought I was the only one left."

Clapping his friend on the shoulder Eboh dipped his head in remorse for his fallen brothers. After a minute had passed he pointed to the bunks. "Why don't you get some sleep?"

But Tomori shook his head. "Tonight we will sleep well for we are free men. Right now I want to celebrate and get started on our plans!" He paused as he glanced at the bag Eboh had been using as his pillow. "Do you still have it?"

Unwinding the animal hide drawstring from around the hand-woven button, Eboh withdrew the ring of the housekeeper's spare keys that he'd managed to lift from the main house. It was the affirmative act that had set their planned escape into full motion. The keys would surely be missed in time but he was hoping that if they could work quickly to put their plan into action, they could return to the plantation and free as many of the others as they could before Massa had time to change all the locks or set a trap.

The day was spent searching the old plantation and gathering an accumulation of tools and food as well as crafting a series of crude weapons they would use to arm themselves and the others they intended to free. Luckily for them most of the fruit trees on the estate were laden with fruit, and just behind the slave's quarters there was a small patch of planted ground provisions that was stocked with large sandy white yams that the men eagerly unearthed and uprooted with their hands.

As evening fell, the two friends sat around a fire, exhausted and singing songs of their home while they waited for the pot of bubbling yam stew to cook. As their songs faded into the quiet chew of their meal, they began to lay out their plans for the early morning. They would try to get a few hours of rest before heading back to the estate. They hoped to get there in time for the changing shift of guards that patrolled the barracks with their dogs. The window was small, at most a fifteen minute gap, but it would be enough to open the quarters and alert everyone to flee.

The plan was simple but needed to be plotted and played by ear given the variables. Their escape had been a big ordeal so it was likely that the Massa would have ordered double the amount of guards with no gaps between their shifts. If things looked too tense they would have to retreat back to their newly established base and continue to build their defences so that they could return at a later date. Nothing was a guarantee, but Eboh was sure in his heart that things would work out in his favour.

Though they could envision their complete emancipation as they boarded ships back to their native lands, it was but a pipe dream and the reality was that their future was still very much uncertain.

They went to sleep that night under the stars for the first time in years. Their sense of life had been renewed by something as simple as the cool and fresh night air rhythmically flooding in and rushing out of their lungs. In time, after their conversation slowly came to an end, sleep came to them both, and in it they dreamt the things only free men dream. Pleasant dreams of family and home. Dreams of promise and hope...

***

The voice inside his head screamed in warning just moments before the sheer force of a hand clamped itself around his neck and dragged him into a standing position. A startled and pained cry ebbed from Eboh as his eyes came to focus on the sneering face him front of him and he felt his heart drop into the pit of his stomach.

Just behind the overseer the triumphant face of the Massa loomed as he stood with his muddy boot planted on the back of Tomori's head. His friend looked out at him with a terrified gaze and Eboh knew it was all over.

"So this was your grand plan? To come to the old estate and live as if you didn't have a care in the world?" Motioning to some of the men who were standing off to the side they parted and Yele slowly strode forward and stood at the Massa's side. "You know, when your friend here told us about your plan I doubted him. I thought there was no way you were so foolish to think you could pull off such a thing, but my newest overseer here assured me it was true, hell, he even staked his life on it. Seems he was right after all. I can hardly believe it." He paused as he face hardened. "You know, Samuel," the Massa said referring to Eboh by his Christian assigned name, a name Eboh despised with all his might. "You have some gall to stand there as if you don't owe me. I took you in and made you a civil man, gave you a home, fed you, clothed you, taught you the word of our Lord and saviour. I made you. I own you. I think you've forgotten that, but we can rectify the problem. As God is my witness we will." His eyes held the promise of death within them and Eboh's heart sank even lower.

As the newest overseer and long-time friend dragged him through the dense woods, the remains of the old estate burned behind them. It had been one more step in the Massa's determined state to utterly and complete crush any semblance of a life outside of their slavery. A combination of salty grief and bitter anger was stewing within him and Eboh found himself distraught and overcome with emotions so powerful that he could hardly think straight.

You have been betrayed, my son.

The voice in his head was solemn and sounded defeated.

Eboh didn't want to believe it. Not after everything they'd been through and everything they'd hoped to achieve. The sharp yank on the chains jerked him forward and out of his pondering state, and Eboh looked up towards the forward facing and almost militaristic posture of his friend who seemed to hold no remorse for his treacherous actions.

So this was what it had come to? Had this been Yele's plan all along? To betray them for the opportunity of a promotion? And to think that his promotion would lead to him being the one who would commit atrocities against his own kind. Against his own friends. Regardless of if he had been threatened into the position or had planned and accepted it with glee, there was no room for forgiveness. Not after what they'd all been made to suffer through.

The emotions within Eboh began to churn more and more

within him and he felt a blinding rage build. In the distance the roar of the river could be heard, and as they approached the bridge, Eboh devised a new plan. A short-term plan. But he knew that his time was limited. After all, the only reason he and Tomori were even being taken back to the plantation was to be made into a public example so that no one else would dare to attempt what they had.

He needed to be quick to action. Closing his eyes he called upon the power of his ancestors once more, but this time he asked them to lend him all of their power and to help guide him to complete the unsavoury task.

My son, this is not the way.

His grandfather's voice was forlorn but Eboh was determined.

"Would you really condemn me to die at the hands of the white man without even trying to help me?" he asked his grandfather.

The silence echoed in his mind with pregnant pause and Eboh knew what needed to be done. If his own kin wouldn't help him he would call upon other forces to grant him his final wish.

Don't do this, Eboh. This is a dark force you are calling upon. There are other ways…

He silenced his grandfather's warning just as they began to cross over the dilapidated wooden bridge.

For the first time in his life multiple unfamiliar voices rose forth in his mind. Amplified and fuelled by his rage, Eboh felt himself swell with their power as his senses heightened. He could hear and see better and he felt stronger than ever. Invincible almost.

The voices were warped and dark, laughing in demonic glee as he reached outwards in a blur of motion and snapped the chains that had been fastened to his hands around the soft flesh of Yele's neck. Dragging his former friend backwards and cinching the chains much tighter than should have been humanly possible, they both pressed against what was left of the bridge's rail while Yele's arms first clawed at the chains and then at the air in front of him while Tomori, who'd been trailing behind him, the Massa who was in front, and his men, all stepped back and watched in horror.

As the railing gave way, they tottered for a brief moment, suspended in the air like a hummingbird in flight, before they both plunged downwards into the depths of the fast flowing river that pushed them further downstream and swept them away.

The chorus of voices in his mind remained in its crescendo, and his anger exploded like a supernova in a searing blast of white heat as he clawed at Yele and tore at his friend's flesh with his bare hands, intent on ripping him apart limb from limb. Unable to swim or escape Eboh's clutches, Yele clung to his friend and screamed as the waters gushed inwards and filled both his stomach and his lungs. But Eboh was having none of it, Yele's death would be at his own hands, not at the river mother's accord.

Summoning all the strength within him, he could feel his body being consumed with hatred so blinding that his very state of existence was being transformed. Drawing back a hand that was now a claw, he plunged it into the soft flesh between Yele's ribcage and ripped out handful after handful of his former friend's insides.

With Yele's still beating heart in his hand, Eboh bit into the twitching muscle and his sharp teeth tore through it with ease. The voices in Eboh's head exploded into praise and approval and lent him even more of their power as a reward.

He understood it now; the more he ate the stronger he would become. Swimming through the red waters he snapped up the remains of Yele and by the time he returned to the bank his body had grown three times in size. The dense ropes of muscles were covered in a layer of hair so thick the strands looked almost like strips of seaweed.

Walking along the river's bank, Eboh found himself at the shoreline and as he gazed out over the open water, the incoming ship with its load of new slaves and supplies slowly drifted towards the shore in its endlessly bobbing motion.

Eboh's rage swelled up within him once more as the last

traces of his humanity vanished. The voices cooed their approval as they egged him on with promises of even more power. Throwing himself into the water, Eboh found that he could breathe just as easily as he could on land.

His strokes were long and smooth and before long the massive ship loomed before him. Though it was much bigger than he'd anticipated, the voices told him it was no match for them, that they would help him tear it apart as easily as he'd torn Yele apart. Nothing could stop him now, and in the end he would be all that was left. This land and everything on it belonged to him now.

***

The boat sped ahead with its nose in the air. Perched and bobbing at what felt like a precarious angle, Roy felt a chill run through his body as wind dried the warm saltwater spray that bathed the group of ten pork-knockers and left behind a fine layer of sea salt on their already bronzed skins. In the wake of the churning water, the engine roared ahead towards one of many Region 8 outposts where the men would spend the next four months arduously toiling away in an attempt to hit gold.

Chris screamed into the wind, clearly thrilled by the rush of it all, and as he grinned Roy couldn't help but shake his head. This was to be Chris' first run and one good bout of malaria would be all that was needed for him to know what it was like to be a real miner.

Leaving behind his wife—a tall, thin, bird like woman with jet-black, short cropped hair and a penchant for baked goods—and his three year old daughter, Roy found himself looking forward to this stint. He had a good feeling about this time. This time would be the time his take away would be enough for him to retire. But he knew that was a lie, no matter how much he made, he would always be back. The call of the gold would always be one that he would answer to.

The boat captain, a fat-bellied man who reeked of Alcolado Glacial and cumin, navigated the canal with ease as he leaned back in his spot beside the outboard motor. As his arm gently guided the craft through the large channel, he pondered if Madam Margareta at the cathouse would be able to see him tonight. Lost in his daydream, he didn't even notice the alarmed exclamations that came from the miners until Roy, the most seasoned of the lot, frantically tapped his knee.

The water ahead in the middle of the channel was bubbling and churning with such force it sent small streams jetting into the air.

The boat slowed then came to a stop as the men all crowded around the edges, peering into the murky depths of the agitated water.

"Must be one of them steam vent things in the earth that letting go gas." Simon declared.

"You think it have anything to do with the earthquake?" Liam asked, referring to the 6.8 magnitude quake and the accompanying aftershocks that struck the island just two days before.

"Yeah man, it hadda be. It probably make a crack in the earth's crust and the gasses and whatnot must be leaking out." Clint nodded as if it all made perfect sense. But the boat captain wasn't so sure. Suddenly overcome with a foreboding feeling, he began to turn the boat around hoping to get away in time.

"Aye! Where you going?" One of the other men asked, but the captain shot Roy a look of terror and panic. Roy took the hint.

"It have another channel further back that will get us around," Roy said to the other men before adding, "That gas is probably poison to breathe in."

As the captain brought the boat around the water suddenly calmed and its surface went still. Roy's eyes scanned the area as his instincts kicked in that something was very wrong. The engine roared to life once more and they group of pork-knockers got about thirty meters before the first bump rocked the boat.

"What was that?" Chris asked as he peered into the murky water.

Another nudge rocked the boat the other way and the men all dropped down into the boat's bottom in an attempt to steady it.

The captain pushed the engine as hard as he could but it seemed like the boat was doing little more than crawling forward a few inches at a time. It was as though something was holding it back. Abandoning the attempt to get away, the Captain threw open a nearby hatch and slipped on his old, tattered life-vest.

Another bump came, this one more violent, and it was quickly followed by an even more powerful one from the other side. The boat rocked back and forth, taking on water with each dip until one final bump rocked the boat enough to spill the men into the water.

The moment they plunged into the dirty river the water began to churn and bubble around their upturned boat. Some of the men tried to swim to the river bank but something was pulling them under.

The water soon turned red as their screams were drowned out leaving only Roy and the captain alone and clinging to the boat. With the creature distracted with the last of the men the captain made one last desperate attempt to escape. Throwing himself away from the boat, he began to furiously swim towards the nearest bank.

Without warning, a large mass glided beneath Roy and headed towards the Captain. Roy didn't even have time to call out a warning before the thing pulled the Captain halfway under the water with a single violent jerk. With a furious scream he sputtered and flailed his arms before disappearing below.

Roy, realizing he was the only one left, was in a full on panic now and as the fear consumed him he felt his mind go blank and his body completely shut down. Helpless to whatever it was that lurked below his dangling legs he felt something coil around his ankles and drag him downwards.

As the screams of horror were forced from his lungs, the creature wrapped itself around him and it's almost serpentine eyes regarded him with black hatred. Long tendrils of hair that looked more like seaweed covered its body, and for a single fleeting moment Roy knew what this creature was.

Roy could hear the rush of blood in his ears as his bones snapped and popped under the sheer force of the beast's powerful embrace. As his world faded to a merciful darkness, the massacooramaan sucked down the tenth and final pork-knocker before it destroyed their drifting boat and moved on in search of others.

AH BIT OF OBEAH GO FIX THAT!

Flora wrinkled her nose against the sickly sweet smell that seemed to be trapped and drifting in the little circulation of air on her front steps. It was a familiar smell, one that tickled some long forgotten memory that threatened to erupt to the surface of her mind. Standing on her doorstep, she laid her hand against the door to steady herself as she closed her eyes and probed her own conscience, digging down to retrieve the memory associated with the smell.

The echoing sounds of a monotone voice followed by a series of weeping and wailing billowed out from the recess of her mind. Surprised, her eyes fluttered open and the sounds faded and was replaced by that of her suburban neighbourhood. Shaking off the odd experience, she opened the front door and stepped into her foyer and was almost dismayed to find that the smell was now even stronger. Dropping her keys into the little crystal bowl on the table, she slipped off her heels and announced her arrival to her family.

"Mommy!" her four year old daughter came bounding around the corner and plastered herself against her mother's stockinged leg. Looking up, she saw her husband coming into the entryway with a small smile on his face. After a quick kiss, he took the plastic bags from her hands and she followed him into the kitchen where the glass vase of pure white lilies stood proudly on the countertop.

She wrinkled her nose again as she saw them and felt her nausea burn in the back of her throat. "Where'd these come from?" she asked, though what she really wanted to ask was, *"Why are they here, in my kitchen, on my counter?"*

Her daughter was the one who answered. "I found them in the garden! I picked them just for you, Mommy!"

"In our garden? But we don't have any lilies in our garden. They're very beautiful though, thank you sweetheart." She kissed the top of her daughter's head. Feeling drawn to them, she walked over to the vase against her better judgement and stroked one of the ten tall-stemmed lilies with forced a smile on her face. The moment her fingertips connected with the flower's velvety petal, the memory once more surged forward.

A flash of a large building filled with old wooden pews that housed a full house of black clad mourners. She could almost feel the stifling heat of the building as the overhead fans spun slowly and lazily, recirculating the hot, honeyed air. The only reprieve came from the sporadic puffs of wind that floated through the large windows of ventilation blocks that ran along the length of the building's sides. She found herself standing to the back of the crowd as the funeral progressed, staring at the life-sized Jesus that hung on his cross, his expression a cross between utter agony and deep sorrow, and she thought that she could understand how he felt. Just below the Jesus figure stood the podium where the priest continued to drone on, and below that was the reason they were all there. The closed mahogany casket sat, adorned with a contrasting mass of white lilies, and as their smell carried on the air Flora felt a deep gut wrenching sadness washed over her.

As quickly as the image came, it was gone, but much like staring at the sun for a singular moment, the image had seared itself into her mind.

"I know it's strange, they weren't there last night but this afternoon when we got home we could smell them even from inside," David said.

With the same smile etched on her face, she turned towards her husband and nodded as though everything was normal, as though the long forgotten memory of attending someone's funeral hadn't just resurfaced in her mind. Feeling as though her limbs were suddenly made of wood, she shuffled towards the backdoor and pulled it open. Breathing in the fresh pre-spring air that had been warmed under the glow of the Houston sun, she reached for her daughter's hand and widened her smile. "Show me where you found them, pretty girl." The long forgotten memory had surfaced enough to remind her of what the smell represented—death—and she was more than desperate to get away from it.

The patch that bore the snipped-off lilies stood in the middle of the yard, and as Flora examined it she felt her head buzz with the beginnings of a migraine. Going back inside she found that her wonderful spouse had set the table and was dishing out the take out she'd brought home. Looking up he saw her absentmindedly press her fingers against her temple and without being told to, he poured her a cup of coffee.

Their unspoken bond was one of the first things that had drawn them together. They understood each other and each other's needs without even needing words. The last five and a half years had been utter bliss that had been completed by Carol's birth four years ago.

Taking the cup from him with a grateful nod she sipped the bitter brew and felt herself relax a little. "How about we put the lilies outside on the patio, that way they can get some sunlight," she suggested to Carol who frowned in contemplation and appeared to muse over the suggestion. With a determined nod, she carefully picked up the vase and disappeared outside.

"Is the smell too strong?" David asked.

Flora once more forced a small smile and nodded. "Just a bit."

"How was your day?" His voice was tender, braided and laced with genuine concern.

She sighed. "Harder than it needed to be. If only people

would stop worrying about socializing so much and just do the jobs they're being paid to do my work would be so much easier. And now that we're being audited, you know we have to be on top of everything. I think I might even have to go in this weekend for a few hours just to make sure we're getting done what needs to be done."

He placed his large warm hand over hers and she looked down at it and smiled. His milky white skin perfectly contrasted her brown skin with its almost autumnal orange-red undertone, and she rotated her hand to interlock her fingers with his. His comfort made the tension in her head to melt away into nothingness, and by the time they all sat down at the table life had resumed its usual routine.

As the alarm went off the soft singing picked up in intensity, spurring her sleepy mind to awaken. As she smacked the off button with a groggy swing, she heard the button connect but the song on the radio continued on. The choir was on the chorus of *Amazing Grace*, a song she hadn't heard in years, and their low mournful tones caused her entrails to tighten and her skin to crawl. Turning off the alarm once more, she was dismayed to hear the song still playing and her annoyance quickly turned to agitation as she picked up the clock and slammed it down, once, twice, yet the sorrowful choir continued to mourn.

"What are you doing?" David asked as he rolled over.

"The alarm doesn't want to turn off," she said as she slid her hand down the length of the cord and unplugged it from the wall.

"What are you talking about?" He sat up and looked at her with concern.

That saved a wretch like meeeeee...

"You don't hear the music?" she asked slowly, cautiously, as though she was afraid of his answer.

"No. I heard you press the button the first time and it went silent...what are you hearing?"

She shook her head and made no response. "I think I'm just overtired. I didn't sleep well last night."

"Was it the nightmares again?" His voice ebbed with sympathy.

She nodded and sighed.

"The same one with the blue?"

Flashes of the dream rose in her mind—her struggle to breathe as she drowned in a world of blue while the cold hands of dead things grabbed at her, dragging her deeper down into...what? She never really knew, the dream never ended or progressed, it was always the same.

"Yeah. The one with the blue," she mumbled. Shuffling off towards the bathroom, she got ready for her work day on autopilot while the song continued to play quietly in the background of her mind.

***

"So I looked him dead in the eye and said, 'Richard if you think you can just call me up whenever you feel like, then you need to think twice!' and his eyes popped open as his mouth dropped open!" Alicia's salacious laughter echoed through the hallways and Flora absentmindedly laughed along with her as she thumbed through the report to make sure all pages were in order. Stopping in front of her boss's door she tugged on her skirt to straighten herself out and squared her shoulders. "Just give me a minute, I'll be right back."

She knocked and pushed the door inwards, peering inside to make sure she was welcome. Mr. Ramesh was on the phone but he waved her in. Placing the massive stack of bound papers onto his desk, she motioned her departure and he waved her off without breaking his conversation.

Once outside, she felt her shoulders slump forward and the tension in her body receded. It was done, and if her work was as immaculate as she prided it being, it had been done *right*.

Alicia clapped her on the shoulder. "Let's go get some lunch!"

She blinked twice and stared down at what was supposed to be her cordon bleu chicken, but the ugly blackish-blue armoured fish stared back up at her with its glassy dead eyes making her stomach churn. She hated fish.

"Was blind but now I seeeee…"

She looked up at Alicia. "What did you say?"

Her friend stared back at her wide-eyed before she laughed. "Like you in another world Flor. I said, I really need to find a man who's good for me."

Without replying, she looked around for the waiter.

"Something the matter?" Alicia asked.

"I didn't order this."

Her friend paused, her fork mid-way to her mouth as she frowned. "The fish? Yeah you did. I thought it was weird but whatever." She shrugged.

Flora paused. "No, I ordered chicken…"

"Chicken? Girl, you sure you feeling okay?"

Pressing her fingers to her temple once more Flora pushed back her chair and stood up. "I think I going home to lie down. If you need me call my cell."

Without another word she walked out of the restaurant as the throbbing pulsed behind her eyes and threatened to overwhelm her. She heard Alicia rise and make a start after her but she just didn't want to see or deal with anyone right now. Making her way through the parking lot and towards her car as quickly as she could, she could feel that something was very much wrong. As she pulled open her car door and slid into the driver's seat she hoped she would be able to make it home in one piece. As the car started, the radio flipped on and the low tones of that funeral march began playing. Stunned, she turned off the radio and sat looking at it with utter disbelief. There was no way that was possible. She had to have been losing her mind.

Her heartrate had tripled making the pounding in her head almost debilitating. As panic began to set in, she could feel her chest tightening as though she was being asphyxiated. She didn't know how, but someone or something was stalking her or haunting her or…or *something*. Her mind babbled on about the possibilities. Reaching for her cell, her first instinct was to call the police. But what would she tell them? That someone had planted lilies in her garden? That she thought she'd ordered chicken but they brought her fish? That that she was hearing that blasted hymn everywhere she turned? The truth was that nothing was really *wrong*. Yet still her instinct assured her that something was indeed very much wrong.

Taking a deep breath, she reversed out of the parking spot as a sense of surreality swarmed and buzzed below the surface of her headache.

It was as though she'd blacked out because the next thing she knew she was standing in her driveway, staring at the two peach trees in her front yard that were covered in their bright pink blooms. Blooms that had attracted a swarm of jet-black butterflies. It shouldn't have even been possible but she could almost hear the soft flutter of their wings as they danced and twirled around in the air. The sight was eerie and as the cloyingly saccharine smell mingled with the cool, crisp air she once again felt herself overcome with the vaguest sense of a long forgotten memory. Looking over her shoulder, she made her way inside and closed the door behind her, sliding both the deadbolt and the security chain into place.

The house was silent as she kicked off her shoes. She was alone but the feeling of unease didn't leave her. As she walked down the hallway a single white feather fluttered and drifted through the air before her. Reaching out her hand, she allowed the soft plume to settle in her palm before she pinched its end and held it up against the stream of sunlight that was flowing through the high set windows.

As she gazed at it, another falling feather drew her attention to the snowy smattering of white feathers that hung in the air and drifted to the ground where they bloomed against the dark oak floors. The trail of feathers were marking a path that disappeared around the corner that led to her and David's bedroom. She followed them without a second thought as the memory pushed its way upwards.

The large gris-gris bag was laid out on her side of the bed, opened down the middle like a body bag to reveal a mound of dark, heady dirt. As her trembling fingers reached out, the unplugged radio began to play the now familiar rendition of Amazing Grace once more as the sounds of wailing in the background reached her ears.

Brushing the damp dirt aside, the white skeletal bone of the corpse's shoulder jutted out and Flora stepped back with a gasp.

Is time to come home, girly. The voice in her head was strong and she could feel the pull of it, beckoning to her.

"No." She bumped into the closed closet door as she backed up. "Is not time yet."

"Yea, when this flesh and heart shall fail, and mortal life shall cease…" The radio bellowed as she slowly slid to the ground and covered her ears with her hands as she screamed and screamed and screamed...

***

"Flor! Flor! Wake up!"

Her eyes snapped opened and she came to sitting upright in bed with a scream still on her lips. As her eyes adjusted to the darkness of the night she could feel David take her in his arms.

"It's okay. I'm here. It was just a bad dream."

Even though she knew they were outside, the smell of the flowers were stronger than ever and Flora could feel it permeating her very pores. She breathed out sharply, trying to get away from it. "David, I don't want those flowers on the property anymore. They is dead people flowers."

Without a word he threw aside the sheets and disappeared out of the room. An uncomfortably long time went by and for a moment Flora was afraid that something bad had happened to him…maybe those flowers were cursed, maybe they were haunted. But the moment the thought took form in her mind, David emerged from the darkness of the doorway with something in his hand.

"Sorry I took so long, I ran down the block to throw them into one of the neighbour's bins. Hopefully no one saw me." She could almost hear the smile in his words as he walked towards her. "Here, drink this. It was my mother's remedy for making me sleepy and making bad dreams go away."

Taking the glass of warmed milk from him, she drank it all in one go and handed it back with a smile. "Thank you. I feel better now." But the truth was that she didn't. She was disturbed. Something was happening to her, something was after her. She didn't know how she knew that, or what it was, or even what it wanted, but she knew that it was happening. That dream had felt more like reality than real life did. It had been an omen, and worse yet, it had been an omen that was slowly uncovering bits and pieces of a memory she'd long since forgotten, one she had buried six feet deep and didn't want to face again.

She didn't go back to sleep that night just in case the dreams returned, and as dawn began to lighten the night sky she slipped out of bed and left the house to go for a run.

Edgebrook was extremely peaceful and quiet in the morning time, and as she jogged on the side of the empty roadway she felt herself relax a little and her mind clear. Aside from the nightmares which could easily be attributed to stress from work, nothing bad had really happened to her. She was letting herself get all worked up over nothing. Making up her mind to carry on like normal, she finished her run and went home to make her family an early breakfast.

Her bubble of normalcy lasted until she arrived at her office. There in her cubicle standing tall and proud was a vase with ten snow white lilies. Flora froze and felt her hand reach up to cover her mouth. Hanging from one of the long stems was a little card, and with a trembling hand she reached out and turned it over.

What was once lost shall soon be found.

"What's that supposed to mean?" Alicia was behind her reading the card over her shoulder. "Did your man send those? They smell so good! You lucky, yes!"

Flora turned to her friend and shook her head. "I don't know who sent them but I'm sure it wasn't David."

"Oooooh! Secret admirer! Even better!" Alicia cackled.

"Alicia…" Flora began but stopped.

Her friend's expression dropped. "Flor, what happen? Something wrong?"

Flora sat down in her chair and stared at the flowers. Being the only other Caribbean worker in the office, she and Alicia had hit it off almost instantly. Without realizing it, Alicia had been her comfort and her reminder of home, but the more she thought about it, the more she realized she struggled to remember her life in Trinidad.

She remembered leaving Trinidad in a hurry and the last person she'd spoken to had been an old man. Had he been her father? She couldn't remember. The old man had been telling her something, something about herself…that she was sick? That she should be careful? Had something happened? Had she been running away? She could see the memory, almost touch the edges of it, but it was like smoke, and the deeper she probed the more the memory blurred and slipped away.

She had so many questions and knew that she needed the answers to them. How could she have gone for so many years without giving a single thought as to who she was and where she'd come from. What about her family? Her friends? Surely she'd had a life in Trinidad. And what about David? Why hadn't he even asked her about her life before she'd met him? But the truth was that he had, at least in the beginning, and her response had been a sobbing statement that she didn't want to talk about it, that she couldn't. He never brought it up again after that.

"I forget who I am." She was talking more to herself but Alicia pulled the chair from the empty cubicle next to Flora's and sat down.

"What you mean?"

"You ever hear me talk about home? About Trinidad? About what I used to do there?"

Alicia shook her head. "Not really but that's no big deal."

"It's because I can't remember anything."

Alicia sat back. "For true? Nothing at all? Like something bad happen there or what?"

Flora shook her head. "Maybe. I don't know, but I think I

have to find out... Actually I think someone or something wants me to find out." She motioned towards the now ominous vase of lilies on the desk. The little square card twirled and danced in the draft from the AC vent and as the silence fell between the two women Flora knew what she had to do.

***

David hugged her to him and their kiss was long and deep. When it was over he looked at her with nothing but kindness in his eyes as she squatted down and picked Carol up. "Baby girl, I will see you in a few weeks, ok?"

Her daughter nodded and smiled as Flora set her back down. "You be a good girl and take care of Daddy for me, you hear?"

The overhead PA system made a last call announcement for a different flight but Flora took it as her cue to leave. Leaning forward, she kissed David once more. "I'll see you soon," she promised. And with that she was off.

A funeral. Her uncle's to be exact. That was the reason she'd told David she was going back to Trinidad. She had a feeling that he knew it was a lie but if he did, he made no indication of it and she appreciated his support. He'd only asked her one question; *would you like me to come with you?* To which she'd shook her head and hugged him. "This is something I just need to do and be done with so I can get back."

The five and a half hour flight blurred by and as she exited customs with her luggage in tow, she found herself being accosted by three overeager taxi drivers.

"Where you want to go, miss?" One of them asked as they stepped directly in front of her and offered to take her bag.

Without thinking about it she looked at him and replied. "Mayaro." She had no idea how she knew that but now that she was back here on her native soil she could feel the answers calling to her, leading her on to what she hoped would be resolution.

The drive down was silent and the closer she got to her destination the more clarity she gained about what was happening to her. As she drew closer to where she needed to be she could almost feel a thrumming deep within her. Directing the driver to drop her off on the corner she paid him with a handful of US bills and stepped out of the car with her duffel bag in hand.

The car drove off leaving her standing below the blistering heat of the midday sun and as her pores opened up and slurped in the sunlight, she found that the feeling was deliriously familiar.

'Tis Grace that brought me safe thus far, and Grace will lead me home...

The song echoed in her head as she stepped off the roadway and began following the small dirt track. The houses that lined the tracked path were the typical board houses she'd grown up seeing and might of even lived in. Walking on, she found that she could sense the area. It was as though she knew who these people were. Passing by a blue painted plywood home, she peered in through the open door as the blowing breeze caused the curtains to billow outwards into the porch like a sail. She could smell the dhal, rice, and smoke herring they'd had for lunch lingering in the air, and she could hear the hum of the low playing TV set. Without knowing how she knew, she counted off the family members who dwelled there; mother, father, and two teenaged sons who weren't home at the moment. Moving on, she felt her resolve grow as the tingling sense of déjà vu that had plagued her for days solidified into what used to be her memories from a life gone by. She now knew where she had to be now and why she was here.

The house was similar to those she'd passed on her way in but the only difference was that there were no power lines that ran to the house, and its yard was divided into little garden beds that were neatly sown. Various crops and herbs were being cultivated and as she moved past them she walked right up to the white, six-panelled front door, turned the shiny golden handle and let herself in.

The house was well lit and smelled of pleasant earthy spices. The room she stood in felt much larger than the house's exterior indicated. To her right, a couch and two arm chairs were arranged around a small carved wood table that looked handmade. To her left, an assortment of items lay scattered over the top of a large work bench. The old man smiled an almost toothless grin as she entered. The deep creases on his weathered face smoothed out some as he stood up and set a handmade doll he'd been fiddling with aside. It was evident from his overall demeanour that he was thrilled to see her.

"Flora!" he greeted her. "Long time no see, doux-doux! How you doing? Come, come, sit down." He motioned to the floral patterned couch that stood against one wall.

Flora wasn't interested in his formalities. Her memories had returned to her now in full and she was sure there'd been some mistake. "What you calling me for?" she asked, her tone cold.

"Ah girl," he waved his hand in the air. "It was time for you to come back home."

"No." Her tone was firm as she straightened up and squared her shoulders. "I still have four years left. Is only six years gone by."

"I know, I know, but that's just how it is." He shuffled off towards the large hutch that stood in the corner near to the entrance way that led to the kitchen beyond it, and produced a little ring of keys. Opening the doors that stood at the centre of the hutch, he took out two long necked glass bottles, one green and the other a dark blue, along with two sparkling crystal glasses. And from the second to last drawer he withdrew a brown accordion folder. Locking the hutch once more, he walked past her and sat himself down in the armchair and placed the items on the little wooden table. "Sit down and let we talk."

Flora stepped over a wooden box and sat on the couch, staring at him with a quiet intensity.

He poured them both a vile drink from the green bottle

that smelled of rotted fruits and rubbing alcohol with an almost earthy undertone of burnt sugar. She wrinkled her nose. "What is that?"

He chuckled and dropped her a wink. "Only the finest Alabama Scotch!"

She shook her head and set her glass back down on the table.

"Suit yourself," he said as he knocked his drink back. "Whoo-boy! That is a good drink!" he wiped his mouth with the back of his hand in a garish display and she felt revulsion ripple through her.

"Listen, ten years didn't pass yet, so why you calling me?" she asked once again.

"I know ten years not done but nonetheless, my dear, is time."

She felt herself taken aback. "But how? You promised me ten years! Was it because of the baby?" That would have made sense. Carol was four years old now, if she'd split her time by having the child then that would have been a total of ten years.

But the old man shook his head. "Is not the child fault." He opened up the rust brown folder and rummaged around until he produced a sheet of paper. "This was your contract. Look, you sign it in your own blood." He pointed to the corner of it and continued. "I told you that you can have *up to* ten years. I never guaranteed you ten years."

"So you lied to me!" Her tone was indignant as she stood up. "I want my last four years, I don't care how, but I want them."

The old man shook his head. "That's not how this works. The deal was that you'd come when I called you back. Don't forget you living on borrowed time. I took life to give it to you. You was done dead and cold in your grave. Don't forget who make you sweet again."

"I not letting you turn me into a jumbie for you to use!" She screeched. "To hell with your deal and to hell with that damned contract!"

"I wouldn't be so hasty, chile." His voice was eerily calm

and she could see him smiling as he ran his thumb over the handmade doll he's been playing with earlier.

"Is that supposed to be me?" she asked cautiously, but he only cocked his head to the side.

"Only partially."

"What that supposed to mean?" Her indignation was smouldering now.

"It mean is time because I say is time."

She could feel him provoking her, toying with her, trying to make her angry and she refused to give in. Sitting back down she tried to regain her composure so that she could ask him what she wanted to know. "So why didn't I remember anything? How was I able to go six years without even thinking about it?"

"You chose to not remember because you didn't want to remember. Can't say I blame you really."

"So why bother at all? Why not just take my soul when I died the…the first time?" Her voice was low, almost a whisper.

"Because the universe demands balance. Nothing is done for nothing, what you take you must give back. There has to be a push and a pull. You get me? I wanted your soul and you wanted more time, I gave you what you wanted and now in return you give me what I want."

"Except you didn't give me what I wanted…you only gave me *part* of what I wanted. I wanted ten years, you gave me six." The petulance was evident.

He smiled. "You wanted to live again, you wanted to have a family, you wanted to see foreign land and live in happiness. Did you not do all that? Sounds to me like you did so my part of the deal is done."

She'd had enough of his games. "You is a dutty, stinkin' liar." She spat at him. "You never said I would have *up to* ten years. You promised me ten years and then you said I would die of something natural."

"Ah, semantics." He waved his hand in the air. "Tuh-may-toe, tuh-mah-toe, is all the same really."

"No *is not all the same*!" She snapped. She was well on her way to being worked up now. "You feel you have all the power in the world, eh? And if I walk away? You is an old man, what you go do? Stop me? Chook a pin in your little doll there?" Her eyes were narrowed, challenging him. Daring him to give her a reason to do what she hadn't yet thought of.

That lazy half-cocked smile turned into a full cackle. "You have a real fire spirit in you, oui!"

"ANSWER MY QUESTION!" she could feel the rage building in her and threatening to burst forth with explosive force.

Reaching over, he picked up her glass and swallowed the fetid contents. Digging through the accordion folder once more, he placed a small gris-gris bag onto the table and allowed its top to fall open. Inside she could see that it was filled with dirt and bones and what looked to be mottled tufts of hair. "If, my dear, you choose to walk away, you will start to fall apart bit by bit until you die. I'm sure doctors will call it leprosy or something like that. It will be long, it will be painful, but you will die. And when you do, I'll still get your soul because you agreed that it would be mine."

"So you knew I only had six years?" She forced herself to control her rage and her words came out through clenched teeth.

He shrugged. "You could have had fifty years if I wanted you to. There was no limit except for when I decide it is time. I have a client who paying me good money to do him a deed and out of all my people you were the one I know go do it best." He grinned at her and reached over for the blue bottle and held it cradled in his lap.

As the realization sunk in that she was nothing more than his pawn and that he intended to turn her into a jumbie one way or the other she knew what she needed to do. If she could kill him then it would be over. She and whoever else this wretched man had chained to him would be free.

Her skin burned as if it were on fire and sweat poured freely down her face and her back as she contemplated her position. It was true that she'd died, it was true that he'd brought her back to life and promised her ten years if she agreed to sign herself over to him in the end. And at the time ten years had seemed so long, but now. Now she'd been cheated, deliberately deceived. And to know that he was ripping her away from her family…

"Is there no one else who can take my place?" It was her last attempt to plead her way out of her predicament and she hated having to bow to this horrible demon of a man.

He paused as the mulled it over. "I can give you another ten years if you sign your daughter over to me as well. I'll even *guarantee* that I will keep you both together for all eternity once your time is up. Sign your man over to me and I'll add another ten years for the three of you and then you can all be a family forever."

She could practically taste the deception in his words and she bit her tongue until she tasted blood. The heat under her skin boiled so intensely that she half expected herself to burst into flames. How dare he even suggest she use her daughter and her husband as leverage for his crooked deal! It was more than she could stand and as her anger at being both fooled and made a fool of exploded, she allowed it to consume her.

She launched herself at him, her mouth opened in an almost feral scream as her hands clamped down around his neck. But the old man didn't even flinch. Instead he calmly popped the cork of the bottle and held it out before him.

She immediately felt all her energy drain from her body. Letting him go, she staggered backwards in an attempt to get away but the bottle pulled her in closer, sucking and slurping at her soul with a series of wet vacuous pops. And when it was done, he corked the bottle and sealed it with a hex. This had gone a lot better than he'd anticipated. The angry ones were always were tricky to deal with, but man did they work the best obeah. Milder emotions like sadness and happiness worked for simple spells and ailments, but for the big hitters nothing worked better than rage.

Adding the blue bottle to his collection, he moved to the living room and picked up the skin she'd left behind. Oiling it with a mixture of coconut oil and bay rum, he rolled it up in a thin layer of cotton and bound the package up with brown twine before he placed it in the bottom of his wardrobe with the others for future use. Going back to the drawing room, he extinguished the bird pepper incense that had been burning in the corner and recanted his charm that intensified and amplified emotions.

He knew he could have goaded her even further to the point he needed, the point where he emotions boiled so fiercely that anything could be accomplished by using her, but time was of the essence as the Minister was scheduled to arrive at any moment.

The obeah man had no doubt that his magic would work flawlessly for the Minister. As he replaced Flora's brown accordion folder into the hutch, he took out another and placed it on his work bench. A drop of blood would seal this contract and give the Minister everything he wanted, but when his time came, the obeah man would claim his payment as he always did. He shook his head and chuckled. Ah, the lengths people were willing to go to get their way! No one ever cared about what came after. Now was all that mattered, until there was no more now. Then they cared. They cared very much.

The approaching sound of footsteps on the gravel pathway outside drew his attention away, and with a toothless grin, the obeah man sauntered over to the doorway to greet his new customer.

Lyrics to the song "Amazing Grace" (1779) by John Newton is used under the public domain clause.

SLIGHT COMPLICATIONS

As the waves of agonized screams reverberated through the small room, Lalita stepped away from between the woman's splayed legs and frowned. Something wasn't right. Either the baby was breached or something else had gone horribly wrong. Her dilation seemed to be beyond what it should have been yet there was no signs of crowning, and her stomach, when pressed upon, was as hard as rock. The woman screamed in pain once more as she rocked her upper body back and forth in an almost pumping motion as if to eject the child from within her womb.

It was the middle of the night when Lalita answered a frantic pounding on her front door and was asked to come at once to this house. She knew nothing about this woman or how her pregnancy had progressed. She didn't even know if this was the woman's due date or if the baby was premature or why her midwife wasn't here. All she'd been told was that the baby was coming and they needed her, and so far all of her other questions had been lost and carried away amid the torrent of screams.

A woman who Lalita assumed was the mother-to-be's sister, hustled into the room with an armful of towels that tumbled from her hands in her frantic attempt to put them down. As she stood back her eyes were wild.

Lalita nodded and offered her a thin smile as she dug into her bag and pondered what the best solution would be. As she rifled through her various bottles of herbs and balms and devices, a piercing scream drew her immediate attention back to the scene before her just in time to see the woman who'd brought in the towels collapse to the floor.

Though the scream had come from her, Lalita looked back towards the mother-to-be who was still rocking her upper body back and forth and saw something she'd never seen in all her forty years of being a midwife.

A small arm that was a so black that it seemed to be absorbing the light in the room was clawing its way out from between the woman's legs. The woman's stomach heaved and seemed to writhe as the creature, for surely that's what it was, continued to make its way out. For a fleeting moment Lalita found herself rooted to the spot in equal parts of terror, fascination, and disgust.

As a second hand joined the first, the creature gripped the bedsheets and began to draw itself out enough for Lalita to see its long, sloped forehead breaching and as eyes as piercing as steel daggers stared at her with an awareness that most adults didn't even possess she found herself shaking in fright.

Though she'd never seen such a thing in her life, she'd been in the profession long enough to know, at least in theory, what was taking place. She'd only ever heard fourth- and fifth-hand accounts of the phenomenon, but rumours of the *raakhas* was enough to tell her what she needed to do.

Forcing herself to look away, she moved across the room to shut and lock the door. Then, as she cast a wary glance at the mother and her demonic baby, she moved over and pulled up the latch that allowed her to shutter the casement window.

The demon had freed itself up to its waist, its wide maw—complete with jagged, protruding teeth—snapped and gnashed itself open and close in its effort and concentration to gain complete freedom. Taking a deep breath, Lalita stepped up to her place between the mother's legs, just as the wriggling fiend popped free and unleashed a flood of thick, foul-smelling black fluid that immediately jetted outwards and soaked into the sheets and mattress below. The moment the raakhas broke free, its mother went limp and fell back onto the bed. Now it was just Lalita and the demon.

Her intent was to snatch and strangle the creature before it could even enjoy a moment more of this world. She'd been determined to removing its unholy presence from this earth before it had even freed itself, but the stench of the beast and that putrid black liquid was so vile, so pungent, that it filled the sealed room and drove her backwards. Turning to the corner, she dry heaved over and over again, until what was left of her dinner came up with an overbearingly bitter taste.

A deep voice filled the room and Lalita looked up through eyes that burned and overflowed with her tears as the demon child stood on its mother's chest and called out her name.

"Nisha…"

Lalita knew that now was probably the only chance she would get to bring this nightmare to an end. She inwardly cringed at the thought of her flesh making contact with *it* but there was no other choice. She needed to end its life before it ended theirs.

Though her mind was torn between slipping out of the room and locking the creature in, after all it was said to have the lifespan of only a few days, she knew that it would kill both its mother and the woman who'd been carrying the towels. While she let her mind indulge itself in the fantasy of retreating and escaping, she lunged forward before she could talk herself out of what she was about to do.

Her fingers were old and semi-arthritic, but the moment she clamped it around the demon-child's neck the thing softly mewled then went still. She was prepared for a fight, she was ready to do battle with the vile thing, but instead it seemed to have given up without so much as a tremble.

Its flesh was as cool as silk and as soft and delicate as a rose petal, and as her hand squeezed down harder, she could feel the fragile underlying bone structure softly cracking and collapsing. And in that moment a strange thing happened, Lalita began to cry and her grip on the demon-child loosened slightly.

Though she'd never been a mother herself and nothing in her life could have prepared her for this moment of dealing with such a situation, her heart went out to both the seemingly helpless demon-child and its mother. Though she knew it needed to be killed, that it didn't belong in this world and had no place here, though she knew that it was just about to kill its own mother, she felt her heart weep with sorrow for it.

With its air supply removed, the demon-child passed and returned to wherever it had come from and Lalita slowly relaxed her grip and sat before it for almost ten minutes, waiting to see if it would return to life, but the creature remained still.

Cradling it in her hands but keeping it away from her own body, she wrapped it up in one of the towels that had fallen onto the floor and examined the mess that lay before her.

What was she to do now? Who should she call? It was the middle of the night and this wasn't even close to being a typical situation. Should she call a holy man? A doctor? The police?

The window.

She needed to clear her head before she decided her next move. Moving over to the window, she opened it and allowed the crisp, clean night air to filter in. The moment she did, a darkness that she hadn't even noticed had been hanging in the room flooded out and both the mother and the woman on the floor began to stir.

"Where's my baby?" The mother immediately asked as she sat up, seemingly oblivious to the almost tar-like mess that was smeared everywhere from her waist down.

Lalita wasn't sure how to respond.

"Where's my baby?!" There was a note of panic in the mother's voice as her eyes darted between Lalita and the other woman who had picked herself up from the floor and was gawking, mouth agape, at the mess on the bed.

"Somebody tell me where my baby is! I want my baby!"

Her pleading held a note of sorrow in it and for a moment Lalita suspected her hysterics were rooted in her knowledge of what had just happened.

"I...I'm sorry. Your baby...didn't make it."

Her sobbing was so loud and deep she was unable to speak anymore. Wrapping her arms around her body, she rocked back and forth as if trying to comfort herself and Lalita's heart broke for a second time.

"A hand...I saw...it was coming out of...I…"

The woman looked at Lalita with wide eyes and Lalita hoped she wouldn't faint again.

Pointing to the wrapped up towel she whispered, "Is that it? Can I look?"

Lalita didn't think it was a good idea but the woman was already walking across the room on shaking legs. With a trembling hand she reached out towards the towel before she withdrew it and reconsidered. Shaking her head as though she were having an internal debate with herself, she pinched the edge of the towel and lifted it up and peered underneath. With a frown she shook her head in confusion and turned to face Lalita. "I...I don't understand."

Lalita didn't understand either. When the woman had lifted the edge of the towel that clearly held the outlined form of the frail demon-child there had been nothing underneath it.

The voice was clear but soft as it drifted into the room through the open window. With a wide-eyed stare Lalita turned towards the window just as the shadow of a dark void moved within the large rose mango tree that was just beyond it as the demon-child called for its mother who was now lying on her side and whimpering softly to herself.

"Nisha…"

Piggy Back Rides for Mr. Gundy

Marcia felt a slight prickling sensation run along her skin like an electric charge. Her body tensed as a shudder passed through it, putting an odd pressure on the base of her neck as her hair stood on end and her heart rate increased. She looked up from her crocheting, alert now to her surroundings, but the hum of the market place continued on as usual. Trying to take in the whole scene before her, she let her gaze focus on nothing in particular which was easier said than done when the dollops of brightly coloured produce gleaned and begged for her attention.

Ignoring the blood ripe tomatoes that screamed at her, the call of the tranquil greens of the breadfruit and chennette, the sickly sweet hues of the juice-engorged mangoes, and especially the festive party of hot peppers that lay piled in sorted clusters on Zams' plywood table, Marcia gulped the whole scene in. Something had to be amiss. But the patrons all moved around without concern.

Her pulse picked up for seemingly no reason and Marcia let out a slow breath as she allowed her senses take over. Ever since she was a child she'd had the ability to see things that others didn't. But now that she was older she was slowly losing that ability, but traces of it still lingered and always would.

With the sight blending into a harmonious focus, the cacophony of sounds came next. The overwhelming babble of conversations; the clanging and clanking of scales and the meat men's machetes; the honking and guttural engine grunts of the passing cars on the main road; the rustle of re-used plastic grocery bags and the quieter, more subtle sound of the market bags all faded into a muted background sound. All sounds except for one conversation.

Molly rocked back against her stool and snorted. "But aye-aye Mr. Gundy, how you looking magga so? Like you nuh gettin' enough food or-wah? What happen? Like you sick? Look how you head looking picky-picky like a dry up pommecythere seed!" She cackled at her own brash joke, making her big breasts and her even bigger belly jiggle under her hand-sewn floral print dress. An uncomfortable Mr. Gundy chuckled in embarrassment as his hand reflexively moved to brush itself over his hair. Looking at them both, Marcia thought it was like looking at Jack Sprat and his wife, for as fat as Molly was, Mr. Gundy was just as thin and emaciated with his dirty clothes hanging on his body like a rack.

But that wasn't all that had caught Marcia's attention. To the left of them, Marcia observed a mother who stood with her back to Mr. Gundy as she picked through a pile of provisions on the adjacent seller's table. As she selected what she wanted and added them to the scale—which Marcia knew for a fact was rigged to tally to the seller's profit—her little baby peered at Mr. Gundy over her smooth cocoa brown arm and scrunched his face.

As Marcia looked on she heard Mr. Gundy's quiet reply. His voice was hoarse and his words slightly slurred. "I eating well but like the more I eat the smaller I get. I did go to the hospital and they say mih blood pressure high and mih sugar low but I ent know nah! I don't trust them doctors and them. All they know to do is send you for test, test, and more test."

"Like yuh ketch something at the cathouse or-wah?" That belly rumbling laugh bubbled out once more and rose to a scandalously high cackle that everyone nearby turned to look.

Everyone including the mother and her baby, and the moment her child was facing Mr. Gundy, he began to squirm and fuss. Surprised at the baby's reaction, the mother bounced him slightly in her arms in an attempt to quiet him, but the forlorn glances the baby threw at Mr. Gundy made the mother smile apologetically to the old man before her.

No. Marcia thought. The baby had not been looking *at* him, but rather *above* him. The child had been gazing at something just above Mr. Gundy's head.

Suddenly she knew what the child was seeing, and though she couldn't right see it herself, she knew. There was a duppy sitting atop poor Mr. Gundy's head!

How the duppy landed up there was a question in and of itself, but the more pressing matter was: what was Marcia going to do?

***

It was early one dreary morning and Mr. Gundy was out back tilling his land to plant his crop of pigeon peas. The rainfall the night before had made the earth perfect to till and it was time to once more complete his ritual planting.

Turning the soil up with his pitchfork, he moved in a meticulous manner, creating row after row of upturned dirt. As he neared the tree line where the dense forest wall kissed the edge of his lot, he paused and wiped the sweat from his brow, listening to the early morning silence that was punctuated by the calls of the insects who were beginning to wind down, while the sounds of the morning birds grew more frequent. The rumble of a single passing car out on the main road brought him back to the moment, and as he was about to resume his work he heard a sound come from directly above him.

From up in its treetop perch the jumbie bird called its warning once more, and as Mr. Gundy stopped and rested his arm against the worn wooden handle of his pitchfork, he looked up into the surrounding canopy.

His eyes met those of the feathered bird whose snowy

white chest was marred by streaks of muddy brown feathers that seemed to ruffle in an everlasting movement like flowing current, though the bird itself remained motionless. Its wide yellow eyes remained transfixed upon him. It called again. Slightly louder this time, and with what Mr. Gundy assumed was some form of urgency.

The old man knew better than to ignore the call of a jumbie bird and he took its presence as an omen. Sticking the pitchfork into the ground, Mr. Gundy turned to move towards the house but his gait was slow and his feet felt heavy and sluggish. As he slowly dragged himself across the yard, he felt a building pressure on his chest that quickly evolved into a burning, crushing sensation as if some great weight had fallen on him and trapped him under it. Mr. Gundy fell to his knees but was determined to make it to the phone, so with everything he had in him, he clambered up the five short back-steps like a four-legged animal and spilled himself into the kitchen. This tale would have ended here if only Mr. Gundy had looked over his shoulder just once before he entered his home...

***

Silencing the blasted bird with a wave of his hand, a weakened Iku chittered from behind the nearby tree and slithered forward. The foolish old man had heeded the bird's death call but it was too late, he should have been listening since yesterday when the bird had made its first appearance and called its warning...

Nevertheless, the call had spurred the man into going inside which was what Iku had been waiting for. And as long as the man didn't turn around and face him, Iku knew that he would be eating richly tonight.

The man stumbled and began crawling towards the door and Iku followed boldly behind, sure that the fragile old fool would never even sense him amidst his heart attack. It had been a long time since he'd been summoned to this village and it seemed like a lot had changed since his last visit. The place seemed…nicer. There was more people, and more importantly, more food.

Iku's belly growled, its bottomless chasm calling out to be fed now that his slumber had been disturbed. The old man made it through the door and his arm blindly reached out for the phone. Iku grinned, baring his teeth that jutted out every which way like the spiny bark of the gru-gru tree, as his spindly limbs propelled him forward and through the doorway. He had been invited in by a most gracious host, and as he landed he attached himself to a dying Mr. Gundy.

***

Sitting up from the cold linoleum floor, Mr. Gundy's back ached in protest and his vision was blurry as if he were staring at the world through wet cobwebs. The sun was just beginning its decent and the mosquitoes buzzed in and out through the open door and swarmed around his head, sounding like the zingers on the mad bulls that were tied to the ever-windy Easter skies. Giving the mosquitoes fierce competition were the crickets and cicadas who were out earlier than usual, screeching their mating calls in the hopes of luring in their true loves.

Everything hurt. And as he picked himself up from the floor he marvelled at just how much pain he was in. His throat was raw and dry, his chest felt compressed, his spine felt bent, the very marrow in his bones felt dried up and brittle. Each breath expanded his lungs that felt charred and burned up, but worst of all was the pain in his neck. No matter how much he tried to lift his head straight, his neck would lock at a forty-five degree angle and go no further. It was truly a miracle he'd survived the heart attack. Reaching up to grab the phone from off its cradle, he dialled his son's number and asked him in a voice that felt as though he were speaking through a mouthful of glass shards, to bring the car around to take him to the hospital.

The wait at the Point Fortin Area Hospital was almost two hours despite there only being a handful of people waiting and him being classed as a triage level two. When they finally took him in, the nurse—a stocky no-nonsense woman who looked sick to death of her job—took his vitals as he sat in the tiny boxed-in area that was sectioned off by office cubicle walls. With Errol at his side, he sighed. "I don't know what happen, nah. I can't remember. I was tilling the lot and then I did hear the jumbie bird calling so I make to go inside. Next thing I know my chest start hurting and I pass out on the floor."

Errol remained tight-lipped now that they were in public though equal parts worry and anger surged through him. His father was eighty years old, and instead of moving in with him and his wife and their two daughters, he stubbornly insisted on living on his own in that ratchety old house.

Another two hours dribbled by before an older, skeletal man with badly dyed slicked-back black hair and a too-white doctor's coat sauntered into the room. Looking at the chart in his hand he grunted as he sat down. "Alright Mr. Gundy, so you say you had a heart attack?"

Mr. Gundy began to reiterate his story for the fourth time but the doctor held up his hand to stop him. "Based on your vitals and the tests we ran I don't see any sign or indication of a heart attack. Your blood pressure is a bit elevated and your blood sugar is quite low, plus you showed signs of dehydration, but aside from that, I can't find anything seriously wrong with you."

Mr. Gundy frowned and Errol exhaled in relief. "So what now, doc?" Errol asked.

The doctor pursed his lips for a brief moment. "I think he'll be fine as long as he takes it easy. I'm going to recommend you go in to San Fernando hospital tomorrow to get a few tests done just to be sure, but really I think two days of bed rest will make you right as rain."

The argument in the car on the way back to Mr. Gundy's house was one-sided with Errol doing enough ranting and raving for them both. The yelling was however suddenly interrupted by a loud rolling grumble that echoed throughout the car.

Errol turned towards his father in surprise and Mr. Gundy grinned meekly. "I ent eat since last night. I hungry fuh-so!"

"What you want, papa?"

Mr. Gundy paused for thought. "We could stop by KFC?"

Errol's shock extended into watching his father devour the fried chicken with such ferocity that he'd twice bitten clean through the bone. The biscuits were gone in two bites, the fries shovelled in at an unprecedented rate, and the drink chugged down in one go. Errol was so mortified by his usually reserved father's greedy and barbaric display he found himself laughing uneasily. "Take care you don't choke!" he cautioned.

Licking his greasy fingers dry, Mr. Gundy sat back and his sheepish smile returned. "I don't think I've ever been so hungry in all my life!"

By the time they made it home Mr. Gundy was hungry again, and as he pushed his son out the door with endless promises of consideration for moving in with him, all he could think about was defrosting all the meat in his freezer and cooking it up.

Late into the night Mr. Gundy worked at the stove, scarcely waiting for the food to cool before he dug in. And when his stew pot was empty he sat back and belched. Iku the invisible had been satiated for now, but come morning the hunger would start up once more and he'd have to go off in search of more food.

It had been almost a month since that fateful day, and the truth was that he knew something was wrong with him because his pains had only grown worse. And it seemed that the more he ate, the thinner and thinner and the more bent over and crooked his body became. Even more alarming was the fact that his copious eating produced only tiny smears of black, tar-like stool that smelled foul enough to make him gag. Yet still his stomach grumbled.

Cooking quickly became a tedious affair since it took too long to go from garden to plate with all the prep in between, so after a few days he'd begun to keep a perpetual hunter's stew going. Mr. Gundy would have gladly kept on going just as he was but the problem was that both his garden and cupboards had been bled dry.

Being in need of some meat and provisions, he pocketed the last of his pension money and headed off to the market. His plan was to ask the market vendors for any throwaways, anything that was too bruised or ugly to sell. Even fish heads and fish guts would do. It didn't matter what he ate anymore, he just needed to eat and eat and eat. And he had his story ready too! If anyone asked he'd tell them he wanted to start a compost for his garden. It was a fool-proof plan, but the moment he'd entered through the open market gates big mouth Molly had cornered him and he was struggling to get away from her cantankerous bellowing.

Turning his attention to the fussy little child in an attempt to be free of Molly's line of fire, he felt himself swoon and teeter forward, guided by some force beyond himself as the entity on top of his head lifted his arm like a marionette and reached out its own long spider-like limbs to sample the woman and child before him.

The woman took an instinctive step back though her expression remained kind, and without warning, the baby began to bawl unlike anything he'd ever heard. It began soft, then almost like an air raid siren, it built up to a full-scale howl that ricocheted around the market and bounced off of every possible surface. It was hard to believe that such a sound could come from such a tiny creature.

Mr. Gundy stepped back in shock and reflexively covered his ears with his hands. The whole scene was so bizarre that for once Molly was left in stunned silence as both the mother, bearing a now mortified and apologetic expression, and Mr. Gundy shuffled off in different directions.

***

Marcia could feel the duppy recoiling at the child's wails. The hair on her head stood on end and her skin broke out in goose-pimples as she rose to her feet and prepared to intervene.

"I wouldn't if I were you. It's getting stronger and will be looking for a new host soon, if it sets its sights on you that might be real trouble."

She'd been so transfixed by the scene before her she hadn't noticed the man who now stood at her side, but she recognized him at once and her blood ran even colder. Speaking through a mouth that had suddenly dried up as if she'd bitten into a cashew apple she asked, "How you mean?"

Clem's face was stern and an almost eerie darkness simmered in his eyes as he spoke. "Is best you just leave it be. It ent have nothin' you can do, and anything you do go only make it worse. You are much younger and stronger than he is and that is what it like."

He was known to all as the scholar. He was a man of high education who believed in both science and the higher powers and worked endlessly to unite the both. Rumour was that he had done it too, and that because of his research he'd gained the ability to transcend his form to be whatever he needed it to be. He was regarded with both awe and fear and though he seemed benign and would often offer his help to anyone he could, come night time the villagers made sure to lock their doors tight. Only the burnt out vagabonds and drunkards who were up at ungodly hours could relay their midnight sightings of Clem as he moved through the village, and lucky for Clem, most of them never even remembered seeing him the next day.

Finding her voice she asked him the only thing that came to mind. "What is it?"

"Never you mind. All you need to know is that it will soon be over." And with that he moved away from her before she could ask anything more.

Mr. Gundy moved through the market at a snail's pace unaware that he was being both watched and followed. As he moved through the maze of tables, Marcia watched in awe as the people in his immediate path all moved out of the way without even realizing it. Those who glanced at him would shrink back and even the vendors all seemed to be making an unconscious effort to have no contact with the old man.

As the fishmonger bagged up all the throw away fish heads Mr. Gundy's stomach grumbled. He chuckled uncomfortably as he cradled his concave stomach and reached a trembling hand into his pocket to pull out a balled up wad of green and purple bills. Holding them out before him, he offered the bills to the fishmongers who were all unconsciously standing as far back into their booth as they could.

"No grandpa, is alright. You keep your money."

With a grateful and seemingly oblivious nod, Mr. Gundy shuffled off to a provisions vendor with his money still clutched in his hand. Marcia could see that the duppy was in full control and that it was slowly draining him of everything he had. Her blood boiled but she forced herself to remain cool and heed Clem's words. There was really nothing she could do without endangering herself. Her sense was weak. She couldn't even really see the duppy, just a slightly wavering shimmer above Mr. Gundy's head like a heat wave coming off a galvanize roof or a hot pitch road.

Looking around for Clem, she spotted him watching from the upstairs part of the market where all the tailors and seamstresses worked. His gaze was fixed on Mr. Gundy but now he wore a smile on his face. Marcia shuddered.

***

The little board house stood in the centre of the lot, looming and foreboding despite its humble size. In the backyard, near the now overgrown peas patch and under the cover of the immortelle the Lagahoo stood, his breathing steady as he connected to the earth. With his massive canine head cocked to one side and his yellow slit eyes glittering in the darkness, he listened to the sounds of the house. Inside the lights were on and the smell of simmering meats and provisions drifted through the gaps between the board walls.

The lagahoo focused on the movements *inside* the house. He could hear the sounds of the eternally bubbling stew and the quiet clinks of the pot spoon against the side of the large round bottom cast iron pot that was followed by an almost excited exclamation of victory as *it* greedily retrieved a fish head from the depths of the brew.

He could hear the snap as Mr. Gundy's teeth sank into the head and began tearing away the flesh from the bone. And the wet slurping as he puckered his lips against the eyes and vacuously sucked them down. *It* moaned in delight as his belly welcomed the food in exchange for a chorus of unsavoury belches. *How disgusting and crude.*

Without moving, the Lagahoo stood amidst the forming dew, waiting until the time was right. He had nothing but patience when it came to dealing with his brother. Behind him, the thick chains that were wrapped around his waist stretched out and came to rest in a series of coils on the coffin he carried. With nothing but the croaking crapauds and the screeching crickets for company, he rolled his eyes and breathed in the night air, allowing himself to observe his surroundings without straying from his target. *Family reunions were always so complicated.*

The moon drifted and settled in the clear night sky, securing itself a three a.m. seat for the event that was about to unfold. Lending its moonbeams to the witching hour, the Lagahoo came to life and grew animated once more. Reaching his arms upwards, he listened to the soft jangle of his chains and smiled as he sensed Mr. Gundy go still. He could hear the old man's heartbeat pick up while his breathing stopped completely as *it* listened.

Seeing the curtains crack slightly, the Lagahoo grinned revealing his teeth and a trickle of saliva fell from his lips to join the dew below. He softly jangled his chains again, drawing out the old man.

The backdoor flew open on its hinges with an almost unnatural force and old Mr. Gundy emerged with a machete in his hand, his eyes wild with fury. He paused on the back step and the Lagahoo could feel Iku's rage.

"Is you who come to meet yuh death here tonight?" Iku snarled, using the body of Mr. Gundy to relay his words.

"Hello, brother. Long time no see." The Lagahoo was calm

and unimpressed.

Mr. Gundy roared. "I is not your *brother*! You is a disgrace to us, a joke! Helping people, eating only fowl and fish…you weak and nasty!"

The Lagahoo sighed at Iku's arrogance and ignorance. "I see you ent change one damn bit. But you know, I find you looking tired. I think you need to take a rest, brother. Feeding off a dead carcass isn't good for your health, you know."

"How you find me anyways?" Iku asked as he sauntered down the steps and closed the distance between them.

"How could I not when you smelling stink of death so?"

Iku laughed and seemed to relax for a split second but the Lagahoo was ready. Without warning, Iku was in motion and the limbs of the old man seemed to grow to an unnatural length almost like that of a four-legged spider. His eyes rolled upwards, white and sightless, as he launched himself through the yard to slash out at the Lagahoo who swung one of his chains and knocked the machete out of Mr. Gundy's clawed hand.

With his other wrist he flicked this thickest chain, one that was rusted beyond measure, and watched as it sailed through the ait with an almost musical tinkle before the Lagahoo brought his arm sharply down. The chain cracked, the sound rolling like thunder across the yard, as Iku was cast from Mr. Gundy's body.

The spider-duppy yelped in surprise as it tried to skitter across the yard and disappear into the nearby culvert, but the Lagahoo was having none of it. With yet another flick of his wrist he wrapped one of his chains around Iku's bulbous midsection and dragged the spider-duppy towards him. Iku howled in rage, clawing through the loose, wet dirt as he tried to break free.

"Is how you so strong?" he asked, the fear and panic evident in his voice.

The Lagahoo wasted no words as he drew his chain in one link at a time while the wooden lid of the coffin behind him opened in anticipation like a dark gaping maw.

Iku screamed as he snapped his poisonous teeth at the chain and wriggled his food-bloated body, but the more he struggled the more the chains tightened around him giving him an hourglass look that would make most women envious. He choked and gasped for breath but it was no use. Dragging him up into a standing position, the Lagahoo held him steady.

"Brother, please, I didn't mean no harm, the man was dead already! I didn't kill him, I just see an opportunity and take it because I was so *hungry*. Look, I will leave him alone and go off on my own, ok? I have some strength back now so I go find someone else. Please, spare me, brother." Iku babbled on and pleaded in his most sincere tone.

The Lagahoo snorted. "Oh-ho, now I is your brethren? At any rate, I understand you well, dear *brother*, because you see, I'm hungry too…"

And with that the coffin jumped up into a standing position and snapped itself shut around Iku. Falling to the ground with a soft thud, it bucked up and down a few times as the spider-duppy struggled and then finally stilled. The Lagahoo drew in a deep breath and sighed as his chains rattled with Iku's power. It was a small meal but it would keep him satiated. Besides, he knew there would always be more.

***

Marcia shifted her faux-leather bag on her lap feeling slightly embarrassed at the peeling flakes that fluttered around the handle. Sitting in the front seat of the PH taxi she leaned against the seatbelt and looked out the windshield, marvelling at the driver's finesse in manoeuvring his car around the pothole-filled road before them. In the back seat sat one man and two women, one of whom had liberally sprayed herself with a cheap knock-off perfume that tickled Marcia's nose with each inhale. Breathing through her mouth, Marcia's finger tapped along to the radio as Lord Kitchener sang about Audrey's sweet sugar bum bum and how it would get him into trouble when she would wiggle, and out of the corner of his eye the driver saw it and smiled.

There was a traffic jam up ahead and the blue flash of lights off to the side, signalled that something bad had happened. The car slowed to a crawl and then a stop as the passing cars slowed down to rubberneck at the scene.

"Watch how everybody studyin' to macco people business!" the driver exclaimed. "Just now yuh go see accident happen!"

Marcia barely heard him, her attention was focused on the flashing blue lights inside the side street and as they passed she saw the crowd that had gathered in front of Mr. Gundy's house.

"Driver, stop the car please."

He twisted his mouth to the side in disappointment as she dug into her purse and fished out a handful of red bills. Counting out the amount, she handed it over to him while she freed herself of her seatbelt and simultaneously opened the door.

The crowd was thick and the murmuring passed over them like shudders. Shouldering her bag, she made her way to the front and peered through fence and into the backyard where the mass of officers seemed to be. They were squatting around a body and Marcia's heart dropped as her instinct told her that it was Mr. Gundy laying on the ground between his plants. Just what had happened?

The coroner's van pulled up with a series of honks as the crowd parted and closed in around the vehicle. Twenty minutes later no one had any answers since no one could get a clear view of what was going on. All the crowd knew was that Mr. Gundy had died. With his body loaded up into the back of the hearse and the solemn faced officers ordering the crowd to break up, Marcia was forced to resume her journey to work.

It didn't take long for the talk to hit the market in a series of harsh whispers and Molly was the first one to hear the gossip. Marcia sat at her table listening in rapt silence.

"Yuh know he was here just the other day!" she exclaimed with a shake of her head. "But is true what they saying? That he body was dry up like he dead long time?"

The woman standing before her nodded and relayed

something she'd heard from someone who knew someone who worked in the hospital.

"Schimps! And you know when he was here I did tell him he looking magga and dry up!" Her face feigned concern but her eyes were alight with the gossip. As the woman paid for her goods and moved off, Molly leaned over and began the discussion with the vendor next to her. Marcia didn't want to believe it. There was simply no way something like that could have happened. Her mind flashed to Clem and what was whispered about him. There was simply no way…was there?

***

Much to the disappointment of the crowd the casket lid had been firmly closed with a picture of a youthful Mr. Gundy sitting on top of it. The service was short on account of the light but unrelenting rain that fell in a sheet over the area.

With black umbrellas dotting a section of the cemetery, the gravediggers, adorned in their dirty clothes and muddy boots, wove a series of intricately laced white rope through the coffin's handles and shifted it into place. Into the ground went Mr. Gundy while the crowd stood watching. Those closest to the grave threw in a handful of clumped wet clay and then moved off to the nearby standpipe to wash the dirt of the dead from under their nails.

When it was over, only Marcia was left standing at the base of the grave while the diggers' shovels whacked the rounded mound into place.

Suddenly the hairs on the back of her neck prickled and she realized she was no longer alone.

"You know, you can train your gift to be stronger," Clem casually remarked.

Marcia felt fear and revulsion fill her but it faded as quickly as it came. If the rumours were true Clem had done old Mr. Gundy a favour. But then what had happened to the duppy?

"He was already dead for a long time, probably a heart attack or something." Clem's voice was soft, almost reverend, as he leaned forward and set a white lily on top of the dirt mound.

That prickling sensation bubbled up once more and she felt her heart beat just a little faster. "So who was that in the market talking with all the vendors?" She asked as she glanced at Clem's saddened face. She knew the answer but she had to ask anyways.

"It was wearing him like a skin."

Clem's lips hadn't moved but she'd been sure she heard him say the words.

"What you say?" she asked as her face morphed into a look of horror.

He turned to look at her with a sad smile. "If you ever want learn how to use your gift come see me anytime, alright?"

He turned and walked down the hill of the Point Fortin cemetery, black suit against the grey sky and even greyer headstones that jutted out of the ground like teeth from gangrenous green gums. Following after him she asked what she most wanted to know.

"What happen to the duppy, Clem?"

Clem turned to face her and studied her as if she was one of his experiments. She felt herself squirm under his gaze but forced herself to meet his eyes dead on.

He nodded. "Don't worry, it not going to be bothering anyone anymore."

"You kill it?" The words left her mouth before she could stop herself.

He smiled. "We go meet again soon enough, I sure of that." A darkness danced in his eyes for a moment before he turned away and left her alone to ponder his words.

Stunned and unable to make heads or tails of the bizarre conversation, Marcia was drawn out of her thoughts by a gurgle and growl that came from the depths of her stomach.

Ah, boy! She was hungry fuh-so!

Crick-crack!
Monkey break he back
Fuh ah piece ah pomerac.
Wire bends.
Story ends.

GLOSSARY OF TERMS AND PHRASES

A

A-A! : An exclamation of surprise or indignation.

ah: A word meaning "I" or the article "a."

ah chut! : An exclamation of disgust or even anger or exasperation that is used to replace its harsher and more profane counterpart. It can also be used to silence someone.

ah ent able/ I ent able: Meaning "I am not able (to deal with that)."

ah go do for she/he: A term meaning that revenge will be sought on a person.

Alabama Scotch: A term that refers to babash (pronounced *bah-bash*) It is an illegal alcoholic beverage, similar to moonshine, that can be made from just about anything organic. Its high proof content makes it a well-known and well-feared drink. Typically babash is sold "under the counter" and is most common during the sugar cane harvest season.

allyuh: (pronounced *awl-yuh* or *al-yuh*) All of you (people).

Amerindian: The term is used to refer to the indigenous peoples of the Caribbean and the Lesser Antilles (namely the Caribs aka Kalinagos or the Arawaks aka Tainos).

away in foreign: This term refers to someone who is currently away (living or visiting) in a foreign country (typically the UK or the US).

B

back-a-day: "back in the day" A term used to refer to a time that has passed.

bazodee: (pronounced *bah-zoh-dee*) This word originates from the French term *abasourdir* and it refers to the feeling of being in a dazed or confused state. Often used to refer to love and a state of mindless bliss, it tells of someone who is so lost and caught up in the moment they are not paying attention to the world around them.

behique: (pronounced *beh-he-kuh*) The shaman of the Taino/Arawak tribe.

bhoot: An East-Indian word that refers to a deceased person's spirit.

bird: This word can be used to refer to the animal or it can also be used as a slang term to refer to a man's female companion or girlfriend.

board house: A house constructed out of wood and plywood.

bo-bo: A term referring to a minor mark on one's skin, an injury or scratch. It is similar to the North American term "boo-boo" that is commonly used by young children.

breadfruit: A large, green, round, starchy fruit that must be peeled and cooked. It is similar in texture to a potato or other ground provision when cooked. It is best known in a dish called "oil down," (pronounced as "*oil dong*") which is a stew of breadfruit in coconut milk, combined with some type of stewed or salted meat.

broughtupsy: This word refers to the manner in which one was raised (or brought up) and how that person behaves and conducts themselves.

buck-man: A term used to refer to one's father.

C

callaloo: (pronounced *cah-lah-loo*) A thick soup made from dasheen leaves, ochroes, coconut milk, and often contains crab. Typically served with rice, red beans and stew chicken or by itself as a soup.

cascadura: (pronounced *cas-cah-doo-rah*) also known as *cascadoo* or *hassar* – An armour-plated species of fish related to the catfish. They typically grow to be an average or nine to ten inches in length. Legends tell that those who eat the cascadura will return home to the Caribbean island of their birth when their time to die is upon them no matter where they are in the world.

cathouse: Slang term for a whorehouse or location where prostitutes can be found.

catspraddling: A term used to refer to the manner in which someone loses their footing or balance and dramatically falls and ends up in a splayed position.

cavalli: Another word for the Crevalle jack fish (also known as the jack crevalle, common jack, black or yellow cavalla or trevally) who is known to populate the warm waters of the Atlantic Ocean.

chac-chac (also called shak-shak): A type of rattle or maracas traditionally used to produce music. It is typically made from dried and hollowed out gourds filled with seeds or beads that produce sound when shaken.

chain up (yuh head): Refers to being manipulated or lied to by someone. The terms means that your mind has been tied up and is no longer free to see the truth.

chip-chip: Also known as *Donax*, it is a small edible saltwater clam. This mollusk is used and prepared as a delicacy that is most often available in February and March and collection of it is an arduous task given their small size.

chile: Child.

chirren: (pronounced *chih-ren*) Children.

chook (also known as *jook*): To poke, prod, or stab.

choonkaloonks/choonkoloonks: (pronounced *choung-ka-loonks*) A term of affection of endearment typically reserved for children.

coco-tap: A coco-tap is an open handed hit one typically sustains on the back of their head (their coconut) usually from your mother.

cocoyea broom: (pronounced *co-key-yay broom*) A broom made by stripping the leaves off the coconut palm fronds, leaving behind the thin centre shaft (mid-rib) which is then collected and banded together. Newly made brooms are green and soft (pliable) but in time they dry out and become much harder.

couyah mouth: (pronounced *coo-yah mowt*) A gesture made by pursing the lips and "pointing" it to one side or another (or at someone who has made a statement). It's typically used as a gesture of indignation, scorn or disbelief. In some instances, this action is done behind someone's back after they've said something that may be a lie or hard to believe and is usually accompanied by a rolling of the eyes or a frown.

coverlet: The top sheet or flat sheet of a bed set that one uses to cover themselves with to keep warm.

crapaud (crapo): (pronounced *crah-poh*) French for toad.

cricket pitch: The cricket pitch refers to the flat strip of field between which the two wickets are situated for a game of cricket.

crocus bag/crotus: A burlap bag or sack that is durable and able to carry a lot of weight without breaking. The sack is commonly used for things such as rice, potatoes or even manure. The bag form is commonly known as a "*market bag*" as many people opt to use it since it is reusable and durable.

cunumunu: (pronounced and also known as *Coo-noo-moo-noo*) Someone who is of a simple mind, someone shy, someone stupid.

cut-eye: A look all Caribbean mothers have mastered! To give a cut-eye is to look at someone "with daggers in your eyes." It is a look of anger that also conveys disapproval and disappointment. It is done by narrowing the eyes so that they are squinted. The mouth is usually twisted into a scowl or a thin hard line, and should you hear the deep intake of breath you know a good cut tail is sure to follow!

cutlass: (also cutlash) A machete.

D

dasheen: A large variety of the Taro root. A common ground provision that is used in many meals in the Caribbean. The leaves of this plant are used to make callaloo.

dat: That.

de: The.

dem: Them.

den: Then.

dey: "They" or sometimes "there."

deya (also diya, deeya): A small clay lamp that looks like a small bowl. It is used by Hindus especially around the Hindu festival Divali (also spelled "Diwali") which is known as the festival of lights. It is filled with oil or ghee, and a cotton wick is dipped in the diya and one end of it is lit. Diyas that are used in Hindu temples to bless worshipers are known as *aarti*.

doh: Don't.

doux doux: (pronounced as *doo-doo*) This is the French patois term of affection which translates to sweet-sweet. It is a term of endearment that is similar to sweetheart, darling or dear, and it is usually accompanied by the world darling (doux doux darling – sweet sweet darling).

doubles: This is a Trinbagonian delicacy. It is usually served from food carts. It consists of a layer of curried channa (chickpeas) that is sandwiched between two yellow (saffron) pieces of fried dough known as a *bara*. Often time it is accompanied by a *chutney* (a spicy East Indian sauce that is used as a condiment. It can be made from either half-ripe mangoes, tamarind, or cucumbers – Note that chutney is also a genre of music that is well known in Trinidad)

dotish/dotishness: (pronounced *dough- tish*) Silly, dumb, stupid. Another word commonly used is "chuppid" (pronounced ch-uh-pid). Dotishness conveys a stupid act or action or even a foolish thought that one has or is considering doing.

donkey years: A term used to mean "many years".

dutty: (pronounced *duh-tee*) Dirty.

E

ent: (similar to ain't) This word means "not." Depending on the context it is used in, it can also mean "right" or "don't you"
Example 1 (not): I ent going there!
Example 2 (right): You know what I mean, ent?
Example 3 (don't you): Ent you know what I mean?

F

'fraid: Afraid

feel a-how: To feel weird or strange or suspicious.

fig: In the Caribbean, this word is used to refer to bananas and not the traditional fruit most people know as "figs." There are many types of figs (bananas) that can be found from silk fig (known as manzano), Chiquito, Lacatan, Cooking fig, Mataboro, Gros Michel, Giant Governor, Red or Green Moko (note that there is also Moko Plantain which is different), among many others. When these bananas are on the tree they're referred to as a bunch, when they've been picked and each section separated they're known as a hand, and when you remove a single one, it's known as a grain.

flambeaux: (pronounced *flam-bow*) This is the plural form of the word "flambeau" which

fried bake: Also known as floats (due to their penchant for floating to the surface of the hot oil when ready) and similar to the Johnny Cake, is deep fried bead disc made from a basic flour dough consisting of flour, water, salt, sugar, baking powder and sometimes butter. There are various types of "bakes". A typical bake is made on a *tawah* (baking stone) while a roast bake is made in the oven.

fuh: For.

funny: Used in the traditional sense to refer to something hilarious, but it can also mean something that is weird, strange or odd.

G

go-bar: This phrase is used to mean nonsense. Originally go-bar referred to a mixture of cow dung and mud that was used to plaster walls and floors. The addition of the mud would keep the plaster from cracking upon drying. The dung was also dried and used for fuel.

Golden Ray: A flavoured vegetable butter that is bright orange in colour. It is created by the brand *Blue Band*. It is said to "add that rich creole flavour" to your savory dishes.

gris-gris (also spelled gri-gri): (pronounced *gree-gree*) This term is African in origin and refers to both the hexed/charmed item as well as the process of hexing/charming the item. A gris-gris bag is said to be a handmade bag containing an assortment of other gris-gris items. The bag itself is charmed and protects whatever is contained within it. The bag and items can be harmless or harmful depending on the intent for which they were created.

gru-gru tree (also known as grugru palm): The *acrocomia aculeata* is a palm tree whose bark is covered in long hard needle-like black spines. It produces grugru nuts and is cousin to both the grigri and *peewah*.

gundy: (pronounced *gun-dee*) This refers to the large claw of the crab.

There is a Caribbean joke that goes: What did the Indian crab say when it fell off the cliff? He said, "*Mih hut mih gundy!*"

H

hustle: This term has multiple meanings 1. It can refer to speed and energy in completing a task 2. to swindle someone or 3. to go out into the world and work hard and arduously to achieve success.

harden: Stemming from the idea of being "hard of hearing" it is most often used in relation to children to refer to disobedience or their tendency to not listen to the rules or guidance of adults.

hunter's pot (also known as a *perpetual stew* or a *hunter's stew*): A pot that is kept on the fire at all times and replenished with whatever is on hand. Ingredients are added to the pot and allowed to simmer into one ongoing stew.

I

In the river, on the bank: This is a game of elimination where a leader is chosen to give the command of "in the river" or "on the bank". An established boundary of where the river is and where the bank is is determined. The players, standing side by side in a line, must then quickly obey the direction of the two commands by jumping over the boundary "into the river" or back over the boundary "onto the bank". The commands are called out at random and can be repeated multiple times in a row. Those who fail to jump in the right position are eliminated from the game and must stand out. The last man standing is the winner who then takes the place of the leader and calls out the commands as the game begins again.

J

jagabat: A slang term used to refer to a promiscuous woman (similar to a *sketel*) or one who is stupid, meddlesome or tiresome.

Jab-Jab: (Carnival character) The Jab Jab is a character who is best known for the whip he carries; a thick, pleated hemp whip which he cracks in a threatening manner. In a display, he can crack this whip, reducing the clothing of other Jab Jabs to ribbons. The costume of a Jab Jab is comprised of satin knickers and a satin shirt with cloth points from which bells hang. A panel on the front of the shirt is typically decorated with swan down, rhinestones and mirrors. On his head, he wears a hooded mask with protruding cloth horns and on his feet he wears cloth shoes and stockings. In the modern-day Carnival, Blue Devils are commonly referred to as Jab Jabs for the jabbing motion they make with their pitchforks.

jalousie windows: (pronounced *jah-loe-see windows*) A window made of horizontal slats of glass louvers that are set onto a track so that they can be opened to a desired angle simultaneously to allow for airflow.

jack spania (also known as jack Spaniard): A type of wasp native to the Caribbean and parts of North America. It is reddish-brown in colour and tends to be peaceful unless provoked or their nest is disturbed. Their nests are built in cool, sheltered places typically around eaves and overhangs of roofs.

K

Klim: A brand of powdered milk that typically came in a brown and yellow tin.

L

let we make quick: A term used to mean "let's hurry up".

licks/licking: Often used in the traditional sense, this word can also mean a beating (that is typically given as a form of discipline) in a fight.

lime/liming: To casually hang out with a friend or (typically) a group of friends.

lingae: (pronounced *ling-gay*) Skinny, thin, malnourished.

M

macco: (pronounced *mack-oh*) To mind someone else's business. To pay attention or involve yourself in events and affairs that does not concern you. Someone who has a habit of *maccoing* is said to be a *macocious* person.

mad bull: A large octagonal kite that is known for flying in erratic zig-zag and spiralling motions. Mad bulls typically have zingers (noisemakers) attached to them that allow them to be heard from great distances.

magga: (pronounced as *mag-ah*) Thin, skinny, malnourished.

Mammee (also Mammy): Mother.

mango chow: Though not exclusive to mangoes, a chow in the Caribbean refers to a dish made of well-seasoned fruits. The fruits can be green, half-ripe or fully ripe and is often cut into bite sized pieces and seasoned to taste with salt, pepper, garlic, chadon beni (culantro), and other optional ingredients such as a touch of lime juice or ketchup. Typically mangoes, pineapple, and pommecythere are used to make a chow.

mapepire: (pronounced *ma-pi-peere*) Also known as a pit viper, it is one the four poisonous snake species that inhabit the island of Trinidad.

mash up: Destroy

meh/mih: Me or in some cases "My" (depends on the context of the sentence).

N

nah (also nuh): This word can be used in place of "no". It can also be used to express dissatisfaction or added to the end of a request or statement.

nana: (pronounced nah-nah) An East-Indian term used to refer to your grandfather, on your mother's side.

nani: (pronounced nah-nee) An East-Indian term used to refer to your grandmother, on your mother's side.

'Nansi Story: (also "Nanci Story or Nancy Story) This term refers to the make believe stories of Anansi the spider. It is used to refer to stories that people don't believe in or that they believe are fictional.

O

Obeah: (pronounced *Oh-bee-ah* or *ohh-year*) Usually refers to black magic or voodoo. Practiced by an Obeah man or Obeah woman, it is based on African rites of magic and calls upon various spirits to ask for a variety of favours for their clients.

Oh gawd /Oh-god-oye: A common exclamation of surprise or of astonishment.

ole/ol': Old.

ole talk/ ol' talk: Useless or idle chatter that has no merit and achieves nothing. Hearsay.

Old mas: (ole mas) This refers to a form of mas that is played during the Carnival season. Considered to be the old-style Carnival, it consists of a display of a variety of traditional characters such as the Baby-Dolls, Bats, Burrokeets, Cow Bands, Dame Lorrianes, Pierrot Grenades, Sailors, Fancy Indians, Jab-Jabs, Midnight Robbers, Minstrels, etc.

Om dum durgayei namaha: A Hindi mantra honoring the Divine Mother that is repeated to help calm and still the mind. *Om* is the cosmic vibration of all creation, *Dum* is the sound of the energy of the goddess Durga, *Durgayei* is the formal name of the goddess, *Namaha* means "I bow before you."

Or-wah? : Or what?

oui: (pronounced *wee*) French for "yes".

P

papa-yo: An exclamation of surprise or shock.

parlour: A small corner shop usually run and managed by a single person (the owner) that sells various dry goods.

patois: (pronounced *pat-wah* or *pat-wuh*) The local dialect. French Patois is a language in and of itself and is still spoken in certain areas of Trinidad, such as Paramin, Valencia, Blanchisseuse, Toco, Arima, Santa Cruz and Moruga.

peewah: This fruit is a member of the palm family. It grows in bunches and is only edible if boiled and peeled. The texture is dry, crumbly and fibrous with little flavour. The seed inside each peewah is hard and black and roughly the size of a marble. The seed can be cracked open to reveal a whitish nut that has a flavour similar to dry coconut.

pelau: (pronounced *pay-la-wuh*) A very popular one pot dish also known as a cook up. It is made of rice, pigeon peas, stewed meat and coconut milk. Typically taken on outings to the beach due to its portability and convenience.

PH taxi: A private, unregistered car that is used as a taxi. Typically the fixed fares are significantly cheaper than that of registered taxis and the system of carpooling or picking up and dropping off passengers along the way is employed.

Picky-picky / picky-head: A crass and derogatory description of short kinky hair that is unkempt.

pigtail (salted): The tail of the pig is preserved in buckets of brine water. Typically sold in *parlours* by the pound, pigtails were once the poor man's meal but have grown to become very popular and common especially in soups and stews.

pitch: It can be used to refer to asphalt that is used to pave roadways. It can also refer to the act of throwing something (similar to pelt).

pomerac: (pronounced *pom-er-rack*) Known by many names including Rose Apple, Bell Apple, Malabar Plum, Malay Apple, Otaheite apple, Plum Rose, Sumutoo, Water Apple or Wax Apple, this bright red, pear-shaped fruit has a thin, waxy skin and a soft white flesh that holds an inedible round pit (similar to an avocado). It is known for having a sweet and juicy taste and though it looks similar to the cashew fruit there is no relation between the two.

pommecythere (also known as golden apple): (pronounced *pom-see-tay*) A fruit that can be eaten when still green (salted or in a *chow*) and when ripe becomes sweet and juicy and bright yellow (hence the name golden apple). A prominent feature of the fruit is its single thorny seed in the middle.

posey: (pronounced *poe-zee*) also known as a chamber pot, this is a large potty-sized enamel basin usually kept under the bed in homes that possess outdoor plumbing. It is used at nights to avoid having to go outside if one wishes to use the toilet.

puja (also pooja): (pronounced *poo-jah*) A Hindu prayer ritual for blessings and spiritual cleansing and protection.

Puncheon (fire water): (pronounced *punch-in*) A high proof, heavy-type rum containing 75% alcohol by volume manufactured by Forres Park. Its origins can be traced back to

1627 when plantation slaves discovered that molasses can be fermented into alcohol.

pundit: A Hindu holy man. Typically pundits are Brahmins who are scholars and teachers. They are skilled in the Sanskrit language and have mastered Hindu law, rituals and philosophies under a Sadhu or Guru.

Q

quenk: (pronounced kwenk) A term used for a wild hog.
quashie: a derogatory name for a person of African descent meant to dehumanize and make them feel insignificant.

R

red-man (male) reds/red skin woman (female): A light-skinned person of mixed or African or Spanish descent (though the term is widely used to refer to anyone with a lighter complexion regardless of actual ethnic origin).

Region 8: This refers to the Potaro-Siparuni. It borders the region of Cuyuni-Mazaruni to the north, the regions of Upper Demerara-Berbice and East Berbice-Corentyne to the east, the region of Upper Takutu-Upper Essequibo to the south and Brazil to the west. Most notably it is a region in Guyana that is known for its gold mining operations

running racket: Making trouble or creating drama.

S

sada roti: (pronounced sah-dah roh-tee) A thick, flat, round bread (similar to a flat bread) that is cooked over an open flame or on a hot baking stone (tawah). It is also commonly referred to as *Bake.*

samaan tree: A massive tree that is native to the tropics with a wide, flat, and symmetrical crown. It is also referred to as the "rain tree" because its leaves close in during the rain. When the tree flowers it bears pinkish-red or creamy-gold flowers

satwick: A non-vegetarian/meat offering made to some Hindu deities.

schimps: A milder word used in place of a more profane one. Used to denote shock or disapproval. Example: Ah schimps! I forgot to bring in the laundry and now it's raining!"

scruntin' / scrunting: Poor, penniless and broke. Someone who is struggling to make ends meet.

shoo-shooed: Whispered/gossiped

shoulda: Should of

standpipe (stan'pipe): This is a water pipe that supplies the public with water. Sometimes it remains as a standing post with a tap affixed, and other times it is simply a metal pipe with a tap. It can usually be found along the main road and it is a common sight. In some areas, it is the only source of water within the village, and it is not uncommon to see people filling up large containers or buckets with water, or even bathing at the site.

St. Ann's: This is used to refer to the lunatic asylum / mental health hospital located on St Ann's road, Port-of-Spain.

steups: (pronounced *stew-ps*) A sound made by sucking one's teeth. It denotes displeasure or anger or disbelief.

T

Tanty: (also spelled Tantie, Aunty, or Auntie) A term used to refer to your Aunt, or a word used for any older woman who you don't know, or who is, in some cases, is a friend of the family.

tatu (also known as tatou): An armadillo.

tawah: (pronounced *tah-wah*) (also known as a baking stone) This is a round, flat griddle originally made out of stone, though modern versions are made out of metal. It is used for baking flat breads (cassava bread and roti).

torchlight: A flashlight.

twenty-four hour lizards: Known as night lizards for their penchant for appearing at night, these common lizards are said to "stick" to your skin and will not come off or leave you alone for twenty-four hours if you come into contact with them.

V

Vita Loaf: Produced and manufactured by CBI Coelho (also known as the Kiss Baking Company), it is a common brand of sliced bread that can be found on many Caribbean islands.

W

whey: Where (or depending on the context it can also mean "what" for example: whey yuh say!)

whey-boy!: An exclamation of disbelief or shock.

wild meat: (also known as *bush meat*) It is a common delicacy that is highly sought after during the hunting season (October to March). It involves the meat of animals such as the deer, iguana, *manicou* (opossum), *tatu* (nine banded armadillo), *agouti* (large guinea pig), *lappe* (lowland paca), *quenk* (wild hog), and *matte* (tegu lizard).

Y

yuh: You

yampie (or yampee) : Eye boogers, rheum, or mucus found in the corner of the eye.

Z

zingers: Attachments to kites that cause them to make a loud humming sound. Similar to this are *zwills* which are razor blades that are attached to kites and are designed to slash and cut down competing kites.

ABOUT THE AUTHOR

AMBER DRAPPIER (July 1992) was born on the beautiful twin island nation of Trinidad and Tobago. With a variety of passions and interests, she tries to not limit herself to one specific genre. Poetry, art, novellas, and short stories categorized as; fantasy, horror/thriller, and folklore, are just some of the categories under which her work falls.

Living with her husband in Florida, USA, Amber is self-proclaimed foodie who finds great joys in cooking up various brews and stews in her kitchen. An avid reader and freelance editor by day, and a writer and storyteller by night, she keeps herself occupied with a never-ending backlog of ideas and projects.

If you would like to know more about Amber's publications and upcoming works you can visit her website at amber.drappiertech.com or if you'd like to contact the author you can email her at amber@drappiertech.com

Printed in Great Britain
by Amazon